MARCOTTE AND COLLINS INVESTIGATIVE THRILLERS - 2

# CAPTIVES

## TRAVIS TOUGAW

Black Rose Writing | Texas

This is a work of fiction. Names, characters, businesses, places, events, and incidents are either the products of the author's imagination or used in a fictitious manner. Any resemblance to actual persons, living or dead, or actual events is purely coincidental.

ISBN: 978-1-68513-425-9
PUBLISHED BY BLACK ROSE WRITING
www.blackrosewriting.com

Printed in the United States of America
Suggested Retail Price (SRP) $22.95

*Captives* is printed in Georgia Pro

*As a planet-friendly publisher, Black Rose Writing does its best to eliminate unnecessary waste to reduce paper usage and energy costs, while never compromising the reading experience. As a result, the final word count vs. page count may not meet common expectations.

*For Carvin and Miles, a constant source of laughter, adventure, and inspiration.*

*And, of course, for Jen.*

# PRAISE FOR CAPTIVES

"*Captives* is an edge-of-your-seat thriller that follows private detective Hadley Collins as she investigates a decade old kidnapping case of a toddler. No witnesses. No suspects. No motive. No hope...Perfect for fans of Laura Dave and John Grisham, this thriller will put Tougaw at the top of your list for favorite thriller authors."
—**Marisa Dondlinger, Author of *Come and Get Me***

"This book kept me up WAY TOO LATE, but I had to finish it. This page-turner was exciting, compelling, and rewarding...The twist was surprising and so powerful, shedding new light on everyone involved."
—**R.C. Mogo, Author of *Innocents of Marbella***

"Warning: Travis Tougaw's *Captives* will hold you captive until the very last page! This riveting thriller takes you back and forth between an unsolved kidnapping cold case and the present-day efforts by private detectives to find the victim and bring him home. The novel's a gripping read you simply won't be able to put down."
—**Sid Meltzer, Author of *Murderer from Moscow***

"*Captives* is a clever detective novel that blends mystery, crime, and suspense. Travis Tougaw's skillful writing takes the reader on an action-packed and high-energy journey...Suitable for thriller fans and crime-solving enthusiasts, this book will keep readers turning the pages! An awesome read!"
—**Readers' Favorite**

# CAPTIVES

# CHAPTER 1

*October 11, 2023*

Hadley Collins never should have taken the call. Or, she should have told Jenny Davidson she couldn't help her, that the agency had reached capacity on its caseload. That would have only been a slight exaggeration.

She already knew the reasons her partners would use to tell her to decline the case. They were all valid; she'd be using them herself if the roles were reversed. Not that there weren't good reasons to take the case, too. There were, but she couldn't share the most important one with them. Maybe someday, but not yet.

Nevertheless, she had met with Jenny. Caught up with her over lunch, talking about how much had changed since high school and then lingering over the empty dishes to get down to the real business. She listened to Jenny's story and told her she'd take the case, knowing she should consult with her partners first. She dreaded meeting with them, but the time had come to tell them what she had committed the agency to.

She rose from her desk and in three quick steps reached the door to her office. The smell of burning coffee greeted her. She crossed the stained carpet with its frayed edges and nearly bare patches to turn off the ancient machine, where a nearly empty pot occupied the burner. She'd asked Eddie to replace the machine with something modern at least a hundred times, but he insisted the coffee tasted better out of the relic.

With that duty complete, she turned and found her two partners seated at a card table with mismatched chairs. In the glory days of the Eddie Fleck Detective Agency, a receptionist's desk occupied that part of the lobby. Those days were long past, as were the days of meeting clients at the agency. Almost every meeting took place over videoconference now, with face-to-face meetings happening in restaurants and coffee shops or, on occasion, in the client's home.

"Top of the morning, to you, Ms. Collins," Eddie said in his best Irish accent. Hadley smiled at him. He wore a wrinkled Hawaiian shirt. His hair appeared grayer than the last time she'd seen him, and it matched the three-day stubble that covered his chin and cheeks.

"Good morning, Hadley," Vince said, from his spot next to Eddie. He wore his typical polo shirt with khaki pants and seemed in good spirits.

"Morning, guys," she answered. "Eddie, we need to talk about the coffee maker."

"Unless you want to talk about how awesome it is, I think we've covered that territory. I can make another pot if you want."

"Forget it," she said, slipping into her chair. They made small talk about the weather growing more fall-like each day and about Broncos and Buffs football.

"Enough about that stuff," Vince finally said. "Let's get this meeting of the Fleck, Collins, and Marcotte Detective Agency going."

"Any new cases this week?" Eddie asked.

"I got a couple cheaters," Vince said. "Standard rate, but I might need help covering one of them."

"What kind of cheating?" Eddie asked.

"The first one is a wife who wants us to prove her husband is having an affair. Suspects his executive assistant at work."

"Tale as old as time," Eddie said, leaning back from the rickety table. Hadley gave him a dirty look. People only hired private detectives when something was going wrong. Rather than showing sensitivity to their clients' struggles, Eddie constantly made sport of them.

"What's the second one, Vince?" she asked.

"It's more interesting, and it's the one where I could use the help. Client is a local paper factory. The foreman at their warehouse had a forklift accident last year. There were no witnesses and the details are sketchy. They just reached a settlement with him last month that includes ongoing disability payment. But, another warehouse worker thinks he saw him rock climbing in Colorado Springs last weekend. If he's healthy enough to scale rocks, he's healthy enough to jump back on the forklift. They want proof that he's violating the terms of his settlement to see if they can get the court to compel him to get an independent medical evaluation. They're paying a little more than the standard rate, plus any travel expenses while we're hunting him down."

"I can suit up for it," Eddie said, then cast a glance at Hadley. "Unless you want to."

"No," she said, "I'll have my hands full with another case." The two men leaned forward, eager to hear the details.

"This isn't our typical case, so hear me out," she said. She took a deep breath. "This one is a kidnapping."

"Kidnapping?" Vince repeated.

"That's a case for the police, not us," Eddie said.

"That's the opposite of hearing me out," Hadley said, scowling at her partners. "The police have had the case for 15 years and haven't gotten anywhere with it." Eddie raised an index finger as if about to interject, but Hadley cut him off with a glare. "I know the victim. Well, not really. I know—knew—his sister. We went to high school together. Her brother was two years old and disappeared from their house one night. Just vanished. No leads, no evidence, nothing. Long story, but the stress and trauma ended up splitting up their parents. Her mom has some health problems, so Jenny, my, uh, high school acquaintance, is desperate to find out something." She looked from Vince to Eddie, wondering which one would jump in first. "I know what you're going to say, but this case is very important to me."

"You can't take the case," Eddie said. "I'm going to be blunt, so forgive my insensitivity. The case is a loser. If it's that old with no leads ever being produced, we have no chance of finding anything now. Most kidnapping cases that aren't solved in the first week end up with the victim dead. This kind of case is a time sink that won't produce results. That's fine when it's a hobby, but when it's your business, you have to be profitable."

"I agree with Eddie on this one," Vince said. "Sorry, Hadley, but this sounds like something better left to a cold case unit with the police."

"In case you've forgotten, we met on a cold case," Hadley said. "And, that worked out pretty well."

"Yeah, but we only got the breaks we did because there was a current case to go with it," Vince responded.

"Like I said," Hadley went on, ignoring his rebuttal, "this case is really important to me."

"That's another reason to turn it down," Eddie said. "If it's too personal, you lose objectivity and perspective. You keep digging until you're in a quagmire you can't get out of."

Hadley blew out a sigh and looked from Vince to Eddie and back. They were right, but she couldn't tell Jenny she was joining the myriad other detectives who had declined the case. She rose and walked back to the coffee maker. She dumped the remaining sludge Eddie called coffee into the sink and rinsed the pot. With her back to the sink and hands on her hips, she said, "She'll pay double our normal fee, even if we don't find new information. And, there's a bonus if we solve it."

"You might have led with that information," Eddie said. "That changes the equation."

"I don't know," Vince said. "A case like this can tie up a lot of resources. And, in case you haven't noticed, we don't have a lot of resources."

Hadley eased back into her seat. "Vince, I hear you. But, we're taking this case. I already told her we would. If the agency can't do it, I'll take a leave of absence and do it on my own."

Vince crossed his arms and stared at the table, his expression somewhere between sympathy and a scowl. "If it means that much to you, let's take it," he said. "Eddie, I'm definitely going to need some help with the rock climber."

Eddie nodded. "You say this kidnapping happened 15 years ago? Was it here in Denver?"

"Yeah," Hadley said. "In the Park Hill neighborhood."

"I was consulting with Denver PD then," Eddie said. "I was working homicide, and Park Hill wasn't in my district, but if this is the case I'm thinking of, we have our work cut out for us. They pulled in detectives from across the city, put the best and brightest on it."

"But not you," Vince teased.

"Like I said, I was in homicide. My point is the case didn't go unsolved because of sloppy police work. They did everything by the book, left no stone unturned. In the end, they couldn't even prove it was an abduction and that the kid didn't just wander off and get lost. The only way we crack this case is if the client can point us in the direction of some new evidence."

"Speaking of the client," Vince said, "when do we meet her?"

"In half an hour," Hadley answered. "At Caruso's. No offense, Eddie, I'd like the initial meeting to be just me and Vince. She's not as convinced as you that the cops did everything by the book, so it might help if she talked to us civilians first."

"That's probably best," he said. "I didn't exactly dress for clients anyway. Besides, Caruso's makes the worst coffee."

Hadley glanced toward the sink but bit back her retort. The meeting over, she returned to her office to gather her thoughts and get ready to meet with Jenny.

# CHAPTER 2

*January 22, 2008*

Hadley grimaced as the tall brunette from the other school spiked the ball between two East High School players. The referee whistled the point, which tied the match at two games each. As the teams huddled around their coaches, Hadley absentmindedly fingered the strap on the school's digital camera. She wondered if she had taken enough pictures to satisfy Mr. Murphy, her journalism teacher, and if any of them would be any good. She'd only signed up for the class to learn the layout and design software; she certainly had not planned on attending sporting events.

To add humiliation to her boredom, the student athletes viewed her as a servant, someone who worked for the team but was decidedly not part of the team. She could say the batteries died and call it an early evening, but Mr. Murphy would freak out. The lecture she'd get from him would be ten times worse than staying for the end of the game.

The whistle sounded again, and the girls from each team took their places. Jenny Davidson lined up to serve, and the East student body cheered and stomped their feet. The bleachers shook as if in an earthquake, and Hadley knew she couldn't get a good shot in the commotion. She ventured away from the bleachers and crept along the sideline.

Most of the students came to see Jenny. She was everything that Hadley was not—tall, athletic, charismatic, and gorgeous. She'd been the homecoming queen in the fall and was destined to be the prom queen in the spring, along with being named valedictorian and most likely to succeed.

Jenny crouched with the ball, a tigress ready to spring into action. In one fluid motion, she tossed the ball upward, exploded off her feet, and rotated her right arm vertically to hammer the ball into the opponent's territory. It sliced through the air toward the left sideline, opposite Hadley. The other school's player tried to return it but couldn't get low enough in time, and the ball bounced off her arms straight to the ground.

The bleachers erupted into more cheering. Hadley looked at Jenny, returning to the server's spot. She checked the camera to see if she'd gotten a good shot of the serve. In her mind, she had captured a frame of Jenny's blur of activity that would define her athletic grace down to the last detail. Instead, she had captured the blur itself. She deleted the image and crept further down the sideline, crossing the net and positioning herself on the East side of play.

Hadley switched the camera mode to take a burst of pictures. It was cheating, of course, and Mr. Murphy would not approve, but it was a lesser sin than not documenting key moments from a tight match.

Jenny served again, once again leaping high into the air and smashing the ball toward her opponents. Hadley heard the whir of the shutter as the camera took multiple photos. She watched as an opponent bumped the ball into the air, another set it high, and the tall brunette spiked it back.

Emily Hayden, another East student, met her at the net and blocked the ball. It flew into the air, cutting diagonally across the court and headed toward the right sideline. Hadley raised the camera and tried to follow the action. She did not see Jenny barreling toward her to save the ball before it landed out of bounds.

Hadley heard voices yelling "Move" and "Get out of the way." She did not realize the comments were aimed at her. Still searching with the camera, she found Jenny in full sprint.

Jenny either didn't see her or thought she would move before the collision. Hadley remained in her crouch, frozen in place.

Jenny smacked into her. The camera flew from her hands. She felt the wide strap pull on her neck as Jenny's shins blasted her ribs. The two girls fell in a heap. In a moment of silence, Hadley heard two sounds. First, the ball struck the ground nearby. A split second later, she heard the double thud of Jenny's upper body hitting the ground, followed by her face.

The referee whistled the sideout, and the East students began booing both the call and Hadley. As she tried to disentangle herself from Jenny, students and players screamed for interference and a do-over.

Jenny shook free of Hadley and stood over her. She glared down at the photographer and hissed, "Stay out of the way!" The coach called a timeout and Jenny took a few steps toward the huddle before turning and glaring at Hadley once more. The hint of a bruise had already blossomed on her left cheek and a trickle of blood ran from her nostril. She ran to join her teammates.

The boos continued to rain down from the bleachers. Hadley collected herself and slunk away, leaving the gym. Outside, she gulped in the fresh air, happy to be free from the anger, from the stench of sweaty bodies, and from the boredom of watching a sport she cared nothing about. Mr. Murphy would be furious with her. She could hear him now, "You broke rule number one. You made yourself part of the story. And, then you left before the game was over."

But, Mr. Murphy didn't understand what it was like to be a Hadley in a world full of Jennys. He didn't understand that Hadley had committed a far greater sin than violating journalism rules by costing the team a point—and maybe the match. These things were a colossal deal to Jenny, her teammates, and all the kids in the bleachers. Hadley's error was unforgivable and unforgettable.

As she trudged toward the bench to wait for a city bus to take her back home, Hadley had no way of knowing that within a few weeks Jenny would forget about their encounter, and the trajectory of her life would change forever.

# CHAPTER 3

*October 11, 2023*

The detective agency of Fleck, Collins, and Marcotte occupied one of four units in a converted house in Denver's Cheesman Park neighborhood. Eddie had secured a ground floor unit years before; their neighbors included a law office and an accountant on the second story and a real estate brokerage in the other ground floor unit.

Hadley and Vince stepped into the crisp fall air. The trees lining the streets had changed colors, an explosion of red, orange, and yellow. A block away, Colfax Boulevard hummed with traffic.

"I'll drive," Hadley said, double-pressing the button on her key fob. Her Grand Cherokee chirped and flashed its lights in response.

"I still can't believe you traded in the Mini Cooper for this behemoth," Vince said. While there were bigger SUVs on the market, parallel parking the Mini had been much easier. The Jeep wasn't practical for their office location in the heart of the city, but since becoming a full-time detective, Hadley felt much safer in the more substantial vehicle.

Caruso's Coffee was only a five-minute drive from the office. By a stroke of fortune, a parking space opened on the street directly outside as they pulled up. Hadley tried not to notice Vince smirking as she maneuvered her way into the space, running over the curb the first time. "One day I'll get the hang of this," she said. Vince held both hands up, palms open, in an I-didn't-say-anything gesture.

A handful of wrought-iron tables and chairs occupied the sidewalk outside the coffee shop. Patrons sat at each, enjoying lattes and an assortment of pastries while scrolling on their phones. The hiss of a cappuccino maker and the murmur of conversations greeted them as they entered. Hadley waved to a woman sitting at a corner high-top, and she and Vince approached the counter to order.

"I take it that's our client," Vince said.

"Jenny Davidson," Hadley confirmed. "Yes, that's her. And, listen. It's hard for her to talk about what happened. I don't think she'll say much about the kidnapping itself."

"Kidnapping?" Vince asked. "Are we reaching conclusions already?"

"Fine," Hadley said, an edge in her voice that she tried to calm. Vince was right. "She probably won't say much about the disappearance."

"Then why are we here?"

"She'll give us her perspective and maybe a lead or two we can follow up on."

The barista handed them their drinks, and they crossed the old maple floor to join Jenny.

Jenny rose as they reached the table. She stood a couple inches taller than Vince, which put her about half a foot taller than Hadley. Hadley and her old acquaintance exchanged a quick hug, and Jenny stuck out her hand for Vince.

"Jenny, this is Vince Marcotte. He's one of the partners at our agency."

Jenny had a firm grip and intense eye contact. "I read about you," she said. "The case with the senate candidate."

Vince grinned sheepishly. "That's usually the first thing people know about me," he said as they took their seats around the tall table. Vince poured cream from a small pot into his cup. He reached for a sugar packet, but Hadley cast him a wary glance and he withdrew his hand.

"I'm hoping you can get similar results for me," Jenny said. "Most detectives won't touch a cold case like this one. Trust me, I've talked to plenty."

"We can't promise anything," Hadley said, jumping in before Vince could say anything. Jenny had turned her attention to Vince, and Hadley wanted to make it clear that this was her case. "But, as we discussed, we will use every resource at our disposal to get the best results we can."

Jenny offered her a sad half-smile. "Where do we start?"

Hadley gave Jenny an overview of their process, how they would start by reviewing any existing documents about the case that they could, and then they'd interview as many witnesses as possible.

"I can help with the first part," Jenny said. "I brought my files on the case; they're in my car. You can take them today, but I'll want them back when you finish your investigation. The second part is more problematic."

"Why's that?" Vince asked, his head cocked to one side.

"There were no witnesses. The day," Jenny paused and breathed deeply. She swallowed hard and dabbed at her eyes with a napkin. "The day Jonah was taken, there was no one else around. He just vanished."

Hadley reached across the table and took Jenny's hand. "Even a potential witness can help. We'll want to talk to people in the family and close to the family. People who can provide us with context for the disappearance. You never know when a minor detail that someone remembers will lead to another memory for someone else, and before you know it, we're adding pieces to the puzzle. Are there police reports in your files? We can start by reinterviewing the people the cops talked to."

Jenny nodded. "A lot of them are gone now. They've moved to other neighborhoods or out of state."

"We're good at finding people," Vince said. "Is there anyone who won't show up in the police report you think we should talk to?"

She shook her head, her short blond hair bouncing against the base of her neck as she did.

"Do you have a theory, Jenny?" Hadley asked. "What do you think happened?"

Jenny pulled her hand back from Hadley's and dabbed at her eyes again. "That's just it. I have no idea what happened or how to explain it. He was just gone."

Jenny led them from Caruso's to her car, parked a block away. She popped the trunk, and Hadley let out a gasp of surprise. "Is that for us?"

"Yes," Jenny said. "I hope it's enough to get you started."

Hadley stared at the two large cardboard boxes, straining at their seams. "That's plenty," she said. She and Vince each lugged a box out of the trunk. Vince took Hadley's keys to pull the Jeep around.

"We'll be in touch soon, Jenny," Hadley said.

A few minutes later, they hauled the boxes into the office, where Eddie sat pecking at his laptop's keyboard with his index fingers.

"Forklift guy doesn't post much on social media," he said, intent on the screen. "But a buddy of his does. Says he's looking forward to visiting Garden of the Gods this Saturday. Guy's a serious rock climber from the look of things. I'll plan on popping down there, see if our guy is with him and I can catch him in the act."

The card table wobbled under the weight of the two boxes, and Eddie finally looked up. "Whoa! What's all this?"

"Our client's files," Hadley said. "Hopefully, something good is hiding in here."

They unpacked the boxes, spreading everything on the table. Jenny had copies of police reports, police interviews, and newspaper clippings in the first box. The second box held stacks of three-ring binders filled with reports from other detective agencies. The largest binder held printouts from a Facebook page, missing children message boards, and a blog about Jonah Davidson's disappearance.

"There's a lot more here than I expected," Vince said. "I wonder how she got the police interviews?"

"It's not uncommon in a case like this," Eddie said. "Denver PD is not supposed to share anything that's not public record, but sometimes a detective will get friendly with a family and make some copies. Off the books, of course."

Hadley flipped through some of the documents and began arranging stacks in a circle on the table. "We'll start here, with the police report," she said. "Then we move clockwise around the table. Police interviews next, then the other private detectives. I'm less interested in the press clippings and social media stuff, so we'll save it for the end."

"We're gonna be here a while," Eddie said. "I better make some more coffee." Hadley rolled her eyes and took her seat. She felt a flutter in her stomach, a mix of excitement about a new case, concern that they wouldn't get anywhere with it, and anxiety over the subject matter. Vince and Eddie took their places on either side of her, and she started reading the police report.

# CHAPTER 4

*March 27, 2008*

Jenny slumped on the couch, enduring yet another day in the most boring spring break of all time. All her friends had gone out of town for the week, spending their vacations on beaches in Cabo, Fort Lauderdale, or San Diego. Allison, her best friend, did not have it so lucky; she got stuck visiting her grandparents in Tulsa. Jenny didn't know which of them had it worse.

Outside, Lisa, Jenny's mother, sat on the front porch steps, watching Jonah, two years old, play while Sara, age six, rode her bike up and down the sidewalk. It was the first sunny day of the week, and they luxuriated in the warmth and blue sky after a string of gray days. Robins chirped and crows squawked. In the distance, the sound of a hammer and nails rang out.

"Not so fast, Sara," Lisa called, watching as the blur of pink sped by, the girl's long, blond hair trailing in the gentle breeze. If Sara heard, she didn't listen. She continued flying at breakneck speed toward the end of the block where she came to a stop with a screech of brakes.

In the small patch of grass that served as a front yard, Jonah's ball rolled away from him toward the sidewalk. Jonah got up to chase it. His unsteady toddler's feet betrayed him, and he fell in a heap, bringing on a storm of tears and wails.

Lisa picked him up and retrieved his ball. He held the ball close to his face as she bounced him up and down. The fall forgotten, she returned him to the grass. She returned to her seat and watched Sara blur by again.

"Last time, Sara," Lisa called. A moment later, the squeal of a sudden stop answered her as Sara reached the other end of the block. Lisa watched as her daughter turned the bike around and started back toward the house, still going way too fast for a little girl who'd been without training wheels for less than a month.

This time, Sara slammed on her brakes directly in front of the house. As the bike skidded, the front tire caught an uneven part of the narrow sidewalk, and Sara pitched forward. She lost her grip on the handlebars and lurched over the front wheel onto the concrete.

She landed with a shriek, and Lisa rushed down the steps. Sara lay on the sidewalk screaming, a current of blood rushing from her scalp down her face.

With Sara in her arms, Lisa rushed into the house. "What happened?" Jenny asked, following them from the front door to the kitchen, where Lisa grabbed a dish towel to stop the flow of blood.

"Ow, ow, ow!" Sara moaned, trying to fight Lisa's hands from her forehead.

"Get me some ice," Lisa said.

"What happened?" Jenny repeated as she dumped an ice tray into a bowl and handed it to her mother.

"She fell off her bike. I need to see how bad this is. She might need stitches. We can't afford a trip to the emergency room." Lisa wrapped a paper towel in ice and applied it to Sara's forehead. Suddenly, she stopped moving. "Jonah!" she shouted. "I left him outside. Go get him!"

Jenny rushed through the living room to the front door. She squinted in the bright afternoon light. She looked across the empty yard and saw Sara's bike in the middle of the sidewalk. She saw Jonah's ball in the grass. She did not see Jonah.

She trotted down the path to the sidewalk and looked up and down the block. She walked into the street and turned around, looking back at the house from the other direction. Still no Jonah. She rushed back toward the house, checking the porch before she went inside.

Sara had finally stopped screaming. Lisa continued to hold the ice to her head.

"Mom, I didn't see Jonah."

"What? What do you mean?"

"I didn't see him out there. Are you sure he was outside?"

Lisa didn't answer. She scooped up Sara and ran to the front door, Jenny close behind. Lisa turned and thrust Sara toward her. "Here," she said, transferring one daughter to the other and racing down the porch steps. She stood in the middle of the yard, hands on her hips, and turned in a slow circle, looking up and down. She called Jonah's name several times.

"Where's Jonah?" Sara asked.

"He's fine," Jenny said, though she felt a lump forming in her throat. She set Sara on the top step. "Keep holding this on your head. I'm going to look inside." Jenny ran back into the house, her fingers sticky with Sara's blood. She looked in the living room and kitchen, then in her parents' room, where Jonah's crib occupied a corner. She looked in Sara's room and then her own. She checked the bathrooms, then went downstairs to the basement. She turned on the light—a single bare bulb in the middle of the space—and looked behind stacks of boxes. She did not find him among the tubs of Christmas decorations, outgrown clothing, and old books. She checked behind the water heater. Unsuccessful, she ran back up the stairs.

Lisa stood in the kitchen with the phone to her ear, Sara clinging to her legs. "I need the police," Lisa said, and tears streamed down her face. "Yes, it's an emergency. My son is missing."

# CHAPTER 5

*October 11, 2023*

"Well, now we know why she said there were no witnesses," Vince said, setting the police report in the middle of the table. "Crazy how he could just vanish like that."

"It was a big deal at the time," Eddie said. "Half the PD's resources were in Park Hill trying to find him. Media circus."

Hadley pushed back from the table and crossed her arms, her brow furrowed in concentration. She took out her phone and typed notes on who the police had interviewed.

"We don't get the police's theory on what happened from reading the report," she said. "But, I'm thinking it goes something like this: mom, daughter, and son are outside. Daughter gets hurt, and mom rushes her inside. She's in such a tizzy that she forgets about the son. Someone sees him unattended and grabs him."

"Sounds reasonable," Eddie said.

"I agree," Vince said. "But, it's a crazy coincidence that a kidnapper happens along at that exact moment."

"Unless the kidnapper didn't happen along," Hadley said.

"What do you mean?"

"Option one, the kidnapper is a neighbor. That raises the chance that he or she is present at the right moment. Option two, the kidnapper has been watching them, sees Jonah alone, and pounces. Grabs Jonah and drives off, never to be seen in the neighborhood again."

"I'm leaning toward option two," Eddie said. "The police canvassed the neighborhood. Hardly anyone was home. The ones who were almost all had multiple people in the house. It would have been hard for someone to snatch Jonah and keep him hidden without raising the suspicions of their family members. And, I don't buy a whole family being in on a kidnapping together."

"The police arrived quickly enough after Lisa called them that they would have noticed anyone leaving the neighborhood while they were searching," Vince said. "That points toward someone moving quickly and driving off before the police arrived."

"So, the most likely scenario is a planned operation, involving surveillance and quick action when the time was right," Hadley said. "We need a list of suspects." She handed Vince and Eddie each a binder. "Here are the private detective reports. Read through those, and I'll read the police interviews. We can compare notes this afternoon and see what kind of list we can build."

With that, she took a sheaf of papers to her office. The window faced the back alley. She stared out at the row of trash cans and recycling bins. She breathed deeply and tried to work out the knots in her stomach. She knew taking a case where she had a personal connection to a victim would be difficult. She knew a kidnapping case, in particular, posed its own set of challenges. She needed to get past all of that and focus on the matter at hand.

Two hours later, she had a list of details about the case—the approximate window when Jonah was taken, how long it took the police to respond, who they had interviewed. From the context of the interview, she made some assumptions about who they considered a suspect in the case and who just had information.

"Hadley, we're ordering lunch," Vince called from the outer office. He had his own office, a twin of Hadley's, on the other side of the anteroom. Eddie, now semi-retired, gladly gave up having a personal space for the privilege of only coming in when the mood suited him.

"What are you getting?" Hadley asked from her doorway.

"I'm thinking cheesesteak," Eddie said, flipping through a stack of paper menus. Hadley turned up her nose at him.

"Think you can find a healthier option?" she asked.

"Come on," he said. "We need thinking food. No one ever solved a case while eating kale. And just look at what you're doing to poor Vince. The guy's wasting away."

"Fine," Hadley said. "I brought a salad. You guys can eat yourselves to death if you want."

Despite Eddie's best peer pressure, Vince changed his order to a salad. When lunch came, they reconvened at the card table to share their observations.

"The police put Neil in their crosshairs early on," Hadley said. The Davidson patriarch, the chief operating officer for a financial planning firm, had been at work when Jonah disappeared. According to his police interviews, he had been meeting with clients all afternoon. According to his executive assistant, Neil had lunch with a client, but his second afternoon meeting had canceled. Neil hadn't returned from the lunch and had never accounted for where he was between the time lunch ended and Jonah disappeared.

"The detective you gave me thought he was shady, too," Eddie said, grease from his cheesesteak dripping down his chin. "This is delicious, by the way. Anyway, the theory in this report was that Neil had a girlfriend and was planning to leave Lisa. He could have taken Jonah to bring him to his new life."

"I got something similar from this detective's report," Vince said. "Doesn't make sense to me."

"Why not?" Eddie challenged. "He and Lisa split up shortly after Jonah disappeared."

"But, Neil never took up with this mystery girlfriend after he left Lisa," Vince said. "And, he didn't leave the area right away."

"Which makes you wonder if something went wrong," Eddie said. "He has a falling out with the girlfriend and has the police on his case about Jonah. Easiest way out is for Jonah to never reappear."

Hadley put her fork down. The thought of Neil murdering his own son made her queasy. "The police never talked to a girlfriend," she said. "At least, it's not in the records here. Do either of you have a name for her?"

Both men shook their heads. Hadley made a note of it as something to track down later.

"Anyone else jump out as a potential suspect?" she asked.

"Not really," Eddie said. "Henry and Pauline Mancuso, the neighbors across the street, were both home when it happened, but they're weak suspects. They still live in the neighborhood, at least they did five years ago, and no one has ever seen an unexplained child with them. From what the private detectives found, they don't seem like the type to sell a kid on the black market."

Hadley glared at him yet again, and Eddie smirked in return. "I'm just saying they're not good suspects," he continued. "For what it's worth, I think the police were right to focus on Neil. There's usually a family member involved in a child abduction, if that's what we're even dealing with."

"What else would it be?" Hadley asked.

"Who knows? According to her statements in the police report, Jenny went outside to find Jonah around 90 seconds after her mom came in. Ninety seconds isn't a lot of time for a toddler to get to either end of the block. But, what if it's not 90 seconds? She didn't start a timer when her mom came in. What if it was three minutes? Five minutes? Now, we're looking at enough time for the kid to wander. Fall down a drain, climb in a dumpster. Who knows? The point is, the police put the best suspect under a microscope and never came up with any criminal activity. We have to at least keep open the possibility that there was no criminal activity."

Hadley rolled her eyes and blew out an exasperated sigh. "We'll keep it open as the least likely possibility," she said. "In the meantime, I'm going to make a list of everyone we want to interview and cross-reference them with who's still living in the neighborhood. Anyone up for walking the scene with me tomorrow? Maybe we'll score a couple interviews while we're there."

"I can go," Vince said.

"I'll beg off of this one," Eddie said. "If I'm going rock climbing with our cheater on Saturday, I need to catch up on a couple other things tomorrow. You can always call me to bounce an idea off me."

With that, Hadley returned to her office, closing the door behind her. She started reading through the police report again, but had to restart twice because she was picturing Eddie's smirk instead of focusing on her work. She closed her eyes, counted to 10, and returned to her notes. When she emerged from the office an hour later, she had a list of potential interviews:

The Davidsons (Jenny, Sara, Lisa, and Neil)

Henry and Pauline Mancuso

Monica Jones (a former babysitter)

Donald and Sheila Rogers and Ty and Bonnie Ferguson (next-door neighbors on either side of the Davidsons at the time)

Gary Brice (the lead detective for Denver Police)

According to her searches, the Mancusos, Rogers, and Fergusons all still lived in the same houses as they did 15 years earlier. She did not have a good address for Monica Jones yet. Gary Brice appeared to have retired from the police force.

She returned to the main office to find Eddie had departed. Vince sat in his office reading the press clippings from the Davidson case.

"Find anything interesting?" she asked.

"Not really. I see why Eddie said it was a media circus, though. There were front-page stories in the *Denver Post* for two weeks, and it stayed on the inside pages for months."

At the mention of Eddie's name, Hadley made a face.

"I'm sensing some tension between you and Eddie," Vince said. He offered a wry grin and followed up with, "I'm a detective, you know, so I can figure these things out. What's up?'

Hadley sat in the chair on the other side of Vince's desk. Like everything Eddie had purchased, the chairs and desk were mismatched and in desperate need of replacement. "His work ethic, for one thing," she said. "He's always punting on cases, letting you and me do the heavy lifting."

Vince bounced his head from side to side. "I don't know if that's fair," he said. "We knew that was the deal when we went into business with him. We're full time; he's part time. And, he always comes through when we need him to."

"I guess." She stood halfway and then flopped back down. "What really bothers me is that he trusts the police so much. It's a struggle to get him to even question if they made the right call, asked the right questions. And, my experience with the police is much different than that."

"That's valid," Vince said. "I doubt there's any changing him, but being aware of where he's coming from and what his biases are will help us keep him from steering things in the wrong direction."

"I guess," Hadley said. "What time do you want to meet tomorrow?"

"How about 10:00? There's a supermarket a couple blocks away from where the Davidsons lived. We can meet there and take one car over to their house."

With a plan in place, Hadley gathered her things and headed for home. As she merged into the interstate traffic, she thought about the case and about Eddie's suggestion that there might not be an abduction. She supposed anything was possible, but that seemed highly implausible to her. True, Jenny didn't know for a fact how long Jonah had been left unsupervised. But, the police responded immediately and had a huge presence on the Davidsons' street and the neighboring roads. She didn't see how an unattended two year old could have wandered the neighborhood without being spotted.

She conceded that in most kidnappings, the best chance for a reunion was to find the victim early. That did not bode well for this case.

But, she couldn't dismiss the idea that there was a boy, almost a man, out there somewhere, and he had no idea who his real family was. He could be a captive and not even know it. She couldn't abandon him.

# CHAPTER 6

*October 12, 2023*

One of Denver's older neighborhoods, Park Hill featured red-brick cottages built close together on each side of narrow streets. The neighborhood had alleys between streets, with garages and parking at the rear of the houses. That freed up the front to feature covered porches and arched entryways. The houses were set back from the sidewalks, with a small yard space in between. The overall effect was a charming neighborhood with loads of curb appeal.

The Davidsons had lived on Gardenia Street. There were 12 houses on each side of their block, and their house had been in the middle, the sixth one in from the direction Hadley and Vince approached from. They parked at the end of the street and walked the sidewalk, trying to get a feel for what it might have been like the day Jonah disappeared.

The air held a chill, and the recently fallen leaves crunched under their feet. "One good thing," Hadley said, "is that the neighborhood hasn't changed much since 2008."

"You grew up here, right?"

"Near here. There have been some changes. Look at how many houses have doorbell cameras and security systems now. It wasn't like that back in the day."

"Too bad. It would have made our job a lot easier," Vince said.

They reached the old Davidson home and stared at it. Like the other houses on the block, three steps led to a front porch that ran the width of the house. A concrete path led from the house to the sidewalk, bisecting the yard.

"Let's walk back to the corner," Hadley said. Vince raised a quizzical brow. "I want to see how long it takes."

They walked at a leisurely pace and reached the corner in just under a minute. As they walked back, still crunching on leaves, Hadley said, "Figure a toddler is at least twice as slow as we are. It would take a minimum of two minutes for Jonah to get from their house to turn the corner and get out of Jenny's sight."

"If Jenny's timetable is right, he wouldn't have enough time," Vince said. "But, don't forget what Eddie said. We have to consider his unsupervised window to be anywhere from 90 seconds to five minutes."

"I don't think it's five minutes," Hadley said. They reached the Davidson's former house again and stopped on the sidewalk. "Jenny and Lisa both recalled their actions when Lisa came in with Sara, and their stories were consistent. Maybe all the chaos of calming a bleeding six-year-old took more than 90 seconds, but I'd say less than three minutes."

"That still gives Jonah time to get out of sight."

"If he left as soon as Lisa and Sara ran inside. That's unlikely. And, figure two minutes to the corner is his absolute top speed. Like if he's a sprinter in the Toddler Olympics."

Vince laughed. "Fair enough. Let's agree that we're looking for a kidnapping suspect and Jonah didn't just wander off. Where do you want to go first?"

"Let's start with the next-door neighbors," Hadley said, walking toward the next house on the block. "This one should be Donald and Sheila Rogers."

They followed a concrete path to a front porch almost identical to the Davidsons'. Hadley rang the bell and took a step back. They waited for half a minute. She rang the bell again. Another minute passed. "Must not be home," she said.

They were halfway to the sidewalk when they heard a door open. Hadley spun around to see a thin, gray-haired man standing in the doorway. Each hand clenched the handle of a walker, and he stood with a stoop.

"You have to give a guy time to answer the door," he said in a voice as thin as his chest.

Hadley led the way back to the porch. "Sorry to disturb you, sir," she said. "My name is Hadley Collins, and this is Vince Marcotte. We're private detectives. Jenny Davidson hired us; do you remember the Davidsons?"

The old man looked skyward and mumbled something. He turned the walker around, so his back was to them. "Come on in," he called over his shoulder. "Let's get this over with."

A few minutes later, Hadley and Vince found themselves seated at the kitchen table with Donald Rogers while his wife, Sheila, made coffee, her hair in a shower cap.

"You shouldn't go to any trouble," Vince said. "We won't stay long."

"Nonsense," Sheila answered as she flitted from cabinet to cabinet gathering cups, saucers, and a package of chocolate chip cookies. "We don't get much company. You might as well enjoy your stay."

Hadley covered the preliminaries while Sheila played hostess. The Rogers had lived in the house for 30 years. Donald had just retired as a mail carrier when Jonah disappeared. They had known the Davidsons fairly well; they had them over for dinner and saw them at neighborhood events like block parties and the annual garage sale.

"It's sad what happened," Sheila said. "A lot of families can't recover from that. I suppose they weren't any different."

"Donald, as we were coming in, you said something about getting this over with," Hadley said. "Do you get questions about the Davidson case often?"

"Donald, you weren't rude, were you?" Sheila interrupted.

"I wasn't rude. I was honest. And, no, we don't get questions often, but it seems like every few years, someone else in the family hires a detective. We don't have any information that can help. I wish we did."

"Were you home when Jonah disappeared?" Hadley asked.

"No," Donald said. "I had to go to the hardware store to get a new seal for the kitchen faucet. Sheila came with me. We stopped at the post office. Had lunch out. Typical day for a couple of retirees. Only reason I remember the details is because the police and everyone else asked about it so many times."

"When did you realize something had gone wrong?" Vince asked.

"We couldn't get into the street or the alley," Sheila said. "The police had everything blocked. When we told them we lived on the street, they let us get a little closer, but we still had to walk home from the end of the block. When we passed the Davidson house, a police officer followed us home and asked a bunch of questions about Jonah and when we last saw him."

"Did you see anything in the street or the alley when you were walking home?" Vince asked. "Anything that seemed out of the ordinary or out of place?"

"There were police everywhere," Donald said, a sarcastic edge in his voice. "That was certainly out of the ordinary."

"We didn't see anyone we didn't know," Sheila said. "No strange cars, no repair vehicles or delivery trucks."

"Before that day," Hadley said, "did you ever sense or observe any tension with the Davidsons? Anything that might have signaled all wasn't well in their home?"

"No," Sheila answered quickly.

"Well," Donald said. He stroked his chin thoughtfully. "These houses don't have air conditioning. Some people have had it added in the past few years. Global warming and all that. We use a swamp cooler. Back then, we kept our windows open at night in the summer to let the house cool down. Closed them in the daytime when the temperatures rose. The Davidsons did the same thing. Some nights, we'd hear things."

"What kind of things?" Hadley asked.

"Hard to say. Nothing specific. Raised voices. Angry voices. I took it that Neil and Lisa fought a lot."

"The week that Jonah disappeared, did you hear them fighting?" Vince asked.

"No, but we kept the windows closed. It had been a dreary week. The day he disappeared was the first nice day we'd had in a while."

They thanked the Rogers for their time and the refreshments. Donald stayed at the table while Sheila showed them out. Hadley gave her a card at the door. "My cell phone number is on there; call me if you think of anything that might help us out."

They skipped the Davidsons' old house and visited the Ferguson home next. It had a smaller front porch that only ran about half the width of the house, but otherwise looked similar to the Rogers' house. Potted plants and flower boxes occupied all but a small area around the door. A sign reading "No Solicitors. Children Selling Cookies Welcome" adorned the wall just above the doorbell. Hadley rang it and they stepped back and waited.

Ty Ferguson answered the door much more quickly than Donald Rogers had. A black man, standing around five foot four, he wore a crisp white dress shirt with a navy blue tie. He looked from Hadley to Vince and back, furrowing his brow. "Can I help you?"

Hadley gave her standard introduction and explained they were detectives hired by the Davidsons. "Do you mind if we ask you a few questions about Jonah Davidson's disappearance?"

Ty glanced at his watch. "I only have about five minutes before I have to join a conference call. Let me make this easy for you. We don't know anything. We barely knew the Davidsons and we were out of state that entire week."

He spit the words out rapid fire, and Hadley struggled to keep up with him. He explained that he was a lawyer and his wife a schoolteacher. They had moved to the neighborhood a few weeks before Jonah disappeared. They were newlyweds, no children, and Bonnie's mother had been in poor health. They took advantage of Bonnie's spring break to take a trip to North Carolina to spend a week with her.

"Once we got back to town, we found out what happened. But, we never talked to the Davidsons about it. The father moved out of the house within the year, and I don't think Bonnie or I ever said more than a 'Good Afternoon' if we saw them in the yard or alley. Now, I've got to get going."

"Last question," Hadley said, stopping him from closing the door. "Do you know the people who live in the Davidsons' house now? Do you think they'd talk to us?"

He leaned his head back and squinted at her like she was crazy. "They definitely weren't around when Jonah disappeared. But, their names are Darren and Gina Barrett. Good people. I'm sure they'll talk to you."

Hadley let go of the door, and Ty retreated inside. They backtracked on the sidewalk to the Barretts' house. "Why do we want to talk to them?" Vince asked.

"I want to see inside the house," Hadley said. She looked at the expression on Vince's face. "I don't know why. I just try to place myself in the scene as much as possible, and I'd like to know what the inside of the house is like."

Vince shrugged, and they headed up the walk to the Barretts' front door. In contrast to the Fergusons, they had two chairs and nothing else on their porch. Hadley rang the bell. No answer. She rang again. Still no answer.

"Hey!" They heard Ty Ferguson's voice and turned to see him leaning out a window. "They're both at work. You have to come in the evening. Like after 6 p.m." He disappeared back inside the house.

"What are you doing tonight around six?" Hadley asked.

"I guess paying another visit to Park Hill," Vince said.

"Good answer. Let's try the Mancusos."

No one answered the door at the house across the street, either, so they added Henry and Pauline to their agenda for that evening.

"Any other neighbors you want to look for while we're here?" Vince asked.

"No. There aren't a lot left who lived here in 2008. I hope we get something good tonight because, otherwise, this has been a bust."

"Not a total bust," Vince said. "We figured out the timing for Jonah wandering off and agreed it wouldn't work."

"Good point. That's why I enjoy walking the scene with you. You always find a silver lining." She didn't add "unlike Eddie," but she definitely thought it.

# CHAPTER 7

"I didn't notice all the decorations when we were here earlier," Vince said.

"Yeah, it gets spooky around here after dark," Hadley answered as she navigated through Park Hill toward Gardenia Street. They passed a house with orange and purple lights lining its roof and a collection of inflatable witches and gargoyles in the yard. The next house had a large jack-in-the-box in the yard, a clown wielding a bloody knife springing from it.

They parked as close to the Barrett house as they could, three doors down. As they walked by the house on the other side of the Rogers, an eerie moaning emanated from a three-foot-tall werewolf wearing a flannel shirt stationed on the front steps.

"Halloween wasn't like this when I was a kid," Vince said.

"OK, Boomer," Hadley teased. They reached the Barretts' door, and she rang the bell. She heard footsteps, and the door swung open, creaking on its hinges. She smelled dinner cooking inside; they came on taco night.

A man in his mid-30s appeared in the doorway. He stood around six feet tall and wore jeans with a black V-neck T-shirt. Tattoos covered both arms, and a tattoo of a snake climbed its way out of the V of his shirt and up and around his neck.

"Are you Darren Barrett?" Hadley asked.

The man scowled at them. "Yeah," he said. "Whatever you're selling, I'm not interested." For the second time that day, Hadley stopped a door from slamming in her face.

"We're not selling anything," she said. "We're private detectives." That got his attention. "We were hired by the Davidsons, the family who used to live in this house."

Darren opened the door wider, but didn't invite them in. He continued to scowl. "What's that got to do with me?"

"We're trying to help the Davidsons find out what happened to their son, Jonah, and I thought it might help if we saw the inside of the house."

"How could that help?"

"I just like to understand the crime scene as much as possible."

He took a step forward and folded his arms across his chest. "I don't have time for this," he said.

"We could come back..."

"No, you can't," he interrupted. "Look, I don't want to be rude, and I'm sorry about that family losing their son, but all of that was years before we bought the place. You know, they didn't put anything about their son's disappearance in the disclosures. About a month after we moved in, a producer for some true crime TV show knocked on the door and wanted to film inside the house. Every couple of years something like that happens. TV show reenactments, private detectives, plain old gawkers...they all want to come inside the house. I'm tired of dealing with it. Now, I need to tend to dinner."

Hadley held out a business card, but he shut the door in her face. This time, she let him. "If you change your mind, you can call us," she said, stuffing the card between the door and the weatherstripping.

They crossed the street. The light in front of the Mancuso house flickered on and off. They didn't have any Halloween decorations out, but the strobe light effect did plenty to set the mood.

"Everyone's slamming doors on me today," Hadley said as she rang the bell. "Why don't you lead this one?"

A woman in her early 60s answered the door. She wore a purple silk blouse with black pants and a strand of pearls around her neck. She cocked her head to the side, as if trying to figure out why these two strangers had appeared on her porch.

"Mrs. Mancuso?" Vince asked. "My name is Vince Marcotte, and this is Hadley Collins. We're private detectives." He explained that they'd been hired by the Davidsons and were investigating the disappearance of Jonah. She invited them in.

"Henry," she said, as she led them through the living room and into the kitchen. "These two want to talk to us about Jonah Davidson." Henry stood at the sink, washing dinner dishes. In contrast to Pauline's elegance, he wore blue sweatpants and a gray Denver Broncos sweatshirt. He dried his hands on a dish towel, shook with both Hadley and Vince, and joined them at the kitchen table.

"Were you home the day Jonah disappeared?" Vince asked.

"We were," Henry answered. "I had a cold and had called in sick from work. Pauline was a real estate agent—still is, that's why she's dressed up tonight—but she didn't have any showings that day. We had gone down to the basement to watch a movie."

"Did you hear the Davidsons outside playing?" Hadley asked.

"No," Pauline answered. "Henry installed surround sound speakers in the media room. We couldn't hear any outside noise."

"When did you know something was wrong?" Vince asked.

"We thought we heard someone at the door," Henry said. "I paused the movie, and we heard a gruff knocking. I went upstairs and the police were at the door."

"In the days before Jonah disappeared, did you see anyone unusual hanging around the neighborhood?" Hadley asked. "Maybe watching the Davidson house?"

"No, can't say that I did," Henry said. Pauline shook her head.

"Have you lived in the neighborhood long?" Vince asked.

"Thirty-plus years," Henry said. "I enlisted in the army out of high school. Married Pauline at my first assignment. Did my four years and got out. Used a VA loan to purchase this place in 1987. Only house I've ever owned."

"So, you would have been here the entire time the Davidsons lived across the street," Hadley said. "What do you think happened to Jonah?"

"Oh, I wouldn't have any idea," Pauline said.

"I always thought Neil had something to do with it," Henry said. "He was always a little off. Kidnapping his own son then divorcing his wife wouldn't surprise me."

"A little off in what way?" Vince asked.

"It's hard to say. He had a weird sense of humor. Laughed at things that weren't funny. Always seemed nervous. Sweated a lot, even in the winter." Pauline cast a wary glance at him. "What? It's true."

"What would he have gained by kidnapping Jonah?" Hadley asked.

"Everyone knows he would have lost a custody case," Henry said. "As I said, the guy was strange. Plus, it probably would have come out that he was having an affair. I heard that when they finally divorced, he didn't ask for custody of the girls at all. Maybe he had Jonah stashed somewhere and he's been raising him ever since."

"What do you know about his affair?" Hadley asked. "Do you know who it was with?"

"You really shouldn't talk about this," Pauline said. Henry waved her off.

"I'm not sure what her name was. She worked at the investment firm with him. A financial analyst of some sort. He never told me he was having an affair, mind you. He'd probably deny it. But, there were plenty of rumors about it."

With no additional questions, Hadley thanked them, and she and Vince made their way back to her car. She pulled into a spot in the grocery store parking lot next to Vince's ancient Subaru. They sat in the Jeep for a moment.

"We didn't get very far today," she said.

"No," Vince agreed. "Not exactly a banner day. Any luck in tracking down the babysitter yet?"

"No," Hadley said. "I think we need to talk to the family next. I'll see what I can set up."

"Sounds good. I'm interested in what Neil has to say."

"Me, too," Hadley said. She had a feeling that if anyone had a clue that might break the case open, it was Neil.

# CHAPTER 8

*April 4, 2008*

The snow started falling sometime after midnight. By the time the shouting in the kitchen woke Jenny up, a foot and a half had fallen, crippling the city. The morning sun bounced off the sheet of white surrounding the house, lighting up the sky as if it were the middle of the day.

Jenny shivered in her bed. She put her palm near the window and felt the draft seeping into the house. The voices continued, lower now, but undeniably angry. A door slammed. With a sigh, she pulled her hair into a pony tail and stepped onto the cold of the wood floor. She grabbed a pair of wool socks and padded down the hallway toward the kitchen.

Her mother sat at the table, her head in her hands. Jenny sat down next to her and pulled on the socks. "What's going on?"

"Your father," Lisa answered. "He's being impossible."

"What now?" Jenny asked. Before Lisa could answer, the door from the garage opened and Neil burst into the house, a pair of snowshoes in his hand.

"Neil," Lisa said, "I appreciate what you're doing, but there's no point. It's too cold and snowy, no one else is searching today, and..." her voice trailed off. Jenny knew that the next words would have been something like, "if we haven't found any sign of him in the past week, we won't today in the blizzard."

The color rose in Neil's face and anger flashed through his eyes. He saw Jenny next to Lisa and calmed down. "I won't stop looking until Jonah's home." Jenny watched as he bundled up in a coat, ski mask, and hat. He secured the snowshoes to his boots, pulled on his gloves and stomped out into the snowstorm.

Lisa returned her head to her hands. "He's going to freeze to death out there."

"He just misses Jonah, Mom," Jenny said. "He's trying. Go easy on him."

Lisa looked at her, the circles under her eyes more pronounced than ever. She took a deep breath, then blew it out. "You're probably right."

Jenny peered into the refrigerator, looking for the yogurt among all the casserole dishes sent by friends and neighbors. "Want some breakfast?"

"No thanks."

Jenny gazed at her mother. She hadn't seen her eat since Jonah had disappeared. She'd lost weight and looked frail. "How about some toast?"

Lisa shrugged; Jenny found the bread and dropped two slices in the toaster. While it heated, Jenny wandered to the living room and peered out the blinds. Two news vans sat outside, snow piled high on their hoods and roofs. A camera man struggled to brush snow from a windshield. A gust of wind blew a pile of snow off the house; it fell in front of the window creating a momentary curtain.

"Some of the reporters left," Jenny said.

"Yeah," Lisa answered. "I think the blizzard is going to be the big story today instead of Jonah."

Jenny came back to the kitchen to finish making the toast and saw the tears streaking down her mother's cheeks. Jenny wondered if their lives would ever return to normal. She wished she could go back to the day of the disappearance and run outside as soon as Lisa came in with Sara. She wished she could lock her eyes on Jonah and never let him out of her sight.

The tears welled in her own eyes and spilled down her face as she wondered where Jonah was and prayed he was alright.

# CHAPTER 9

*October 14, 2023*

"I know he's not your favorite person right now, but I wish Eddie were with us for this one," Vince said as he moved a chair next to Hadley's and squeezed behind her desk. "He always has a good perspective."

Hadley didn't respond. She raised the cover of her laptop and hit the power button. The machine whirred to life. Vince's phone chirped with a text alert.

"Speak of the devil," he said. "He says he has a breakthrough on Fork Lift." A moment later, his phone chimed again. This time, Eddie sent three photos. The first showed the former fork lift operator climbing out of a Jeep Wrangler, dressed in tactical shorts and a bright red T-shirt. He wore Oakley sunglasses and shouldered a backpack.

The second photo showed him at the base of a red rock formation. He knelt next to his pack, withdrawing a helmet and coil of rope.

The third photo was further away, but the red T-shirt halfway up the rock face was unmistakable.

Another text came in. "Got some better action shots with the telephoto lens. I'll have to send them to you once I download the card."

Vince texted back. "Great work! That should wrap this one up!"

He filled Hadley in on the development as she navigated to Zoom and signed in. "He does good field work," she conceded. She clicked the link for their meeting, and the camera came to life, displaying an image of the two of them. Vince adjusted his chair to bring his face fully into the frame.

A second box appeared on the screen, followed by the image of a fit-looking man. Neil Davidson was in his early 60s. His dark hair had gone gray at the temples. He wore a pair of rectangular-framed glasses. He had tanned skin and wore a navy blue blazer with a light blue, open-collar shirt underneath.

"Good afternoon," he said. "Thanks for meeting with me over Zoom. Since I moved to Fort Collins to run our branch here, I've had to work every day. I don't know when I'll get back down to Denver."

"It's not a problem," Hadley said. "It's the way of the world now." She introduced herself and Vince and explained that they had been retained by his daughter, Jenny.

"Before we start," Neil said, "I just want you to know that I'll do anything in my power to help you find Jonah."

They started with basic questions, establishing how long the family had lived in Park Hill when Jonah disappeared and that he'd been working the day that it happened.

"According to the police report we read, your firm couldn't account for where you were that afternoon," Vince said. "The report says your afternoon appointment canceled." Hadley thought she saw a cloud of anger pass over Neil's face, but he recovered quickly.

"That was a miscommunication," he said. "I had a client cancel, but while I was across town, I met with another client in the area. I was with him when I got the frantic phone call from Jenny telling me to come home."

"I apologize if these next questions are uncomfortable," Hadley said, "but they'll help us understand the context surrounding the case."

"I think I know where you're going, and as I said, I'll do anything I can to help you."

"We've heard rumors you were having an affair with a co-worker. Have you heard those rumors before?"

"Yes," Neil said. "They aren't just rumors. They're true."

Hadley cast a quick glance at Vince, who looked as surprised as she felt.

"I'm not proud of it," Neil continued. "But, things weren't great between Lisa and me. They hadn't been in a while. We had talked about separating before Jonah was kidnapped. People think losing him is what ultimately drove us apart, but we were destined to split."

"We haven't been able to find the name of your, um, the woman you were having an affair with," Hadley said. "Could you share that information with us?"

"No," Neil said. He took off his glasses and wiped them on the inside of his blazer. He stared into the screen with his slate gray eyes. "I said I'd do anything I could to help you find Jonah. So, answer this for me. What bearing does my affair or who I was cheating on Lisa with have on the case?"

"It's another person with a connection to you and your family," Hadley said. "That's one more person who might remember something, any little detail, that will point us in the right direction."

Neil put his glasses back on and shook his head. "She didn't know my family. Didn't even know where we lived. She knew I had kids but didn't know their names or ages. We weren't planning on getting married or running off together. The fact is, the police used the allegations of me having an affair to focus the investigation on me, as if I'd kidnap my own child. And, while they were focusing on the absolute wrong person, an actual kidnapper escaped and the trail got colder every day. The police failed in their investigation because they got distracted by something that had no bearing on the case. Don't make the same mistake." He jabbed a thick forefinger at the table, punctuating each word in the final sentence with a tap.

"Can you think of anyone else who might have had a reason to abduct Jonah?" Vince asked.

"No," Neil said. "And, that's the point, isn't it? Very early on, the police decided it was a family-involved kidnapping and refused to look for suspects in a random case. But, that's what this was—a random crime that could have happened to anyone."

Vince nodded and bit the end of his pen. "I get your perspective," he said, "but, bear with me a moment longer. What about at work? Any clients or co-workers who had a problem with you in the days or weeks leading up to the disappearance?"

Neil shook his head. Then he gave a short chuckle. "There was this one client, but it was after the kidnapping. Jeremy Costas. He had some money when he came to us, and I helped him build a portfolio that made him rich."

"You don't mean *the* Jeremy Costas?" Hadley interrupted. "The guy in the solar industry?"

"Same guy," Neil said. "I never had a problem with him until after Jonah went missing. As I said, I made the guy rich, and then he took that money, invested it in himself and his solar panel business, and became a gazillionaire. Well, when Jonah was taken, I took a leave of absence. I spent the first week with the search parties, combing every inch of the neighborhood, going to nearby parks and playgrounds, abandoned buildings. Work was the last thing on my mind. One day, I get a call on my cell, and it's from Jeremy. I'd been ignoring work calls, but this is our richest client, and in the back of my mind I was hoping he'd help. Offer a reward. Buy us a helicopter or a team of dogs. Something.

"But, no. He wanted to talk about his portfolio. I told him I couldn't and referred him to a colleague who was covering my clients. I explained what happened to Jonah. He said he was taking his money and getting away from the firm. He wanted to go somewhere else where he'd be the top priority. He had a lot of nerve. Last time I talked to him. Only client I ever had that kind of confrontation with."

Hadley thanked him for his time and concluded the interview. "You have my contact information," she said. "If you think of anything else that might help, anyone else we should talk to, please let me know."

Neil nodded. "Can I ask how the investigation is going?"

"Not a lot we can tell you at this point," Hadley said. "But, we're finding what the police found 15 years ago. There aren't clues. There's just not much to go on, and to be honest, it feels like we're grasping at straws."

Neil nodded again, the sadness apparent on his face.

She clicked off the call, and Vince moved his chair to the other side of her desk. "What do you think?" he asked.

"I think Eddie wouldn't have liked what he had to say about the police."

Vince laughed. "They're polar opposites on that. But, do you think Neil has a point? Are we wasting time by investigating the family-involved angle?"

Hadley leaned back in her chair and looked up at the ceiling. The water stains in the plaster had always bothered her. "It's always worth re-investigating what the police looked at, in case they missed something that could open the case. And, if it was truly a random, spur-of-the-moment thing, then I don't know where we'd even start. There's no physical evidence. No surveillance video. No eyewitnesses. We've got nothing to go on."

"So, what are our next steps?"

"I'm setting up interviews with Lisa and Jenny. I'm hoping we can do them both at Jenny's place. I'd like to talk to Sara, too, but Jenny told me she hasn't cooperated with previous detectives. Says she doesn't want to relive the trauma from that day."

"Understandable," Vince said. "And, I wonder how much she'd remember that could help. But, it's worth a shot. I'm going to need a few days to work on that infidelity case."

On the drive home, Hadley racked her brain for ways they could expand the investigation to account for a stranger abducting Jonah. She thought back to true crime podcasts she'd listened to and discussion threads on the Citizen Detective website. She continued to come up empty.

Normally a meek driver, she laid into her horn when a BMW pulled directly in front of her and she had to tap her brakes. The frustration from the case tightened her shoulders and neck.

As she neared her exit, she saw a billboard for JC Alternative Energies, complete with Jeremy Costas' face smiling down at her. She thought back to Neil's story about him. Jeremy didn't come across as a jerk in any of the commercials she'd seen him in, but that was just TV. Or, maybe he'd grown up some in the past 15 years. She didn't see how his insensitive behavior toward Neil had anything to do with the case, but it was an odd detail for Neil to hang onto all these years. She knew that's how tragedy worked, though.

She pulled into her street determined to spend the afternoon getting Lisa and Jenny scheduled and looking for Monica Jones, the babysitter, and Gary Brice, the retired police detective. After that, she'd put the case away for the rest of the weekend and use Sunday to relax. She needed a day away from the case to approach it with fresh eyes.

# CHAPTER 10

*October 17, 2023*

Jenny Davidson lived in a condo in Denver's posh Cherry Creek neighborhood. The complex had a controlled entrance, so Hadley pressed the button to call Jenny's unit and waited to be buzzed in. Once inside, she strode toward the bank of elevators, her footsteps echoing on the dark hardwood floors. Everything about the place, from the floors to the artwork on the walls to the crystal chandeliers, said it was expensive.

An elevator dinged, and Jenny stepped out, accompanied by an older woman who Hadley assumed was her mother.

"I thought we could meet down here at the coffee bar, as long as no one else is around," Jenny said. "This is my mom, Lisa. Mom, this is Hadley Collins. We went to high school together, but I don't think you met her back then."

Hadley and Lisa shook hands. Hadley could have responded that while she and Jenny went to the same school, they certainly didn't go "together" and she absolutely would not have been introduced to Lisa in those days. She let it pass and followed Jenny down the corridor to the coffee bar.

It looked like a miniature Starbucks, minus the barista. A counter along the wall held oversized urns, labeled as dark roast, medium roast, decaf, and hazelnut. There was also an espresso machine and a single cup coffee maker with a variety of pods.

The refrigerator was stocked with milk, heavy cream, half and half, oat milk, almond milk, and a variety of flavored creamers.

"What would you like?" Jenny asked. "I like the dark roast best, with the ginger bread creamer."

"Dark roast is fine," Hadley said. "I'll take it black."

While Jenny and Lisa filled coffee cups, Hadley turned to the seating area. A long communal table ran the length of the far wall, with four tables for four between it and the coffee station. Hadley took a seat at the end of the long table. Jenny and Lisa followed.

"If you don't mind, I'd actually like to talk to each of you separately," Hadley said, withdrawing a notepad from her purse.

"There's nothing you can ask me that I can't answer in front of Jenny," Lisa replied.

"It's not that," Hadley said. "Sometimes, two people will remember the same event differently. And the difference could end up being a clue or highlighting a detail that might get overlooked. We have a better chance of uncovering those differences if I interview you separately."

Lisa did not look convinced. "It's okay, Mom," Jenny said. "I need to make a couple of work calls, anyway. I'll go back upstairs and you can come get me when Hadley's ready."

With that she strode out of the corridor. Hadley heard the elevator chime a moment later. She looked at the woman in front of her. Like her children, Lisa had blond hair, though it had started to gray. She had deep crows' feet around her eyes that showed despite the considerable amount of makeup she wore. She dressed in jeans and a T-shirt with the Colorado flag emblazoned on the front.

"Thanks for meeting with me," Hadley began. "Some of what I need to ask you today might bring up unpleasant memories or be difficult to answer, and I apologize for that in advance. I ask that you trust me, though, and answer thoroughly and honestly."

She asked Lisa to walk her through Jonah's disappearance, starting with going outside. Her story matched the police report and the reports from the previous detectives. "Any idea how long you were inside before you remembered Jonah and asked Jenny to go get him?"

Lisa closed her eyes and took a deep breath. She turned her body slightly away from Hadley, as if trying to protect herself. When she opened her eyes, Hadley saw that they brimmed with tears, so she fished a packet of tissue from her purse and extended it toward Lisa.

"I don't know how I forgot about him," she said. "I'm his mom. It's my job to protect him."

"You had your hands full at the moment," Hadley reminded her.

Lisa fumbled with the tissue packet until she withdrew one and dabbed at her eyes. "It couldn't have been much more than a minute. Maybe a minute and a half? It wasn't long."

"When you were outside with the kids, did you notice anything unusual? Any people or vehicles that seemed like they didn't belong?"

She shook her head. "We were alone out there. I remember thinking that was weird because it was spring break and the first nice day. But, most of our neighbors with kids went out of town. We had planned a trip to San Diego, but Neil called it off because he was busy with work."

Hadley made a note of that. They hadn't heard that detail before. "And, after Jenny said she couldn't find Jonah, did you notice anyone outside? Anyone near the house?"

Lisa touched the tissue to her eyes again. "No," she said. "I was in a panic. Jenny was looking in the house, and I ran down the street, down to both corners. I didn't see Jonah, and there wasn't anyone else around. If there had been, I would have asked them to help or if they had seen Jonah."

"What do you think happened?" Hadley asked. "I'm sure you've thought about a lot over the years. Where should we focus?"

Lisa turned her body some more; she was nearly perpendicular to Hadley at that point and didn't attempt eye contact. "It's all I think about," she said. "Every day, I replay what happened and think about what I could have done differently and how we can get Jonah back. I think you should focus on Neil."

Hadley usually kept her composure, but she was not expecting that response. She drew in a sharp breath.

"It doesn't make sense that a stranger would do it," Lisa said. "It doesn't make sense that someone with no connection to us would just happen to be around the one minute that Jonah wasn't in my sight. I think Neil arranged for someone to take Jonah. Probably from our room during his nap. And the kidnapper was watching us to decide when to make the move. And, I made it easier for him."

"But, why would Neil do that?"

"I think he wanted to start over again with Jonah."

"But, he never did that."

Lisa finally turned her body back to face Hadley. "I think something went wrong. If I'm totally honest with myself, that's the only thing that makes sense. Something happened, and Jonah didn't make it." She looked down and her shoulders began shaking as she silently sobbed. She grasped a handful of tissues, tossing the empty wrapper aside, and blotted at her face. When she looked up again, she was a mess of mascara and splotchy foundation.

"Something bad happened to Jonah, and Neil walked away from the whole thing."

Hadley reached across the table and gave Lisa's hand a light squeeze. "I appreciate you sharing that with me," she said.

"That's not easy to say. Have you shared that theory with anyone else? The police or other private detectives?"

Lisa shook her head. "The police were already looking at Neil. The detective, Gary, told me he was their number one suspect. That was after Gary had been taken off the case. And, with the other private detectives, what was the point? It wouldn't bring Jonah back."

The two sat in silence for a long moment. Hadley finally spoke. "I appreciate you taking the time to meet with me today. Here's my card if you think of anything else that might help us investigate the case." She slid her business card across the table. Lisa stared at it without moving, and Hadley thought she might refuse it, but she finally clutched it. "Before you go get Jenny, there's one other thing. Do you remember Monica Jones? She used to babysit for you. We can't find her anywhere."

Lisa smiled. "I always liked Monica. She was a few years older than Jenny. Moved to Denver for college, and she and a few of her classmates rented a house a few blocks over. We met at the farmers market one weekend, and I started hiring her when Jenny wasn't available to watch Sara and Jonah. Didn't use her very often; it's not like Neil and I were having many date nights. That's a whole other story. Anyway, I lost track of her after Jonah. No idea where she went or what she's up to now."

"Did you do a background check on her? Anything like that?"

"Heavens, no! We were neighbors. I trusted people back then. I guess I shouldn't have."

They sat in silence again, the awkward tension growing by the moment. "I'll go get Jenny," Lisa said. She walked toward the elevators, leaving a coffee cup and a pile of tissues at her place. Hadley gathered the trash and threw it out while she prepared for the conversation with Jenny. She refilled her coffee and settled in, turning her notepad to a fresh page.

The ding of the elevator and the tapping of footsteps announced Jenny's arrival. She poured another coffee and took the seat Lisa had been in a few minutes before. Hadley gave her a brief update on the case, explaining who they'd talked to so far and who was left to interview. She told Jenny she didn't have much hope they'd gain any new leads that would help with locating Jonah.

"How was the interview with my dad?"

"It was okay," Hadley said. "He was helpful, for the most part. He definitely has a perspective on what happened."

"And my mom's was totally different."

"Exactly."

Jenny took a long sip of coffee. She furrowed her brow and then relaxed. All expression had left her face. "I should have warned you that the family doesn't like the idea of a detective re-investigating the case. I mean, we all want to find Jonah. Every single one of us thinks about it every day. But, there's a lot of pain that gets revisited every time someone asks questions."

"So, why hire us?" Hadley asked.

"I read about the case you all solved with the senate candidate. It was a cold case like this one. I thought, why not try? I can't think of a better way to spend my money than on the possibility of finding Jonah."

She stood and paced in front of the table. She paused and gripped the back of a chair with both hands. "My dad must have told you that he thinks a stranger took Jonah. And, from the state my mom was in when she came upstairs just now, I'm sure she told you that she thinks my dad had it done. Whoever took Jonah didn't just kidnap him; they ruined a family. They split my parents up, derailed my senior year and college plans. I think Sara still sees a therapist about the whole thing. And, while my dad and Sara have both moved, my mom and I can't leave Denver because what if Jonah shows up out of the blue one day?" She paced some more, her gait taking on a frenetic energy. She stopped again, shoving a chair out of the way and leaning on the table, both palms down, her face just inches from Hadley's. Her voice came out in a strangled whisper.

"I hate to think of what Jonah's been through. I hope whoever took him has given him a good life, but I've read enough about kidnappings to know that's a fool's hope. My heart breaks every day when I think about him being captive. But, he's not the only captive. All of us are, the whole family. We live normal lives on the outside, for the most part, but inside…we're all prisoners chained to that moment when I went out the front door and he wasn't in the yard."

"Jenny," Hadley said. "I get it. I really do. I probably understand what you're saying right now better than anyone else. So, believe me, I will do whatever I can to break this case open. Now, is there anything you haven't told anyone before, the police or the other detectives, that might help me out? No detail is too insignificant."

Jenny slumped into a chair and took another sip of coffee. "No," she said. "I went outside. There was no one there. I mean, no one. Not Jonah, not another soul. I looked around the sides of the house, and I went inside to tell my mom. She ran outside, and I searched inside the house, in case he had wandered in behind her."

"You never saw or heard a car during the time you were looking for Jonah?"

Jenny shook her head no.

"So, what do you think happened?"

"What am I supposed to think? One of my parents thinks the other one did it. I don't know how to wrap my head around that. I have a hard time believing my dad could have been involved, even if he was a jerk to my mom."

"Why do you say that?"

"Just that he was cheating on her. He was always rude to her. Took her for granted."

"So, if he didn't do it…"

"Who did? No idea. My theory has always been that a stranger took him, but I can't make that make sense. The odds of a kidnapper being on our street at that exact moment. Especially since no one else saw or heard anything."

Hadley nodded. "This is tricky. Everyone we've talked to has been cooperative, except Sara. I haven't been able to get her to return my calls or texts. Oh, and the Barretts."

"Who?"

"The people who moved into your old house. In Park Hill."

"How could they help? They didn't move in until years later."

"I wanted to see the inside of the house. Just to put myself in the moment. They wouldn't let me."

"I could see if we have any old photos or anything that show what the inside looked like."

"Yeah, that might help."

Jenny looked up and a smile crossed her face. "Wait. Two birds with one stone. I think Sara has a video that would show you what the house was like." She took out her phone and scrolled through her contacts. She held the phone to her ear. "Hey, Sara. How's it going?" She listened for a minute and laughed. "That's good to hear. Listen, and I mean it, don't hang up. I'm here with Hadley Collins, who's a detective, and we think you can help with her investigation. Remember that home movie from your birthday party? We need it."

The smile evaporated from her face, and a patch of red, like a heat rash, began crawling up Jenny's neck as she listened to her sister. "I don't know why you won't talk to her. You can do it over the phone." She listened for another moment, then snapped, "Well, you were there when he disappeared. You never talk about it; maybe if you did, you'd remember something that would help us find him." She looked at Hadley, a fury in her eyes, as Sara talked on the other end of the call. "Well, you can at least share the video with us."

She swung the phone so the mouthpiece was no longer near her lips, while keeping the earpiece pressed to her head. She mouthed, "She doesn't want the tape to get lost" to Hadley.

"Put her on speaker," Hadley said.

"Sara. Sara, stop talking for a minute and listen. I'm going to put you on speaker, so you can explain to Hadley why you don't want to help." She set the phone on the table between them. Sara began talking, her voice thin and reedy over the phone's speaker.

"I watch that video a lot. Maybe once a month, sometimes more. I still have a VCR so I can play it. I'm not sending it to you. Nothing against you. I'm sure you'd take good care of it. But, things get lost in the mail. Packages get damaged. There are porch pirates. I'm not doing it."

"Sara, this is Hadley. The last thing I want to do is lose or damage something that means that much to you. I think I can help you out. If I can get you in touch with a place in your area that will convert the tape to a digital file, would you do it? I'd pay for it, and you'd be welcome to a digital copy, too. Then you don't have to mail anything; you could email it. And, you'd have a backup in case anything ever happens to your tape."

Sara didn't respond. The silence hung in the air. Hadley checked the phone to make sure they were still connected. "There's no risk to you," she said. "The bigger risk is that your VCR will break and eat the tape one day." She felt like a high-pressure saleswoman as soon as she said it and hated herself for it.

"Okay," Sara said, her voice small and the angry tone gone. "If you send me the information, I'll do it."

"Hadley will text you. You need to take the tape in right away when she does," Jenny said, sounding like an older sister bossing her younger sister around.

"Fine," Sara said. "I'll talk to you later."

With that, the call ended. Hadley promised to be in touch again soon and departed the condo. The wind had picked up while she was inside, and she could feel a cold front blowing in. She wished she'd brought a jacket or sweatshirt.

Safely inside her car, she opened the notes app on her phone and made a to-do list. Up first was to find VHS-to-digital conversion near Sara's place in San Diego. Second was to look for Monica Jones. Knowing that Monica had been a college student renting in Park Hill helped. She could search alumni newsletters for the Denver area colleges to see if she could find what Monica was up to these days. If she'd taken a married name, it would be helpful to learn that, too.

She needed to find Gary Brice, the police detective. She added that to the list with a groan, knowing what she'd need to do. And, the fourth thing was to talk to her partners about Neil Davidson canceling a vacation that would have taken the family far away from the kidnapping site.

She started on the first and third items before she left. She opened a web browser and navigated to the Citizen Detective website. Logging in as MileHighMarlowe, she posted a new thread on the discussion board:

"Hey, guys! MHM here. It's been a while, and I need a favor. I need someone in the San Diego area, preferably near the Gas Lamp District, who can convert a VHS tape to a digital file. I can't over-stress how important it is that the tape be returned to the owner in pristine condition. If you know someone who could do the work (and fast), let me know."

She hit post and opened her text messages. She started a new message to Eddie. "Still trying 2 track down Gary Brice. Can u help? Anyone at DPD who can help?" As much as she hated to admit it, having a former police officer for a partner came with some distinct advantages. He could often get information that she and Vince never could, no matter how clever they were.

The reply buzzed seconds later. "Sure thing. I'll jump on it right now since it's for my favorite private eye (don't tell Vince I said that)."

She didn't know why, and she knew Eddie meant well, but comments like that grated on her nerves. She was thankful for his help, but she wished she didn't need to ask for it.

She started the car, turned up the music, and began the drive home. By the time she got there, she had three replies from Citizen Detective. Two of them recommended A-Plus Digital Marketing. PadrePete, a Citizen Detective member she'd given advice to on a couple of cases in the past, said that if she told A-Plus that Pete Morales had sent her, they'd make the job a priority. She wondered what kind of relationship PadrePete had with a digital marketing company that would carry that kind of cachet. She copied the business's contact information and pasted it in a text message. She hoped Sara would follow through. She knew she was putting a lot of effort into something that might not produce a lead, but working cases over the years had taught her to cover all bases.

The interactions on Citizen Detective made her miss the days when solving crimes was her hobby. She could take the cases she wanted and didn't have to answer to anyone. And, she belonged to a great online community that always offered help and support when she got stuck. Not that she didn't love doing detective work full time, but she felt like some of the magic had disappeared. Maybe solving this case would bring it back.

She pondered posting a thread about Jonah's kidnapping and seeing if any amateur sleuths out there had any bright ideas. She ultimately decided against it. She didn't like giving out too many specifics on a case, especially early on when she still didn't know which details mattered.

She set her laptop on the kitchen counter and placed a kettle of water on the stove. She tossed a bag of chamomile in a tea cup.

While she waited for the water to boil, she started up her laptop and opened a web browser. She had a list of Denver-area colleges on her notepad. She started at the University of Denver's alumni page. It was a long shot she'd find Monica this way, but at least it was something she could do on this case that felt productive.

# CHAPTER 11

*April 9, 2008*

Hadley took her sack lunch to an open spot at the end of a long table in the school cafeteria. Many of her classmates had opted to eat outside and take advantage of the sunny afternoon, leaving plenty of empty seats inside. She had long given up on anyone joining her for lunch, so she opened a paperback, a guide to coding and programming, and emptied the contents of her sack onto the table. She had a turkey sandwich, an apple, and a bag of chips. She started with the sandwich, absent-mindedly chewing as she flipped through the book.

A chair scraped on the linoleum floor; she looked up to see Jenny Davidson directly across from her. "Do you mind if I sit here?" Jenny asked. She looked different, older, than she had the last time Hadley had seen her. She had a heaviness in her eyes that Hadley always associated with people her grandparents' age. Hadley shook her head.

As Jenny settled into the chair, Hadley said, "I'm surprised you're not eating with them." She nodded her head toward a noisy table filled with female athletes—basketball, volleyball, and soccer players.

Jenny gave a half smile and replied, "I'm not in the mood for all the excitement today."

Behind them a girl screamed as a boy chased her with a water bottle. "I guess there's no escaping the excitement here," Hadley said. Jenny didn't answer. Hadley continued, "How have you been?"

She had followed the story of Jonah in the news. It had been on TV for nearly every newscast for two weeks, though the stories were coming later in each broadcast and getting shorter. They'd stopped doing live shots from outside the Davidson house. They always ran the photo of Jonah, the one of him smiling open-mouthed in his high chair, a cupcake in front of him and chocolate icing on his chin.

"I'm okay," Jenny said. "I'm way behind in all my classes. I thought about not coming back to school at all, but being here is…" She trailed off not finishing the sentence. Hadley thought she was going to say that coming to school was better than being at home. She couldn't imagine the tension running through the Davidson home.

They sat without saying anything else for a few minutes, the silence interrupted only by the crunch of Hadley's apple. She noticed that Jenny had brought a sad-looking sandwich, two pieces of rubbery lunch meat on mushy bread. She didn't see any other food at Jenny's place, so she slid the bag of chips across the table.

"You can have these," she said. "My mom worries that I'm not eating enough, so she throws things in my bag when I'm not looking."

"Thanks." Jenny opened the bag, the wrapper crinkling in her hands. She nibbled at a chip. "You're the photographer, right?" she asked after a moment. "For the school paper?"

"I'm one of them," Hadley said. "I didn't know I was going to get stuck doing stuff like that when I signed up for journalism."

"I always thought it looked like fun," Jenny said.

"It can be," Hadley said. She looked away for a second. "When I'm not tripping the star athlete in the middle of a play."

Jenny laughed. Her eyes lit up, and for a moment she looked like herself again. It didn't last long. The old-woman eyes returned. Jenny looked down and rested her forehead on her hands. "I feel guilty when I enjoy something," she said without looking up. "Like I'm doing something wrong."

"Your brother would want you to be happy," Hadley said. Jenny didn't move. Hadley thought about telling Jenny her story but held back.

"Thanks for the chips," Jenny said, standing suddenly, the half-empty bag clutched in her hand. She picked up her books and trudged out of the cafeteria. One of the girls from the athlete table noticed her and called after her, but Jenny trudged on, out the door.

Hadley didn't see her at school for another week.

# CHAPTER 12

*October 20, 2023*

Eddie's booming laugh announced his presence in the office. Hadley smelled the coffee brewing a minute later. Unlike most recent occasions, she was happy to have him there that morning. She needed to get him and Vince to lay eyes on the video. She gathered her laptop and a folder and found her two partners at the card table.

Despite the cold snap, Eddie still wore a Hawaiian shirt, the top two buttons left open, his chest hair billowing out. Hadley bit back a comment. Vince wore jeans and a sweater, much more appropriate for the office. She took her seat between them.

"Well, kids, what do you have this time?" Eddie asked. Hadley looked at Vince, signaling for him to go first.

"Well, our latest Infidelity Guy is definitely up to something. From the looks of things, his co-worker is about half his age. They've spent a lot of time together the past couple of days. I mean, they work together, so that's to be expected, but they had lunch together each of the past two days. Yesterday, he called his wife to say he had to work late and not to wait on him for dinner. He didn't stay at the office. He went to dinner with the co-worker and spent two hours at her apartment before going home."

"Maybe they were working at her place," Eddie said, giving a sarcastic sneer.

"I'd be shocked," Vince said.

"Sounds like he's another Neil Davidson," Hadley said.

"Men are pigs," Eddie said.

"I got pictures of them going into dinner and into the apartment building. I'll hang around for a couple more days to see if I get anything more incriminating, and then I'll turn everything over to our client. I gotta tell you, these cheaters just suck out my soul."

"That's the job," Eddie said. "What about you, Hadley? Any updates on the Davidsons?"

"You go first," she said.

Eddie frowned at her, but said, "Sure. I gave the photos of Fork Lift guy to his company. Here, check these out." Eddie spread a few prints out across the table. Hadley recognized the pictures he'd texted Vince before, but he'd added a few he'd taken with a telephoto lens. It was definitely the same guy, and he was definitely climbing rocks in a way that seemed incompatible with his injury settlement. "They're negotiating with his lawyer now, but it sounds like they're going to get back everything paid to him for the injury in exchange for not making this a criminal matter."

"That's good work, Eddie," Vince said.

"It gets better. They're so happy with us, the company is going to give us a bonus. I love bonuses." He turned to Hadley. "And, I've got something for you, too."

"What's that?"

"Gary Brice. I scored some contact info for him." He pulled an envelope from his breast pocket and slid it across the table. "He's out of the country through the rest of the week, though. Turns out the guy is the literal salt of the earth. He's in Guatemala building an orphanage. How's that for a retirement activity?"

Hadley looked at Eddie's scrawl on the back of the envelope. She had an address, email, and cell phone number for him. "I owe you one," she said.

"We're all one happy team," he said. "Now, you must have something big, if you wanted to go last."

"Well, I don't know if it's big," Hadley said. "Actually, I don't know if I even have anything. Here, watch this."

She opened the laptop and turned it to where Vince and Eddie could both see it. She pulled up a media file and hit play. A grainy video played, showing a ton of kids crammed into a living room. Boys and girls, who looked to be five or six years old, crowded onto a couch and chairs and lined the floor in front of the couch. The camera turned toward the fireplace, where a magician performed.

"This is Sara Davidson's sixth birthday," Hadley said. "Three months before Jonah disappeared. I wanted to see what the inside of the house looked like."

The video continued; the magician made flowers disappear out of a vase, and the kids all screamed their approval. The camera panned from the magician to the kids, taking in a wider angle of the living room than before. Neil and Lisa Davidson stood behind the couch. Jonah was positioned near a wall, sitting in a high chair. A woman stood next to him.

The video played on, the camera panning back and forth from kids to magician. They watched him do a variety of tricks: cutting a rope and turning the two pieces back into one, making a ball levitate over his table, and, finally, pulling a rabbit out of a hat, putting it back, and making it reappear in a cage.

The kids cheered, Neil and Lisa clapped politely, and Jonah banged on the high chair tray. Jenny, who was operating the camera, went from the living room, around a corner, into the kitchen, filming the whole time. She got a shot of the three-dimensional birthday cake, a top hat with a rabbit popping out holding a magic wand, then the video stopped. Hadley looked at the two men.

"I'm not sure you have anything there," Eddie said.

"The kitchen is around the corner from the living room," Vince said. "It looked like you could see the front door from a certain angle on the couch, but if Lisa came running in with Sara screaming and went straight to the kitchen and Jenny followed, they definitely couldn't have seen anything happening outside. Probably couldn't have heard anything, either."

"True," Eddie said. "But, I don't know if that helps."

"Watch again," Hadley said. This time, she navigated to a specific time stamp and covered all but a sliver of screen on the right-hand side with her folder.

"That's Jonah," Vince said. "Who's the woman next to him?"

"She seems really interested in Jonah," Eddie added.

"Keep watching," Hadley said. She jumped forward to another time stamp.

"There she is again," Vince said. "What's that in her hand?"

The video moved away, and Vince and Eddie both said, "Rewind it."

"Can you do slow motion?" Eddie asked. "Move it forward one frame at a time."

Hadley did what he asked. They watched the video move forward frame by frame. The woman wore a dark gray cardigan, and she removed an object from her pocket. Hadley kept the screen on that frame as they all stared at it. In the next frames, the woman turned her body, so her back was between the video camera and Jonah. She was only on the edge of the frame to begin with, so it was hard to see what was happening. The woman's arm bent at a right angle to her body.

"It looks like she's saluting," Vince said.

Hadley advanced another frame.

"Stop!" Eddie yelled. "Look at that, surrounding her face."

"It's like she has a halo," Hadley said. They all peered at the screen.

"Can you grab a screen shot?" Eddie asked.

Hadley gave a quick key stroke and pasted the screen capture on a blank slide. She cropped the photo, so it only contained the woman and Jonah, and blew it up as big as she could. The image blurred as she did so, but there was no mistaking that a ring of light surrounded her head.

"I knew there was something off about this video," Hadley said. "Now it makes sense."

"What would cause that kind of lighting?" Eddie asked, oblivious to Hadley's comment.

"Maybe the magician did something and it's a reflection of that," Vince said.

"You two are detectives, right?" Hadley said. "She pulled something out of her pocket. She moved her hand to her face. Then there's an explosion of light. There's a pretty good bet that whatever she pulled out of her pocket and held near her face is the source of the light."

"Camera," Vince and Eddie said in unison.

Hadley nodded. "I completely missed it when I watched it at full speed. Even at half speed I didn't see what happened. It wasn't until we slowed it down frame by frame that I saw it." She went back to the video and played it from the beginning. On the camera's first pass by Jonah the woman looked up, and her full face was visible. Hadley took another screen capture and pasted it into a slide.

After a moment of cropping and adjusting, she had as clear of a blow up of the woman's face as they would get from the video. She texted it to Jenny Davidson.

Two minutes later, her phone rang. Hadley put it on speaker. "Hey, Jenny. I'm here with Eddie and Vince."

"Where'd you get that photo?" Jenny asked.

"It's a screen grab from the birthday video Sara sent me," Hadley answered. The seconds ticked by in silence while they waited on a response. "Jenny?"

"Sorry. I took the videos at the party. That was my job for the day. I guess it completely slipped my mind that she was there. There were like 30 kids there. I think every kid from Sara's class showed up, so it was hard to focus on anything we were doing with them screaming all the time."

"Who is this person?" Vince asked.

Jenny laughed. "Creepy Mary. Sorry, that's what the kids in the neighborhood called her. I think Mary was her real name, but I don't know her last name."

"Creepy Mary?" Eddie asked.

"She worked as a house cleaner in the neighborhood. There were rumors she hung out in kids' rooms. Looked at their clothes, played with their toys. I don't think there's anything to that. How would the kids even know?"

"What was she doing at Sara's birthday party?" Hadley asked. "Was she a friend of the family?"

"No, nothing like that. I'm guessing Dad hired her to help manage with all the kids there. Maybe clean up as we went. I bet if you showed this picture to him, he could tell you her real name. Or, at least he could tell you who referred her to him. We never hired anyone to clean the house normally, so he probably asked around for recommendations."

They thanked her and clicked off the call. "I still don't know if this is anything helpful," Hadley said, "but, it's a lead to follow up on."

"For sure," Eddie said. "A stranger you hired to work at the party spends the day hanging out with your two year old? And takes his picture? You know what I'd call that?"

"Creepy?" Vince said.

"Bingo."

"Sorry to break up the comedy hour," Hadley said. "But, I'm going to try to get Neil Davidson to join a Zoom, so we can show him the picture. Why don't you two join from Vince's office? I'd like to get a read on his facial expressions when he sees Creepy Mary's photo."

With that, the two men shuffled toward Vince's office, while Hadley set up in hers. She started with a phone call to Neil's office. The woman who answered wouldn't commit to Neil being in the office or not, just that he was too busy to take a call. Hadley tried his cell phone next. He answered on the third ring.

"Mr. Davidson? It's Hadley Collins. I'm the detective you talked to a few days ago."

"I remember who you are, Ms. Collins."

"I'm hoping you have a few minutes to join a quick videoconference with my colleagues and me."

"I have a full plate today. I could text you some times next week that might work."

"We have a potential lead in the case, and we need to discuss it with you."

"What kind of lead?"

"I can explain better in a video call. I need to share my screen to show you what we're looking at."

"I'm driving to a client meeting. I should be there in 15 minutes, and I'll have about 10 minutes to talk to you. Send the meeting link to this number."

He clicked off the call. Exactly 15 minutes later, Hadley joined a Zoom call from her office. A second later, Eddie's face filled the screen.

"Is Vince with you?"

"I'm here," Vince said. "There's not much room in here, so I'm just going to watch over his shoulder."

After another minute, Neil Davidson appeared on the screen. "I don't have much time," he said.

"This won't take long," Hadley said. She clicked an icon to share an image, and the blow-up photo of the woman from the party appeared. "Do you recognize this woman?"

Neil's expression didn't change. He leaned forward, his forehead growing larger as he peered at the screen. He moved back and nodded. "She looks familiar. She cleaned some houses in the neighborhood. I hired her once."

"We got this picture of her from Lisa's birthday party."

Neil took off his glasses. He looked sad, on the verge of tears. "A few months before Jonah disappeared, we had this big party for Sara. Invited the whole class, but we had no idea they'd all show. I hired this woman to help clean up afterward. There was some kind of miscommunication, and she showed up right as the party was starting. We just had her stay through the whole thing."

"Do you know her name?"

"I think her first name was Mary. Maria. Marissa. Something like that. Do you think she has something to do with Jonah?"

"We don't know," Hadley said honestly. "But, it's a lead worth following up on. Did you ever hear any of the kids refer to her as Creepy Mary?"

Neil smirked. "Can't say as I did. Where'd you hear that?"

"Just someone else who remembered her. You don't remember her last name?"

"Sorry."

"Why did you hire her? I know, to clean up after the party. But, why her, specifically?"

"I got a referral from a neighbor. The Mancusos."

"They lived across the street?"

"Yeah. She cleaned their house for a while. They liked her, told me I should hire her. So, I did." He looked off camera for a moment and must have been checking his watch because he said, "I really have to go now."

"Before you go," Eddie said, "I have one more question for you. Why did you cancel your family's planned vacation? You were supposed to go to California, right?"

Hadley tried to keep a poker face in front of the client, but she felt the heat rising. She gave her head a slight shake from side to side, trying to call Eddie off.

"I had a lot going on at work."

"And, who knew that you were canceling your trip?" Eddie asked. "Who would have known that your family would be at home that day?"

"What are you insinuating?" Neil snapped. Eddie didn't respond. Neil leaned back and crossed his arms over his chest. "It wasn't a secret. Everyone I worked with knew we canceled the trip. Everyone in the neighborhood could see we were home. Now, I'm running late." With that, he disconnected from the meeting.

Hadley didn't bother disconnecting. She shot out of her chair as soon as Neil disappeared from the screen and dashed across the shabby lobby. "Eddie, what was that?" she demanded. "This was my interview, and that line of questioning was completely inappropriate."

Eddie swaggered out of Vince's office, a wry grin on his face. "He's your guy. You don't need to waste time trying to chase down this woman."

"I'm leading our investigation, and I'll decide what to follow up on," Hadley said. She felt a vein near her temple throb and wondered if Eddie had ever induced an aneurysm in anyone before.

"Sorry," Eddie said, holding his hands up. "I didn't mean to step on your toes, but the question needed to be asked."

"It didn't," Hadley countered. "We learned no new information from your exchange, but we've definitely made him less cooperative now. What if we need something from him in the future?"

"I've been doing this for longer than you've been alive," Eddie said, and Hadley clenched her fists at her sides. "Did you see how he reacted? I touched a nerve. I'm telling you, he's the guy. Can you prove it? That's what this case is about."

"Are you hearing this?" Hadley asked Vince. He looked uncomfortable, shifting his gaze from Eddie to Hadley and back.

"Eddie, Hadley is right," Vince said. "You shouldn't have taken over the interview like that. We were just there to observe. And, the theory that Neil was somehow involved doesn't make sense. It's not a priority for the investigation."

Eddie shook his head. "I'm just trying to help."

"Maybe you can help better by staying away," Hadley said.

"Hadley..." Vince said, but Eddie cut him off.

"Maybe she's right. Maybe this agency is better off if I'm a silent partner. I'm happy for you two to do the work and give me my cut. You know where to send the check."

He stomped out of the room, slamming the door behind him.

Hadley strode to the kitchenette and unplugged the coffee maker. She picked up the machine and dropped it into the trash can. It hit the bottom with a crash and the sound of glass breaking.

She looked back at Vince, who seemed unsure how to respond. "Sorry about that," she said.

"I'm not the one you should apologize to," Vince said.

"If you think I'm going to apologize to him, you're out of your mind."

"He did save our lives," Vince said. "And, he's been good to us since we went into business with him."

Now it was Hadley's turn to not respond. After an awkward moment, she started toward her office.

"Let's call it a day," Vince said. "We'll need to work this evening."

Hadley spun and cocked an eyebrow at him.

"We need to go see the Mancusos. See if they have a last name on our mystery woman."

Hadley smiled at him, grateful that at least one of her partners trusted her instincts.

# CHAPTER 13

A flock of Canada geese flew overhead, squawking their way south. The air held a chill like it could snow any moment, and Hadley smelled a wood-burning fireplace nearby. She loved fall in Colorado.

Vince parked his Subaru behind her Jeep, and the two of them approached the Mancuso house together. The streetlight still flickered, casting moving shadows on the sidewalk.

Pauline answered the door. This time, she was dressed in jeans and a hooded sweatshirt. She showed them inside, where Henry sat in blue sweatpants and a gray Broncos sweatshirt. Hadley wondered if it was the same one as before or if he had a closet full of them.

"You must be making some progress if you have something to follow-up on," Henry said.

"We have a lead," Hadley said. "We're trying to see where it goes. I'm not sure if it's progress yet or not."

Pauline ushered them toward the kitchen table, and they all settled in. Hadley thanked them for the first interview and promised not to take much of their time.

"We have a picture of a person who might have some knowledge of this case, but we haven't been able to identify her. We understand you might know who she is."

Henry and Pauline exchanged bewildered glances. Hadley opened her folder and withdrew the picture of the woman. She showed it to the Mancusos. Pauline drew in a sharp breath. Henry wrinkled his chin in confusion, drawing his mouth into a tight frown.

"What would Mary have to do with this?" Pauline asked.

"We don't know," Hadley said. "But, we'd like to talk to her to see if she knows anything that might help. It looks like you know her."

"Yes," Henry said. "She cleaned our house for a couple of years."

"Did you know her well?"

"No. She usually came when we were both working. We'd see her from time to time. She was always friendly."

"She must have been good at cleaning if you kept her on for two years?"

"Yes, she was excellent. Until the end."

Vince cocked his head to the side. "What happened at the end?"

"She stopped showing up," Pauline said. "She would miss her scheduled days and not call. She was supposed to come every Monday. I think she showed up twice in six weeks, and that's when we told her we'd have to let her go."

"When was that?" Vince asked.

Henry looked at Pauline, as if seeking permission to answer. She nodded at him. "It was shortly after Jonah disappeared," he said. "We called her and told her not to come the first two weeks after it happened. The neighborhood was crawling with police, media, search party members, and gawkers. We didn't want to add to the chaos by having another person come in. After those two weeks, she became sporadic. As Pauline said, we had to let her go. But, I can't imagine that she'd have anything to do with your case."

"Do you know her last name?" Hadley asked.

"Taggert. Her name is Mary Taggert."

"Have you seen her since you let her go? Maybe at the supermarket or somewhere in the neighborhood?" They both shook their heads.

"Neil Davidson said you recommended Mary to him?"

"That's true," Henry said. "He knew we hired a cleaning person, so he asked me for her name and number."

"Did you ever recommend her to anyone else?" Hadley asked.

"I'm sure I did," Henry said. "It's been a while, so I don't have any specifics."

"Well, there were the Fergusons," Pauline offered. "Remember, shortly after they moved in?"

"That's right," Henry said. "I don't know if anything came of that, but we told them about her."

Hadley thanked them again, and Henry shuffled to the door behind them. "I don't know if we helped," he said, "but I hope you find out what happened to Jonah. If it were my son, I'd want to know what happened."

A gust of wind blew, scattering leaves across the sidewalk and street. Hadley zipped her coat. She looked across the street at the Ferguson house.

"The lights are on," she said to Vince. He nodded, and they made their way across.

Ty Ferguson answered the door, a look of surprise on his face, followed by disappointment. "Oh, it's you," he said.

"Maybe not the greeting I was hoping for, but at least you remember us," Hadley said, smiling at him.

"Sorry. We're expecting a pizza, and then we're watching a movie with the kids." Hadley heard the commotion inside the house. Squeals of laughter and footsteps running.

"We won't take long," Hadley said. Ty stepped onto the porch and closed the door behind him. "Did you ever hire Mary Taggert to clean your house?" She held up the picture.

Ty studied it closely. He rocked back and forth on his heels. "Yes," he said. "Just once, but I remember hiring her."

"What can you tell us about that?"

"We hadn't been in the house long. The people who owned it before us were not the best housekeepers. No matter how much we cleaned, Bonnie always said the place felt dirty. We were going to be out of town for a week, so I hired a professional to do a deep clean while we were gone."

"Was that the spring break trip?" Vince asked. "When you went to North Carolina to see Bonnie's mother?"

"Yes."

Hadley's heart raced. Her fingers tingled. "What day did she come?"

"I don't know. We said she could come any day that week."

"Are you sure she came?"

"Yes. The house had been cleaned. Partially cleaned."

"She didn't do a good job?"

"She did a great job where she cleaned. But, she didn't make it into the bedrooms. They hadn't been dusted or vacuumed. The guest bath didn't look like she'd touched it."

"How did she get into the house?" Vince asked. "Did you leave her a key?"

"No. We gave her the code to the garage door keypad. It was the same code the previous owners had, and we were going to change it, so I just gave it to her and told her she could enter through the garage."

"Did you ever tell the police about any of this?" Hadley asked.

Ty's eyes widened in surprise. "Police? No. Why would they care about our house cleaner?"

"They were investigating a child abduction in the neighborhood. I'm sure they would have appreciated knowing everyone who was potentially in the neighborhood when it happened." She tried to keep the edge out of her voice, but she could hear it breaking through her professional demeanor.

"Well, they never asked if anyone else could have been in our house," Ty said. "They barely talked to us. Once they knew we were out of town when it happened, they lost interest in us."

A pair of headlights swung up the street as a car made its way along Gardenia. It stopped at the Fergusons' curb, and a teenage boy jumped out. He reached into the back seat and emerged with three pizza boxes.

"Looks like our time is up," Hadley said. "This has been helpful."

They stepped to the side to allow the pizza guy to come up the stairs and then walked back to their cars. They agreed to meet at the Park Hill Deli, a few blocks away. On the way, Hadley drove through the alley behind the Ferguson house. It was narrow; just enough room for one car at a time. She paused behind the Ferguson house. There was room to park in a concrete slot next to the garage.

Hadley coasted through the alley and then drove to the deli. Vince motioned her to a table. "I ordered you a salad," he said. "I'm getting the BLT and chips, and I won't feel guilty about it."

"I'm not your mother," she said. "You can eat whatever you want."

Vince scoffed, and they both laughed. "What took you so long?"

"I checked out the alley. They have fences on the wings of the houses. You can't see the front from the back."

"Or vice versa," Vince said. "And, that would mean a toddler couldn't wander to the back from the front."

"Not without going all the way to the end of the street."

The food came. Vince's smelled delicious, but she wasn't about to tell him that. Once they had their plates settled, Hadley walked him through her new working theory. Mary Taggert had been at the Ferguson house the day Jonah disappeared. She heard the kids outside and looked out the window at them. When she saw Lisa run inside with Sara, she made her move. Ninety seconds would have been plenty of time to get outside, grab Jonah, and come back in before Jenny saw her. While Jenny and Lisa looked outside and then back inside, Mary could have loaded Jonah into the car and drove off while they were inside calling the police. They wouldn't have seen her and probably wouldn't have heard her.

"It's not bad as a theory," Vince said, tomato juice dripping down his chin. He dabbed at his face with a napkin and continued, "But, you have a couple of problems. First, motive. You don't have one."

"She was Creepy Mary," Hadley said. "That establishes motive right there."

Vince laughed. "I don't think that's enough to go to the police. But, maybe there's some truth to it. Maybe she was predisposed to kidnapping."

"What's the other problem?"

"Evidence. It's all a hunch right now. I like it better than a random stranger happening down the street and grabbing Jonah, but I don't have enough proof to buy in yet."

Hadley nodded. "Proof will come. If she's the one, we'll figure it out." She took the last bite of her salad and pushed the plate back. In her best Eddie Fleck imitation, she said, "'I've been doing this for longer than you've been alive.' Maybe if the police wouldn't be so arrogant, they'd solve more cases."

"Plenty of good police officers out there," Vince said. "And, Eddie was one of them."

Hadley scowled but didn't respond right away. Finally, she said, "She was the perfect house cleaner for two years. Jonah disappears and she becomes erratic. She had access to the house next door to Jonah at the time he disappeared."

"I'm not saying it's not a good hunch," Vince said. "I'm actually excited about chasing this down. What's our next step?"

Hadley leaned back in her chair. "Find Mary Taggert."

# CHAPTER 14

*October 21, 2023*

Mary Taggert had no discernible internet presence. No social media of any kind. No news articles about her. No online reviews of her cleaning services. Hadley knew about companies that would sanitize the web for you. They called it reputation management. But, why would a house cleaner in Park Hill need her reputation managed?

The background check sites the agency subscribed to did not turn up much more than that. She located a birth record, but no records of marriage, divorce, or death. No lawsuits filed by or against her. No criminal record of any kind. Mary Taggert existed off the radar.

According to the birth record, Mary was born in 1980 to Dan and Emily Taggert. That put her at 43 years old—28 when Jonah disappeared. Her place of birth was Pueblo, Colorado, about two hours south of Denver.

Hadley found a three-year-old obituary for Dan Taggert. The article claimed he had worked for a construction company and later started a landscaping business. He'd lived most of his life in Pueblo, moving north to Colorado Springs when he went into landscaping. He was survived by his wife and two daughters, Mary Taggert and Esther Morton.

Emily had a Facebook page that hadn't been updated since before Dan died. Hadley did not see any pictures of Mary on the site. She also had left a few online book reviews. Apparently, historic Celtic romance was her genre of choice.

A background check of Esther showed that she was two years younger than her sister. She married Shawn Morton when she was 22 and had a son, Kyle, two years later. That would have made him the same age as Jonah Davidson, Hadley noted. According to property records, Esther and Shawn owned a home in Longmont, Colorado, north of Denver.

Hadley copied an address, phone number, and email address for Esther and continued searching for her online. Unlike Mary, Esther lived her life in public. She had Facebook and Instagram sites, both filled with pictures of her, Shawn, and Kyle. They didn't have a great picture of Mary for comparison, but Hadley saw the sibling familiarity between the two. They had the same brown eyes and pronounced cheekbones. The same slender chins. Esther was taller and thinner. She also looked more than two years younger than Mary, but that could have been because she looked a lot happier. She seemed satisfied and carefree.

The oldest picture on Facebook was posted in 2010. Mary and Esther stood at the railing of a boat, the kind that's used for whale-watching excursions or pleasure cruises. There were plenty of other people crowded around. The sky was blue, and the sun beamed down on them. They both squinted without sunglasses. Hadley imagined the foamy sea spray churning along the side of the boat. She could smell the tang of the ocean mixed with the sunscreen and umbrella drinks of the people around them and hear the chatter of gulls flying overhead. It looked like a good day. They both laughed, leaning into one another's arms, and appeared to be having a great time. The caption read, "My sister and me. I miss the old days. I miss her."

A search of Esther's Instagram did not yield any additional photos of Mary. She looked up Kyle Morton, as well, and found a TikTok page, but it was all reposts of clips of comedians and bad lip reading bits. If he had a relationship with his aunt, it was far away from social media.

Her phone buzzed and she read the incoming text message from Vince. "Something's definitely up with Cheater. Skipped work today, took the light rail toward downtown instead. I'm staking out his car."

A second message buzzed in. Vince again. "Do you think Door Dash will deliver to a specific parking spot at a park and ride? I didn't plan on doing a stake out today."

Hadley smiled. She sent him a reply asking if he needed her to bring him some supplies. He responded, "No thanks. I don't like kale with my stake out." She rolled her eyes, well aware that if Eddie had made a similar comment, it would have set her off. She tried not to think about Eddie. She was making headway on her lead and didn't need any negative thoughts slowing her down.

She tried Esther's cell phone number, but it went straight to voicemail. She left a brief message asking Esther to call her. Then she composed an email:

"My name is Hadley Collins, and I'm a private detective. I believe your sister Mary might have some information that would help me with a case. I'm hoping you can help me find her. Do you have a few minutes to meet this week? We could grab a quick coffee while we chat."

She decided it sounded sufficiently non-threatening and hit send. With that task done, she fished the contact information for Gary Brice from her purse. It was still too early to contact him. He wouldn't be back for a few more days. It wouldn't hurt to send him a note, though.

"Detective Brice, my name is Hadley Collins. I'm a private detective hired by the Davidson family to investigate the disappearance of Jonah Davidson 15 years ago. I'd like to talk to you about your investigation and see if we might be able to help each other out. I heard you're out of town right now, but perhaps we can meet when you get back?" She read it and changed the last line to, "Please reach out to me when you have a few minutes." She added her phone number and email address and hit send.

# CHAPTER 15

*May 1, 2008*

Jenny had gotten used to many of the changes in her family's life since Jonah disappeared. She had come to terms with knowing that most mornings she'd find her father's pillow and a blanket on the living room couch. She'd adjusted to quitting basketball and track so she could spend more time supporting her parents. And, while she would never be okay with Sara's frequent nightmares, being woken by shrieks in the middle of the night no longer surprised her.

Nor did it surprise her to be woken by Sara climbing into bed next to her; her sister's warm body a sharp contrast to her tiny, freezing feet, which she'd grip Jenny's legs with. Jenny actually enjoyed cuddling up to Sara, smelling her clean hair, and the two of them holding each other until they fell asleep. She didn't want to admit it, but she found as much comfort in the arrangement as Sara did.

She could not get used to her parents' constant fighting. For several weeks, her father was barely at home. He joined the search party in the early days. As time stretched on without Jonah being found and with no clues to lead to him, the search party's numbers dwindled, until it was Neil, alone, walking the neighborhood streets, looking in trash cans and peering into the windows of empty houses.

Eventually, he came back home, where the family learned he was just as fragile as the rest of them. Any off-hand comment could ignite a tantrum. Any mention of Jonah was bound to be met by his scorn. He was distraught, as any father would be, and he expressed himself through his anger.

Most often, he targeted Lisa. He would yell at her for no reason and seemed to go out of his way to disagree with her. Sometimes it was Jonah-related, like if he should go to work or spend the day searching. Sometimes it was something as mundane as the kind of bread she picked up at the grocery store.

In her most frustrated moments, Lisa would punch back with accusations of his infidelity and claiming that he had been emotionally absent from the family long before Jonah disappeared. Neil would counter with a haymaker of his own: "If you'd brought Jonah inside with you, none of this would have happened."

That would win the argument for Neil, but it was a costly victory, Lisa locked in their bedroom in tears, screaming at him that she wanted him out of the house.

Jenny arrived home from school one Thursday afternoon, clutching an envelope containing her acceptance to Washington University in Saint Louis. She knew she couldn't go there in the fall but held out hope that she could work out a deferred admission for a future academic year, after Jonah was safely home. The school had one of the top architecture programs in the country. The acceptance gave her a respite from the overwhelming sadness in her life, and she wanted to share that moment with her mother.

She walked in the door to find her parents having one of their many arguments. Her father had left work early, driving the neighborhood for any clue that might lead him to Jonah, before coming home.

"You should have told me you were going to be in the area," Lisa said. "You could have picked Sara up from school while you were driving around."

"How many times do I have to explain that I'm not just driving around?" Neil countered, his voice already raised. "I need to focus on what I'm seeing out there, and I can't very well do that if Sara's in the car with me. I might as well stay at work for all the good that would do me."

"Maybe you should stay at work," Lisa said, her voice now matching Neil's in pitch and volume. "They've been lenient with you, but what happens when they want you back full time? We can't afford for you to lose your job. And, I can't exactly go to work, since I'm the one doing all the cooking and cleaning and shopping." She walked away and then wheeled quickly to look Neil in the eye. "And, I'm the only one doing any of the school drop-offs and pick-ups." She nearly screamed the last line, her cheeks flushed and deep creases crossing her forehead.

"And, I'm the only one trying to bring Jonah back!" Neil roared. "In case you haven't noticed, the police haven't been able to do it. Our neighbors and so-called friends are useless."

As he continued ranting, the phone rang. Jenny crossed through the living room, neither parent giving her a second glance. She picked up the handset in the kitchen, saying "Hello" loudly to drown out the sounds of World War III coming from the living room.

"I know where the little boy is," a nasal voice whined on the other end.

"Who is this?" Jenny asked, scrambling to grab a pen and notepad.

"I know where the little boy is," the person whined again.

"I need your name and phone number and any information you have." She pushed the mute button and yelled, "Will you two shut up?"

The argument in the living room stopped. Jenny listened but heard only silence on the phone. She unmuted the phone. "Are you still there?" she asked. "I need your name and phone number."

Her parents gathered in the doorway, watching intently. Jenny heard a deep breath over the handset, followed by a cackling laughter.

That was the other thing she wouldn't get used to. The police had told them to beware of prank phone calls. The authorities, both the Denver police and the FBI, had fielded dozens of fake tips and prank calls since Jonah's disappearance. Even though she knew not to get her hopes up, the idea of someone being so cruel was beyond comprehension.

"Listen here," she snapped. "I don't know who you think you are, but you just crossed the line." She berated the caller with language that would have put any sailor to shame, not caring that her parents were in the room. It didn't matter what she said; by the time she paused for a breath, she heard the dial tone of a line gone dead.

She let out a primal scream, capturing all her frustrations, anxieties, and fears in a guttural wail that she was sure could be heard throughout the neighborhood. She wound up and threw the handset, stepping into the motion and driving the power through her hips. The phone hit the opposite wall and exploded, raining shards of plastic and circuitry throughout the kitchen.

"You'll have to get the number and time of the call from the caller ID on the other phone," she said. "If you can stop fighting long enough." She stormed out of the kitchen and into her room, where she let herself cry as hard as she had since her brother went missing. Sara crept through the door and climbed onto her lap.

They gripped each other fiercely, rocking until they were out of tears.

# CHAPTER 16

*October 22, 2023*

Hadley pointed her car north on Interstate 25 toward Esther Morton's Longmont home. Her reply had been brief: "You're welcome to come talk, but I don't know how much I can help you." A couple follow up emails later, Hadley had confirmed the address and booked an appointment to see her.

The weather had cleared, the cold making way for a glorious fall day. The sun shone in a brilliant blue sky, and the mountains showed off their recent dusting of snow. As she drew closer to the mountains, she saw patches of evergreen trees broken up by swaths of golden aspens. Not for the first time, Hadley thought about how nice it would be to move out of the city and closer to nature.

"Near Longmont" would have been a better description of where the Mortons lived. Hadley followed the GPS's directions outside of the city and into a wooded area. Hidden inside was a planned community with plenty of room between houses and thick trees to afford privacy to the residents.

The directions took her to a large house with a stone exterior and a circular driveway wrapping around a stand of blue spruces. There were no other cars in the driveway, but Hadley saw a second driveway just beyond the circular one. It led to a three-car garage with a basketball hoop mounted on the roof.

Hadley put her phone in her purse, checked to make sure she had her laptop, as well as a notepad and pen, and approached the front door. The doorbell security camera whirred to life as she approached, and a chime alerted the residents to her presence before she could even press the button.

Seconds later, the door swung open, and Esther Morton stood in the doorway. She looked just like her Facebook photos. She stood about 5 foot 6, a few inches taller than Hadley, and had shoulder-length brown hair that matched her brown eyes. She wore a Longmont High School sweatshirt and blue jeans and smiled broadly as she welcomed Hadley in.

"You didn't have any trouble finding the place?" she asked.

Hadley assured her she didn't. They made small talk about the traffic and weather and the comparison of Longmont to Denver. Esther had Hadley get settled in the living room, and she disappeared into the kitchen to get drinks. She came back with a pair of Diet Cokes and glasses.

"I usually drink straight from the can," Esther said. "But, since I have company, I can pretend to be civilized." She smiled again, and Hadley liked her right away.

Hadley looked around the room. Family photos and trophies filled a shelf along one wall. Hadley saw photos of Esther and Shawn, as well as plenty of Kyle. She assumed the baseball and track trophies were Kyle's, too. There were a few photos of older couples, probably Esther's and Shawn's parents. She didn't see any images of Mary.

"I appreciate you seeing me and on such short notice," Hadley said.

"Well, it's not every day a private detective wants to talk to you," Esther said. "But, as I said in my email, if you're interested in Mary, I won't be able to help you much."

"You never know when something might be helpful," Hadley said, eager to keep Esther from retreating too soon.

"What's this all about?" Esther asked. She leaned close and lowered her voice, even though they were in the house alone. "What has Mary gotten herself mixed up in now?"

Hadley thought it a curious question to start the interview with. She explained that a crime had been committed at a house where Mary was working years ago, and they wanted to find Mary to see if she knew anything that might shed some light on it.

"If it happened a long time ago and you're still looking, we're not talking about something small like petty theft. This must be a big case."

Hadley didn't answer. Instead, she said, "How much did you know about your sister's house cleaning business?"

"I thought it was a waste of talent," Esther said. "Mary had a full academic scholarship to CU, majored in engineering. She was a top student. Started working for a manufacturing company out on the West Coast. Then, all of a sudden, she moves back to Denver and takes part-time jobs. Worked as a barista for a while, then as a cashier at a convenience store. Eventually, she started cleaning houses." Esther took a quick look at her well-appointed surroundings and added, "Nothing wrong with any of those jobs, mind you. But, she worked hard to get that engineering degree, and she loved that kind of work. At least, I thought she did."

"Do you think something happened when she lived on the coast?" Hadley asked.

"I think it started before that. She hung out with some weirdos in college. I think they filled her head with ideas about capitalism being bad and not wanting to work for the man."

A back door opened, and the two women turned to see a teenage boy walk into the kitchen. He paid them no attention, going straight to the refrigerator. He guzzled milk directly from the carton. He stood taller than the refrigerator and almost as wide. Wiping his mouth with his sleeve, he finally noticed they had company.

"Oh, hi," he said, his face coloring slightly.

"You're home early," Esther said.

"Coach canceled practice. Some kind of sprinkler problem with the field. Whole thing's flooded."

"This is my son, Kyle," Esther said to Hadley. "And, this is…" she paused, clearly having forgotten her guest's name.

"I'm Hadley Collins."

Kyle started toward the stairs, pausing to answer Esther's questions about how his day had been, if he had homework, and if he needed to do laundry for the next day. As he thundered up the stairs, Esther turned back to Hadley. "Where were we?"

"Mary had some weird friends in college."

"That's right. They were weird, too. Dressed in flannel shirts in the summer. Didn't take enough baths."

"When's the last time you saw Mary?"

"About 15 years ago."

That got Hadley's attention. "Do you know where she went?"

"I have my ideas. She had started talking to a couple of the guys she went to college with again. They wanted to buy land somewhere and start a self-sufficient community. Sounded like a hippie commune to me."

"You think she went with them?"

"It wouldn't surprise me. Now, do you want to tell me what this is all about? Why are you so desperate to find my long-lost sister?"

"I can't give too many details on an ongoing investigation," Hadley said.

Esther crossed her arms and leaned back into the stuffing of the couch. Hadley wondered how far she could go before she disappeared completely. Esther gave her a sideways glance. "The thing is, there's more I can tell you, but I need to know what you're getting into before I decide if it's worth it."

Hadley was surprised. She'd been leveraged by interviewees before, but she hadn't suspected Esther to be the type to try that.

She debated her options and quickly decided that she hadn't gained any real information; if Esther had more to offer, she needed to hear it.

"Fifteen years ago, your sister was hired by a family in Park Hill, in Denver. They wanted her to help clean up after a big birthday party. Three months later, the family's youngest child was abducted."

Esther's eyes grew wide. "Do you think Mary had something to do with it? Are you tracking down everyone who might have been in the house during those three months?"

"We're tracking down anyone we believe might know something. I saw a video of the birthday party where Mary showed unusual interest in the boy who was kidnapped."

"Define unusual."

"She appeared to take his picture."

Esther mulled that over. She sat forward out of the cushions and said, "I promised her I wouldn't say anything, but she called me. Three years ago on my birthday. We talked for a few minutes. She asked about me and Shawn, that's my husband, and Kyle, who you just met. I asked her where she was, and she wouldn't answer. I asked how she was doing, and she said she was great. She said, 'I never knew it was so nice this far out east.' Then she sounded angry, not at me but at herself. She made me promise never to tell anyone she said that."

Hadley cupped her chin in her hands. "But, you're telling me about it now."

"Yeah," she said. "I'm a mother. There's a kid missing. I don't think Mary would have had anything to do with it, but it's strange that she'd take his picture at his birthday party."

"It wasn't his birthday party; it was his sister's."

"See. That's even stranger. So, if that detail helps you find her, and she helps you find the boy, it's worth betraying her trust."

"She didn't say what 'out east' meant?"

Esther shook her head. "She had a Colorado area code, though."

"Do you still have the number?"

"Yeah. I saved it in my contacts. I've called it a few times. It went straight to voicemail a time or two, and now it says it's out of service. Do you need the number?"

Hadley gladly took it, scribbling it down in her notepad. "One last thing," Hadley said. "The picture I have of Mary isn't the best. It's a screen capture from the birthday party. Do you have any photos of Mary that you could spare?"

"I'll be right back."

Esther disappeared up the stairs. Hadley inspected the wall of memorabilia while she waited. Kyle had won trophies in numerous sports, dating back to his elementary school days. The family had taken a lot of trips over the years. The shelf was dotted with photos of Shawn, Esther, and Kyle in front of various landmarks—the Washington Monument, the Space Needle, the Eiffel Tower, and the Sydney Opera House among them. Whatever Shawn did for a living, he was obviously successful.

There were pictures of Esther at various ribbon-cutting ceremonies and charity events, as well, rounding out the family of high achievers. Hadley could see how Mary's decision to forsake her engineering degree to pursue a career in house cleaning would strike Esther as odd, maybe even incomprehensible.

Hadley wondered what effect the Morton family's public displays of achievement would have had on Mary. Did she ever feel like she was living in her little sister's shadow? Would that have encouraged her to pull up stakes and move to a commune somewhere?

Esther's footsteps sounded on the stairs, and Hadley returned to her seat. Esther carried a scrapbook and opened it on the coffee table. "These are all the pictures I have of Mary and me, since we were little girls."

They flipped through the pages, beginning with a photo of Esther as an infant laying in Mary's lap. There were pictures of them as young girls in Halloween costumes, Mary dressed as a ballerina and Esther as a ninja one year; the next, Esther was more prim and proper as a princess, but Mary had gone as a soldier, her face painted camouflage to match her outfit.

There were pictures of each of them alone, too. Most of Esther's featured some kind of ribbon or trophy, with Mary empty-handed in hers. They flipped through their teenage years, the two of them dressed for homecoming, and into adulthood. Mary's college graduation photo was the only one that came close to the success-laden pictures of Esther. She wore a black gown and matching mortar board, beaming at the camera. Her earrings caught the sunlight and sparkled. She looked like a young woman with the whole world in front of her.

They finally came to the last page, which included the boat photo Hadley had seen on Facebook. Esther's handwriting captioned the photo—"Whale watching in San Diego. Soooo much fun!"

Under that photo was a final shot of Mary. It looked to have been taken on the boat, too. Mary leaned against the railing, a glass of white wine in her hand, and smiled. She looked off in the distance and seemed at peace.

"When was that one taken?" Hadley asked.

"Sixteen years ago. About a year before she left."

"That's a much clearer photo than the one I have. Do you mind if I take a picture of it?"

"Sure, go ahead," Esther said. She paused, then laughed. "I was going to say that you can just have the picture, but I really don't want to take the scrapbook apart."

Hadley nodded her understanding. Using her phone, she snapped a couple of pictures, then looked at them to make sure they turned out. "You've been helpful," she said. "I appreciate you trusting me with the information you've shared today."

"No problem," Esther said, but there was a catch in her voice. "I can't believe Mary could be involved in something like this."

"There's a good chance she isn't," Hadley said. "This case has been investigated and re-investigated over the years. There aren't many clues, so any new information has to be checked out."

Esther closed the scrapbook. She held it to her chest, like a mother holding a baby. Hadley stood to leave.

"One question crossed my mind as we were looking at pictures," she said. "Was there any sibling rivalry between you and Mary? How did you get along?"

"No rivalry," Esther said. "I kind of wish there had been. But, Mary always sacrificed herself to make sure I got what I wanted. Our parents both worked multiple jobs, and in a lot of ways, Mary raised me."

Hadley returned to the Jeep and took the long way out of the community, driving in a circuitous route to take in as much as she could. All the houses were huge; she could fit two or three of hers inside most of them. They all looked fairly new. She guessed the neighborhood was 10 years old at the most. She passed a clubhouse and a pool, closed for the season, and several parks and playgrounds. If Mary really had left town to join a commune, she was probably living a polar opposite life to her sister.

She found the interstate again. Unsurprisingly, it was packed with rush hour traffic. Knowing that she'd be there a while, she dialed Vince.

"What's up?" he answered. She filled him in on the trip to Longmont and what she'd learned from Esther. "Out east is not helpful," he said when she told him about the phone call. "That could be New York or eastern Colorado."

"I'll do some research on the number. Maybe we can identify some candidate locations and go from there." She filled him in on the photos in the house and scrapbook and what Esther said about Mary always sacrificing for her.

"Not to get too psychological, but if Mary was always looking out for Esther and Esther got to a point where she didn't need that anymore, Mary could have felt rudderless. Lacking purpose."

"And, a commune could fill that purpose," Hadley finished his thought.

"It's a big maybe," Vince said. "And, 15 years is a long time." He paused a beat before continuing, "I should wrap up the cheater case tomorrow, and then I'll be able to help you with this one."

"What happened with your stakeout the other day?"

"He stayed gone for a couple of hours; came back with a guitar case and drove it to the coworker's place. They were inside for a while, then he came out without the case."

"Weird."

"Yeah. I'm meeting the client tomorrow to give her my photos and a summary. No smoking gun, but I can confirm he hasn't been telling her the truth about his whereabouts, and he's been spending a lot of time with the coworker."

They ended the call, and Hadley continued to sit in traffic. She opened her notepad and dialed the phone number she had scribbled down. Just like Esther said, she got an out-of-service message. She'd do some more digging. She thought about what she'd say if Jenny asked for an update. Hadley would love to tell her that they had new clues, but she needed to find Mary and determine her involvement before she got her client's hopes up.

# CHAPTER 17

*October 23, 2023*

With Vince getting his paperwork together for a client meeting and Eddie in exile, Hadley had the day to herself to pursue the Davidson case. She started with the phone number. An internet search identified it as a cell phone, but details on carrier and owner were missing or contradictory on each site she looked at.

She logged into a phone look-up service the agency subscribed to and entered the number. It showed that it had been out of service for two years and did not provide detail on the ownership, carrier, or location before that time.

Grumbling to herself about how everything was difficult with the case, Hadley logged into yet another database. She always saved this one for emergencies; she had to pay for each use, and it wasn't cheap. She verified her credit card information, entered the site, and plugged in the phone number.

The service took several minutes to compile a detailed report, which she had to click through screen by screen before downloading the complete PDF at the end. The first screen told her it was a cell phone. The next screen identified the carrier as Mobile2Go, which she knew was a prepaid cell phone service. Up next should have been details about the owner, but because it was prepaid, that screen was blank.

Finally, she got the information she was looking for. The phone had been activated at a convenience store near Limon, about 80 miles east of Denver in the plains of Colorado. Not exactly an idyllic spot for a commune, but it would have plenty of wide open space to it.

She pulled up Google Earth and searched for Limon. She zoomed in enough to see buildings and scrolled around eastern Colorado. She wouldn't find it that way. Many of the images were outdated, and she couldn't tell what might be a farm versus a commune full of Utopia-seekers.

She went back to the phone database and saved a copy of the report to her laptop and printed one for the file she'd been building. For what Jenny was paying them, she wanted to be sure to show an honest effort in trying to find Jonah. Hadley made sure to bill fairly and keep meticulous records of the work she'd done on the case. If they learned something about Jonah, Jenny would surely think whatever she paid was worth it. If they didn't, she didn't want Jenny to think they hadn't done their best.

She texted Vince to see if he had time to talk. A minute later, he called her.

"I hope you have good news on your case because mine has failed in spectacular fashion," he said.

"What happened?"

He told her about meeting with the client that morning. She'd insisted on meeting at his office; she didn't want to meet in public or at her house. He assumed she expected him to present incriminating evidence and didn't trust how she would react with other people around.

"So, I have everything pulled together into an airtight presentation. I can show her how for each day that she told me his whereabouts, whether he was at work or golfing or whatever, he was actually spending time with his coworker. And, from the photos, his coworker is a bombshell and a lot younger."

"The presentation didn't go well?" Hadley asked.

"It didn't go at all," Vince said, exasperation in his voice. "She refused to look at anything that I'd prepared. She just wanted to pay the bill—in cash, by the way—and forget that she ever engaged us."

"She must have had a change of heart."

"Sort of. I asked her what was going on. Told her I'd spent a lot of time trying to get this right for her. She finally confessed to what happened. Her husband's coworker? She moonlights as a music teacher. Voice, piano, guitar. Turns out, her husband wasn't having some torrid love affair. He was learning to play a song on guitar. And sing it. He wanted to surprise her with it on the anniversary of their first date."

Vince sounded completely frazzled, but Hadley couldn't stop herself from laughing.

"I spent half a day watching his empty car in a parking lot. For this." That set Hadley off even more. "That is the last cheater case I'm taking. I don't care if they pay the bills. How's your case going?"

Hadley composed herself enough to catch him up on the latest developments. She told him about locating the convenience store where the cell phone was purchased.

"So, assuming someone didn't buy a burner in Limon and drag it across the country, 'out east' means eastern Colorado," Vince said.

"That's my bet. Now the trick is finding a location for Mary. Eastern Colorado narrows it down a bit, but it's still a big area."

"You made a good choice in partners," Vince said. "You're talking to one of the finest paralegals in real estate law the state of Colorado has ever known."

"You think you can turn up some property records that will help?"

"I don't have access to the right databases anymore. But, I know a guy. I'll call Mason."

They bid each other goodbye and clicked off the call. Her phone buzzed again immediately. She didn't recognize the number but answered anyway.

"Is this Hadley Collins?" The voice sounded thin and faint.

"Yes it is. May I ask who I'm speaking with?"

"This is Gary Brice."

"Hello, Detective. Thanks for returning my call."

"It's just Gary now. And, I'm curious about your interest in the Davidson kidnapping."

"As I mentioned in my voicemail, I'm a private detective who was hired by Jenny Davidson to find her brother. I understand you were the lead detective on the case?"

"I don't want to do this over the phone." He paused and coughed. He must have put the phone down and walked away because the sound grew fainter. Hadley heard footsteps and the sound of a glass being filled. "Sorry about that. Where was I? I'd rather talk to you in person. Where are you located?"

"I'm in Littleton," Hadley said. "But, I can meet you anywhere."

"I'm close to you. I'm in Parker. I'll text you my address."

They arranged for a 2 p.m. meeting. That afternoon, Hadley headed south toward the city of Parker. As she got closer to Gary's house, the neighborhoods gave way to ranch-style homes, spread out on multi-acre lots. Many of the houses had horses, and she spotted a couple of cows, some goats, and even a llama.

Her GPS directed her to Gary's driveway. She didn't notice any livestock on his property. The house was a low, wide building outfitted with light blue siding. Navy blue shutters adorned the windows. Unlike her home, Gary had plenty of room between neighbors. She could picture a lifelong cop, who spent his entire career in the city, settling in for retirement in a place like that.

She rang his doorbell, heard a familiar chime, and saw the device light up. "I'm around back," Gary said through the doorbell. "Just follow the path on your left." She followed a cobblestone walkway around the side of the house, let herself in through a gate, and continued on the path until she was in the backyard.

Gary, she presumed, nodded to her from the deck but didn't make a move to get up and greet her. He wore blue jeans and a long-sleeve pocket tee, with a cowboy hat and boots. He sat at a wooden picnic table, a longneck in front of him and a cigarette in his hand. For some reason, Hadley had been expecting something different, but seeing him for the first time, she realized he was exactly what she should have expected.

"Come on up and have a seat," he said, finally rising. He shook her hand as she reached the deck, his grip surprisingly strong for how thin he looked. "Need a drink? Or a smoke?"

"No thanks to both," Hadley said. "I'm good."

They sat, and she explained again that Jenny had hired her agency and talked about the police work they had reviewed so far.

"I'm assuming Ms. Davidson shared our files with you?" Gary asked.

"Yes, she did," Hadley said. "I hope that's alright."

He waved the comment off. "I gave her the files. Wasn't supposed to, but when I was getting ready to retire, I wanted to make sure she had what she needed to continue her search. Between you and me, it's pointless to keep searching, but I'm not about to say that to a family member. I didn't want all my notes to end up in some cold case box in the basement, so I made copies for her."

"Why is it pointless to keep searching?"

Gary took a long drag on his cigarette and exhaled slowly, the smoke leaking out of his mouth and nose. "The boy's dead."

It took Hadley a moment to recover. "You're sure of that?"

"Nobody can be too sure unless you've found a body, but that's the outcome that fits. Best case is we find an abducted child within 48 hours. After that, it gets dicey. And, when there's a family member involved and the child never reappears, all my years of law enforcement tell me that you're working a homicide and not an abduction."

"By family member, I assume you mean Neil?"

Gary nodded and took a drink from his beer. "Again, that's the best fit. He made sure the family was home that day and not on vacation. He couldn't account for his whereabouts during the abduction. He tried to control the search parties and told us how to do the investigation. He didn't act like a grieving father."

"People grieve in different ways."

Gary snorted. "I always felt like he was trying to manipulate the situation. Like he was steering us."

"But, if Neil kidnapped his own son, why didn't he disappear, too? He never started a new life with Jonah. He never started a new life at all."

"My best guess is he hired a kidnapper. Something went wrong. Most likely the boy died. Neil tried to play it cool, and it worked. In my entire career, that's the one perp I regret not collaring."

"Did you ever look at a woman named Mary Taggert?" Hadley asked.

Gary wrinkled his brow under the cowboy hat and stubbed out his cigarette. "Never heard of her."

Hadley pulled up the picture on her phone and turned it toward him. He studied it, then slowly shook his head.

"The Davidsons hired her to help at a party at their house. She showed an unusual level of interest in Jonah. Took his picture, even. She might have been in the neighborhood the day Jonah went missing."

"That's pretty thin evidence."

"But, it's not nothing."

"No, it's not. You should go to the police with this. I still think my theory is stronger. If anyone suspected this woman, they would have said something while the investigation was active."

"Maybe this works with your theory," Hadley said. "Maybe Neil hired Mary and made sure no one mentioned her during the investigation."

"Now you're thinking like a cop," Gary said. Hadley knew he meant it as a compliment, but she wasn't so sure it was one. "Where is this Mary now?"

"Great question. No one knows."

He pulled his pack of cigarettes from his shirt pocket and offered one to Hadley. Again, she begged off. He lit one up. "The mystery deepens. Take this information to the actual police. Let them see what they can do with it. Probably nothing, but at least you've done your duty and can sleep better."

"I'm not getting much sleep until we find out what happened to Jonah," Hadley said. "If he's still out there somewhere, his family has a right to know. And, trust me, if he's still out there somewhere away from his family, he'd want to know, too."

# CHAPTER 18

*March 2, 2000*

Hadley dreaded the Thursday bus ride home from school. The ride itself wasn't so bad, but at the end of the ride, she'd have to walk home alone and go into an empty house. Her mother worked late on Thursdays. Her sister rode to gymnastics with a friend. Hadley fended for herself.

That particular Thursday was worse than most. The day had been a dreary gray, and as the bus pulled out of the school, a steady drizzle poured down. She watched raindrops cling to the window then streak down, leaving tear stains along their path.

The bus reached her stop, and she got off, dragging her backpack behind her and hoisting it to her thin shoulders when she climbed down the steps. She trudged toward home.

The blue pickup truck with patches of rust along the bottom panels pulled even with her. She looked up at the familiar face.

"Hi, Dan," she said. She liked Dan better than her mother's other boyfriends, although she wasn't sure if he was really a boyfriend anymore. She hadn't seen him at the house much lately, and her mom hadn't been talking about him.

"Need a ride?"

She knew better than to accept a ride from a stranger. But, strangers were people she didn't know and who her mom didn't know. They both knew Dan. She gladly opened the door and climbed into the truck and out of the rain. He offered her a snack.

He had a bottle of Coke and a package of peanut butter crackers, both forbidden in the house. She accepted them readily.

He asked about her day, and she chatted with him easily, like a pair of old friends. She told him about how Isabelle lost a tooth during reading and about how much she hated math. She didn't notice that they weren't going to her house until they were clear of the neighborhood.

"Dan," she said, her mouth half full of crackers, "I think you went the wrong way."

Dan turned and smiled at her before facing the road again. Dan had short black hair and a beard the same length. He had friendly brown eyes. But, Hadley liked his smile the best. It was always warm and reassuring and made him look like the kind of person you could trust with anything. He hadn't smiled much the last few times he'd been at the house.

"We're going to a surprise destination," he said. "Do you know what that means?"

She shook her head.

"A destination is the place you're going. And, you know what a surprise is. So, I'm taking you somewhere you don't know about, but you'll like it when we get there."

He turned and smiled again. This time, Hadley didn't feel reassured. Her stomach had a weird feeling. "Will Mom and Heather be there?"

"They'll meet us there," he said, eyes on the road again. He merged onto the interstate and accelerated. "They might not be there right away, but they'll be there soon enough." He turned the radio to a country station and turned up the volume. He sang along, his voice off-key and most of the lyrics wrong. He adjusted the heater and turned up the fan. Hadley felt a blast of cold air that soon turned warm. She leaned her head against the window, watching the scenery blur by through the rain-dotted windows. With the music playing and the temperature rising, she grew drowsy and soon closed her eyes, drifting off to sleep.

She dreamed that her mom came to the school and told her to come straight home. Her mom said Hadley had to walk home from the bus stop; she couldn't get a ride with anyone, especially not Dan.

When she opened her eyes, it was dark outside and the temperature in the truck had grown much cooler. She shivered and tried to draw her legs up under her coat.

"I have a blanket in the back," Dan said. "I'll get it for you when we stop. We'll have some dinner at the next town."

She looked out the window and saw nothing but vast empty spaces. She saw cows and an occasional farm house. She didn't see any other cars. The clock on the dashboard said it was 6:22. It had been almost three hours since she'd gotten in the truck. The surprise destination that seemed like such a great idea back then didn't sound so great now.

"We've been driving for a long time," she said.

"That's because it's a big surprise."

"My mom will be there? And Heather?"

"Eventually." The word hung in the air between them.

Finally, they approached the lights of a town. Dan pulled into a McDonald's and had her take a seat in a booth while he ordered.

"My mom lets me order for myself," she said.

"We're doing things a little different tonight," he replied. "Now, sit right there where I can see you. I'll be back in a minute."

Hadley watched him stand at the counter, glancing back at her every few seconds. The feeling in her stomach returned. She didn't know what the surprise was, but she knew she didn't like it. She wanted to go home.

# CHAPTER 19

*October 24, 2023*

Vince drove Hadley from their office to his old law firm. He pulled into his usual parking spot and pointed at the yellow Porsche nearby. "Looks like Mason's here," he said.

Hadley was interested to finally meet Mason in person. She'd heard plenty of stories about him, and she wanted to know how much Vince was exaggerating and how much was true.

Vince led her to the front door. Swinging it open, he said, "Welcome to the law firm of Cassady, Ginsberg, Phillips, and Associates."

"I thought Mason was the only partner here?"

"He is," Vince said. "But, he thought Phillips and Associates looked silly on the sign, so he added some names."

They approached the front desk, where an emaciated woman with a bright pink streak in her hair and matching fingernails paged through a magazine. "Welcome in," she said without looking up, her voice flat. "Be right with you."

Hadley looked at Vince who watched the woman, clearly amused. She reached the bottom of her page, flipped to the next one, and said, "How can I help you?" She finally looked up and formed her mouth into a miniature O of surprise before replying, still inflectionless, "It's you."

"That's a fine welcome back, Naomi," Vince said. "We're here to see Mason." Naomi stared at him, making no effort to alert

Mason that he had guests. "We have an appointment," Vince added. "I can show us back."

That prompted Naomi to take action. She flipped her magazine shut and held up a hand in a motion for Vince to be still. She picked up the phone and dialed an intercom extension. "Mr. Phillips, your next appointment is here. No, I won't bring them back." She hung up the phone and glanced at Vince and Hadley before reopening her magazine. "Mason will be right here."

Hadley heard footsteps beating a path down the hall, and Mason Phillips appeared. He wore faded jeans with a rip spreading just above the right knee. He also wore a T-shirt featuring Sesame Street characters in a grid, Brady Bunch-style.

"Vince!" he exclaimed, rushing forward and wrapping his former employee in a bear hug. "It's good to see you again." He let go of Vince and gave Hadley a handshake, his palm puffy and damp. "Nice to meet you. Come on back."

He led them past his office, the door closed conspicuously, and into the firm's small conference room. He already had a folder on the table. He sat on one side and motioned for Vince and Hadley to take the other.

"Vince, you look great," Mason said. "You've lost weight. Gotta tell me your secret." He barked his words in short bursts.

"Remember all those cases where we'd work late nights, trying to finish a last-minute filing?" Vince asked. "Imagine you had a partner who insisted you replace all the pizza and candy bars with kale and celery."

Mason made a face. "Sounds disgusting. I'd rather stay fat."

"For the record, I've never forced him to eat kale."

Mason shook his head and waved his hands like he didn't believe her but that it didn't matter. "I got some stuff for you."

"Thanks for jumping on this so quickly," Vince said.

"Anything for my guy Vince. Let's see what we have." Mason flipped the folder around and opened it. He walked them through pages of reports. "I ran a search for property sold east of Limon 15 to 20 years ago. By east of Limon, I mean anywhere in the state east of that line of longitude. Anyway, I eliminated smaller plots of land—single family units, duplexes, et cetera—and anything that's been sold again in the past 15 years. Asterisk that. What you're left with are large tracts of land that have been in the same hands for at least 15 years."

"Impressive," Vince said.

"I'm not done yet," Mason said. He flipped to a map where he'd drawn three circles in red. "I've narrowed it down to three good possibilities for you, based on what Vince shared with me." He pointed to the first circle, located outside Sterling, Colorado. "This one was purchased by Costas Energy. About half of it is a solar farm, but there are out buildings. Presumably, they came with the property. They could be used for research and business-related functions, but, who knows, right?"

He jabbed his pen at the second circle, in the far southeast corner of the state. "Property two, sold to Paul and Sally Emerson. Used to be a youth camp of some sort, so it's got it all. Housing, bathrooms, kitchen and food prep, common areas. If I were starting an out-of-the-way hippie commune, this is the property I'd buy for it. No idea what the Emersons are doing with it."

He moved his pen to the third circle, drawn about 40 miles east of Limon. "Here's the third one. No improvements listed on the land in the sales records. Looks like it was strictly a land deal. Here's the interesting part. Sold to Costas Energy."

"Wait," Hadley said. "Just like the first one?"

Mason nodded. "Remember that asterisk? This one got sold again 8 years ago. To another corporation. Place called TerraPure."

He flipped from the map to a sales report. Vince picked it up and read it. He put it back down and looked at Hadley, who had no idea why he looked so confused. He turned his gaze to Mason.

"I know," Mason said, shaking his head.

"I don't know," Hadley said. "Care to fill me in?"

"The buyer waived everything," Vince said. "No assessment, no appraisal, no inspection. No declarations. Nothing."

"That's unusual?"

"It leaves the buyer with no legal recourse," Mason said, taking over. "I would never let a client sign that contract. And, look at the price."

He poked his index finger at a box on the report.

"Costas Energy didn't make any money on this," Vince said.

"The sales price was Costas's original purchase price plus closing costs, which there weren't many of," Mason said. "And, get this, I can't view the deed. The only thing in the database is that report."

"Just to be clear," Hadley said. "This is Jeremy Costas, the billionaire energy guy, we're talking about?" Mason nodded. "And, his company owned this land and sold it to another company for what they'd bought it for? Anything illegal about that?"

"No, but it's weird. You know how much land value went up in the time Costas owned the place? Guys don't become billionaires by making bad real estate deals."

"If he's not making the deal for money, there must be another reason," Vince said. "Sounds like we need more information on TerraPure."

"Good luck," Mason said. "I tried looking for them. There's nothing on them."

Hadley collected the materials while Vince thanked Mason for the research. Vince bid goodbye to Naomi on their way out. She stayed glued to her magazine; if she heard him, she gave no response.

"Mason seems like a fun guy to work for," Hadley offered as they drove back to the office.

"He was great. He could be demanding, but he kept things from getting boring."

"Naomi seems like..." Hadley trailed off, not sure how to finish that sentence.

Vince laughed. "She excels at all parts of her job that don't involve people. Unfortunately, most of her job involves people."

When they reached the office, Vince insisted on ordering pizza for lunch, in tribute to the good, old days. To show him she wasn't trying to force-feed him health food, Hadley agreed to share. They brainstormed about the case over slices of pepperoni.

"Property two is the best bet," Vince said. "It was ready made for a group of people to start Utopia."

"We'll need to research the new owners," Hadley said, "and we might be able to find something on it based on the former camp name."

"I don't like property one. The idea of this commune or whatever it is being so close to something as corporate as Costas Energy just feels off."

Hadley nodded as she dabbed at a new slice with a paper towel. "That's my least favorite of them. It shouldn't be hard to research. You'd think if a group of people lived near the solar farm, someone from Costas Energy would have said something about it. What do you think about number three?"

Vince held up a finger while he swallowed. He took a long drink of Diet Coke before answering. "Something's up with it. That sales record was weird."

"Are we going to talk about the Costas coincidence? He's popped up on two of the three candidates, and he had a relationship with Neil Davidson."

"I honestly don't know what to do with that," Vince said. "I don't see a role for him in the kidnapping. It's probably just a coincidence."

"Maybe it's not that big of one," Hadley said. "The guy is rich, and he needs land for solar panels and wind turbines. Manufacturing, too. He may own a lot more of Colorado than we realize." She took a sip of her iced tea and continued, "Here's what I propose we do. Can you start with property two? Try to run down Paul and Sally Emerson. I want to do some research on TerraPure and see if there's anything out there about communes in eastern Colorado."

"Or cults," Vince said. Hadley raised an eyebrow. "We don't know what we're dealing with. Commune might be the polite word for a cult."

"Fair enough. Let's see where we get this afternoon, and then we can compare notes. If it doesn't look like any of these properties are the one, we'll need to review the sales records Mason gave us and see if anything else makes sense."

Back in her office, Hadley confirmed what Mason had found. There was no useful information about TerraPure. She switched from the typical search engines to KryptoSearch. While most portrayals of the "dark web" were largely based on myth and fantasy, there were sites that Google and Yahoo web crawlers did not index. Most of those sites avoided the crawlers intentionally, and KryptoSearch specialized in finding them.

She only achieved marginally better results. She found a message board with a question posed unanswered four years ago: "Hey guys! I've heard TerraPure in CO might be worth looking into. Anyone have any details?" Q&A on domestic militias and anti-government groups filled that message board.

She had similar results from other message board sites, but the questions were never answered. Whoever TerraPure was, they kept a lid on their activities.

She logged into a public records database and found that TerraPure had formed as a business entity eight years ago, right before the sale with Costas Energy. Curiously, the records did not list an owner or any officers. Beyond the business name and the incorporation date, the record did not include anything useful.

She backed out of the record and looked at the database's "about" information. It included a disclaimer saying that some records may be incomplete and that paper records could be acquired in person at county records offices. She sighed her frustration and added a trip to Lincoln County to her mental to-do list.

She began her research into communes and cults in Colorado and found plenty to wade through. She clicked a link that looked promising but groaned when she began reading a description of Colorado's "most populous cult" where 75,000 people gathered in Denver on Sundays in the fall, dressed in orange, to worship a great white horse.

She looked at several more results without better effect and wondered if the public library might have better resources on this. Having already made one field trip that day, she continued to slog through sites.

Her next page of results rewarded her for her efforts. She found a blog that included a link to a documentary about cults in the state and how many sought to victimize women. The link took her to YouTube. The documentary, she noticed, had just 214 views. It had been posted three years earlier. She turned up her speakers and hit play.

The presenter, a woman in her 20s with light brown hair, flawless skin, and perfect, straight teeth looked familiar to Hadley. She looked her up on her phone while the documentary played, and Hadley saw that Teri Vanetta had been a reporter on one of the Denver news channels and now anchored a weekly online newscast.

She turned her attention back to the documentary. While interesting, it didn't give her the insight she wanted until the 28-minute mark. The video cut to a scene where Teri sat in a darkened room with a woman whose image had been blurred and voice had been changed to a robotic sound.

The scene only lasted 40 seconds, but the woman talked about getting caught up with a group in eastern Colorado. The group's mission was to achieve independence—from the government, from corporations, and generally from any outside influence.

"They wanted families there," the woman explained. "My husband, daughter, and I moved in. It was great, at first. But, I found my independence wasn't nearly as important as the leadership's. They used us to get what they wanted. They're so afraid of outsiders that they make it difficult to leave. I snuck out in the middle of the night; my husband refused to leave. I haven't seen him or my daughter since."

Teri segued to a discussion of how the woman's comment rings true across cult-like organizations, that the leaders view the membership as a disposable means to achieve their goals.

Hadley continued watching, but she couldn't get past the idea of how scared the hidden woman must have been—so scared that she wouldn't show her face. Even more importantly, scared enough that she left her family behind to escape the organization. The documentary said she had been in eastern Colorado. What if her location matched one of their candidate properties for Mary's commune?

Hadley closed out of YouTube and searched for Teri Vanetta's contact information. As a journalist, she was easy to find. Hadley dialed her cell phone, expecting to leave a voicemail.

"This is Teri," came the chipper voice on the other end. Hadley explained who she was and that she had just watched "Cults and Patriarchy in the Centennial State."

"Wow," Teri said. "I thought that was some great work, but not many people have watched it."

"I'm glad I did," Hadley said. "I'm looking for a woman who I believe joined some kind of self-sustaining commune in eastern Colorado. I'm wondering how I can talk to a woman from your video." She described the scene to Teri.

"Sounds like a longshot that she'd be able to help you."

"Unfortunately, that's where we are with this case," Hadley said truthfully. "It's long shots or no shot at this point."

"And this woman you're looking for—the commune woman, not my contact—what information do you hope she has?"

"We're trying to solve a kidnapping. From 15 years ago. She had a connection to the victim's family that we recently uncovered." Hadley waited, but Teri offered no response. "I'm desperate to find this woman. If your contact happened to be in the same group that she joined, this could be the break my client has been waiting for."

No response. She heard Teri breathing on the other end of the line and then the sound of nails clicking against a tabletop. "Here's the thing. The woman in the video, she trusts me. It took me a long time to gain that trust. I cultivated a relationship with her for four months. I got 40 seconds of usable video from those four months. I'll reach out to her, but I'll be shocked if she talks to you."

"That's all I can ask for," Hadley said. "I appreciate you doing that." She gave Teri her contact information and thanked her repeatedly.

She heard Vince stirring in the main office and found him and the leftover pizza at the card table. She wanted to lecture him on eating bad for two meals in a row but backed off. "What did you find out?" she asked.

"Property two is out," Vince said. "Paul and Sally Emerson had two special-needs children who both died young. They took their life savings to buy the youth camp that had been owned by the Colorado Baptist General Convention. They brought it up to date and reopened it as a get away for special-needs kids and their families. They don't charge anything to the families. They exist on sponsorships and donations. I guess Mason didn't research this much because there's a ton of information on them."

"His research on TerraPure was more accurate," Hadley said. "I can confirm that there is no public information on them, whoever they are. I'm going to have to make a trip to Lincoln

County to view the incorporation records in person. And, I have a possible lead on a cult of some sort." She filled him in on the documentary and her discussion with Teri Vanetta.

Vince did not seem enthusiastic about her new lead. "I want to solve this case, too," he said, "but at some point, we have to think about briefing Jenny on what we have and seeing how much more money she wants to spend on us. It feels like we're chasing shadows."

"Give me a few more days," Hadley said, knowing he was right. "Let me see if Teri's person gets back to me and what I find out in Lincoln County. By the way, you want to go with me?"

Vince flexed out the veins in the sides of his neck. "Sorry," he said. "I'm going to have to go out of town for a little while. My dad was in a car accident down in Texas, and I need to get down there to help my mom. She has limited mobility, and now Dad does, too. I'm leaving tomorrow; planning to be there about a week."

"I'm sorry to hear that, Vince," she said. "Let me know if I can do anything for you."

"If you want someone else to go to Lincoln County," he said, "you know who you have to call."

"Don't say it."

"You're going to do what you want to do...you don't need me to tell you that. But, you owe Eddie an apology."

Hadley opened her mouth to interrupt, but Vince charged ahead.

"You found a theory that casts suspicion on both Mary and Neil, but you berated Eddie for wanting to focus on Neil. He's a valuable partner. You'll need help on this case while I'm gone, so you should think about calling him. I've got to go get packed. I'll check in with you while I'm in Texas."

After Vince left, Hadley stewed over his comments. She had been harsh to Eddie. But, it wasn't just because he was focused on Neil as the sole suspect. Eddie had interfered with her interview. Vince had no idea what it was like to be a woman and feel like a man was trying to control you.

As she felt her ire turn toward Vince, she decided she needed a break. She packed up her stuff and got in her car. Before she pulled away from the office, her cell phone rang. Teri Vanetta's name showed on the caller ID. Hadley turned off the radio and took the call.

"I can't believe it, but she's agreed to talk to you," Teri said. "Be forewarned. You might make a long trip for nothing. I'll text you the details of where she wants to meet. She said she'll set the ground rules when you get there, but she's already said she won't discuss any specific people with you."

"That's better than nothing," Hadley said. "I'll take it."

# CHAPTER 20

*October 25, 2023*

The mystery woman set the meeting for 9:00 a.m. at a rest area off Interstate 76 near Ogallala, Nebraska. Hadley crawled out of bed at 4:00 in the morning, so she could be on the road before 6:00.

She drove into the sunrise, pink and orange illuminating the plains. As she moved further from Denver, she watched the mountains retreat in her rear-view mirror until they merged with the horizon and disappeared. She still had an hour and a half to go, most of it through a flat, brown landscape dotted with occasional spruce trees or ponderosa pines.

She drew closer to Ogallala and the landscape became greener. The highway took her along the South Platte river, a fertile crescent in the otherwise bleak setting of eastern Colorado and western Nebraska.

She followed the directions to an exit a few miles ahead of Ogallala and pulled into the rest area. Semi-trucks and tractor trailers lined the shoulder along the lengthy driveway leading to the building. Gruff-looking men in company jackets and billed caps leaned against the cabs smoking or drinking coffee from giant metal thermoses. A surprising number of cars had pulled in as well, cross-country travelers stopping for a stretch, a bathroom break, and a cup of coffee.

Hadley made her way inside and found a rudimentary coffee shop. It consisted of a counter, a couple urns, and a bakery case half-filled with prepackaged coffee cakes and muffins. There were a few tables scattered throughout the open area, and Hadley spied a woman sitting alone in a corner.

The woman had a scarf wrapped around her face, covering her nose, mouth, and chin. She wore a pair of oversized sunglasses and had a second scarf covering her hair. Hadley approached the table and said, "I think I'm supposed to be meeting you here. Teri sent me."

The woman turned her head to face her, but Hadley couldn't tell if she was looking at her or not with the sunglasses obscuring her eyes. The woman nodded and motioned for Hadley to take a seat across from her.

"Can I get you a coffee or anything?" Hadley asked. The woman shook her head. Hadley needed to build rapport with her, but it was going to be difficult with all the barriers the woman had put up. "Thank you for..." Hadley started, but the woman interrupted her.

"Before you start, I need to make some things clear." The woman's voice was deep, and it was hard to make out her words with the scarf muffling her. Hadley leaned forward. "No recording or notes of any kind. I won't answer questions about specific people. If I tell you I can't answer something, you drop it immediately."

"Agreed," Hadley said. She'd conducted hostile interviews before, but they were always with people she'd ambushed and was talking to against their wishes. She'd never had someone volunteer for an interview and be this aggressive. She was grateful for her decision not to involve Eddie in this. She'd taken Vince's words to heart and would apologize to Eddie, but not yet. Her instincts had been correct; there was no way she'd let Eddie sit in on an interview with this woman.

Turning her attention back to the woman, she said, "Again, thank you for meeting with me. I think Teri told you that I'm working on a case to locate a child who was abducted 15 years ago. There's a woman who may have some information who, I believe, moved to a community like the one you lived in." She shared a few more details about the case, explaining that Jonah had simply vanished, and there were few leads in the case, which is why she was so intent on tracking down Mary Taggert.

She wished she could read the woman's expression to see if she was softening or not.

"Why did you move to the commune? Is that the right word, commune?"

The woman nodded. "You can call it that. It makes it sound a little friendlier than it actually was." She paused for a long time, and Hadley wondered if she should repeat the question. Finally, the woman continued. "My husband was self-employed as a carpenter. We had some problems with the IRS. Nothing intentional; he thought he had filed everything correctly. They came after us, took us to court, and ruined us financially. We had a four-year-old daughter, and we needed a better life. He had met one of the leaders of this group, and it sounded wonderful. Homesteading, living off the land, not living paycheck to paycheck. Everyone would chip in and help each other for the good of the community. So, we tried it. What did we have to lose?"

"When was this?"

"Sixteen years ago."

"And, you left four years ago." The woman nodded. "What was life there like?"

"It was great, at first. Exactly as advertised. They had some livestock. We had fresh milk and eggs. They grew crops outdoors and in greenhouses, so we had plenty of vegetables and produce, too. Some things were hard to come by. We didn't eat much meat. We didn't get a lot of citrus fruits or bananas. My husband built things for them—houses, storage sheds, whatever they needed—and I helped in the school. It was a great life for a while."

"What happened?"

"I wanted more. We worked hard. We didn't have a lot of comforts. In a lot of ways, it was like going back in time. There was electricity and running water but little technology outside of what was needed for the community to run. No television or radio, no internet. You get used to it, but it's nice to have some entertainment now and then. And, I heard rumors about the leadership." She wrung her hands together and her voice grew softer as she finished the sentence.

"What kind of rumors?"

"That they had all the things we didn't. The leaders lived separately from the rest of us, and I heard they had everything they wanted. They would leave and go eat in a restaurant from time to time. My family was never that much into going out to eat, but when it's taken from you, when you see the same faces and do the same things every single day, you miss things. It didn't seem fair that they could do what they wanted and we couldn't."

"Why couldn't you?" Hadley asked. "Why not just take a long weekend? Go into the city, stay at a hotel, do the stuff you missed?"

The woman laughed a mirthless chuckle. "How could we leave? They took our truck when we got there. One of the conditions of us living there was that property was held in common. They had a strict rule about outside influences, and we were forbidden to leave unless it was a dire emergency, and even then we had to have the leaders' approval."

Hadley made a face like she had smelled something foul. "I can see how the leaders leaving whenever they wanted wouldn't sit well with you." The woman offered no response, so Hadley moved on. "What was day-to-day life like? Where did you live? Did you have your own house?"

"We lived in tiny houses. Like those shows on the home channels, you know? Families either had one or two bedrooms and a small living area. There was a common kitchen, dining, and bathroom building for every six to eight houses."

"You must have gotten to know your neighbors well." Again, the woman didn't respond. She continued squeezing her hands together and tapped her foot under the table. Another woman dragged a screaming toddler past them on her way to the restrooms, and a man with an enormous belly and a long, red beard came in from the opposite direction and ordered a refill of coffee for his thermos. Hadley thought it might hold a full gallon.

"You mentioned families living there. Was it just families? Any single people? Single parents?" Hadley asked.

"Mostly two-parent families," the woman said. "Occasionally, a single parent, but that was rare. I think the leaders were all single, but they lived apart from us."

"Did your husband like it there?" The woman nodded, saying nothing. "Did he know you didn't like it?"

More nodding. She used the edge of her face scarf to dab at her eyes under the sunglasses. "I spoke to the head leader one day and told him that after as many years as we had been there, I felt like we should have more status. More freedom. I was banished from the school after that and we were told to move from our house to a smaller one. We had been fortunate to settle into a two-bedroom, which was unusual for a family of three. They moved us to a one-bedroom. As a punishment for me speaking up, I'm sure. After that, my husband insisted that I stay quiet and enjoy our life there. Those were his words." She moved the scarf up under her sunglasses again, dabbing incessantly. Hadley gave her a moment to regain her composure.

"Is that when you decided to leave?" she asked. The woman nodded. "What did your husband think about that?"

"He didn't know I was leaving. I had suggested to him before that we go, but he said he didn't want to. I think he was afraid."

"Afraid of what?"

"Afraid of going back into the world with no savings, no possessions, and no recent job history, for one thing. And, afraid of what the leaders might do if they found out."

"What do you mean?"

"They wanted no outside influence. That was their mantra. They achieved it by strictly controlling who came in. But, that also meant strictly controlling who went out. They didn't want people leaving and drawing attention to the place. Let's just say we couldn't exactly walk out the front gate. Preserving their precious community was way more important than what might happen to us."

She didn't elaborate, and Hadley didn't want to press her. It was clear from the lengths this woman went to protect her identity that she believed she was in serious danger if the leaders of the commune found her. The next logical questions were about how the woman got away and why she left her daughter behind, but Hadley worried the woman wouldn't want to answer and would end the interview. She changed direction.

"Teri's documentary was about cults in Colorado. I usually think about cults as being religious, but you haven't said anything about that. Was there a religious component to the community where you were?"

"Their politics was their religion," the woman said. "Their political beliefs were that they had the right to withdraw from society. No outside influence. No taxes, no social services. Basically, they believed we lived on American soil but that we had in all other ways declared our independence. They'd often say America wasn't a true nation, that a nation required common culture and beliefs, and only a community like ours could actually achieve that."

"There must have been some taxes. Property taxes, at least."

The woman held her hands out in a who-knows gesture. "I think it was all a bunch of baloney anyway. The leaders were rich and living out some kind of separatist fantasy. Wouldn't shock me at all if they were writing checks to the state for taxes and not telling us about it. That's how they operated; they used their money to solve problems and never told us anything."

"What kind of problems?"

"Could be anything. I mean, you'd think at some point in the time I was there, there would have been some need for the police or county government or someone like that to come by the property. But, they never did because the leaders had the government in their pocket. And, check this out, a few months ago, I learned how to use Google Earth. I looked up the place, just to see what images there'd be. It's fake."

"Fake?"

"The satellite imagery isn't of the compound. None of the buildings are shown. None of the paths between buildings. No greenhouses. How did they do that? It must have cost them a pretty penny."

Hadley wished she had a notepad and determined to commit that detail to memory. It was time to bring things to a close. She could ask her riskier questions.

"So, you started questioning things and wanting more out of life. That's understandable. It sounds like your husband was more bought in to the belief system there?"

"If it really is a cult, he's completely brainwashed by it."

"What about your daughter?"

"She's right there with him. I tried to get her to see things my way, get her to come with me. But, she refused. It's all she's ever known. She thought she had a good life there. I wish I could show her how there's so much better out here."

"It must have been hard to leave her behind."

The woman raised the scarf to her eyes again. She took a deep breath like she was about to speak, but said nothing.

"I know you said we couldn't get into anything too specific, but could I show you a map, and you can tell me if I'm close to where your commune was?"

"No. I won't do that."

"Fair enough. Here's my card; if you ever want to talk more about what it was like there, or if you want to share any other details, you can call me. Day or night." She slid the card across the Formica table top. The woman looked down at it but did not touch it.

"I have one last question," Hadley said. She pulled a printout of Mary's picture from her pocket. Smoothing the paper, she laid it in front of the woman. "Did you ever see this woman in your community?"

"You need to leave. Now." The woman's voice took a steely edge. Hadley didn't even bother thanking her again. She gathered her things and stepped away from the table, leaving Mary's picture on the table.

"You left this," the woman said as Hadley walked off. Hadley didn't turn around. As she exited the building, she stole a glance to see the woman ball up the paper and shove it into the trash can. Hadley rushed out of the building to her Jeep and slumped low in the front seat, to where she could just peer over the dashboard.

She saw the woman exit the building, still in disguise, looking around for anyone watching her. Satisfied, she went to her car, a beige Toyota Camry and exited the rest area. Hadley gave her some space and drove out after her. She turned on her dash camera.

The woman pulled off the road before she reached the entrance ramp to the interstate. Hadley saw her removing the scarves. She could read the woman's license plate number clearly, which meant the camera could, too. The car was registered in Nebraska, as a fleet plate. Probably a rental. Turning her head to avoid the woman seeing her face, Hadley stepped on the gas and sped past the stopped car. She entered the interstate, heading deeper into Nebraska. She had to drive several miles before she could exit, turn around, and begin heading back toward home.

Except she wouldn't be going home right away. She had another stop to make first. She'd be taking the long way back to Denver, and stopping in Hugo, Colorado, first. Hugo was the seat of Lincoln County, and she needed to pay the county clerk and recorder a visit about a certificate of incorporation.

# CHAPTER 21

Hadley arrived at the county clerk's office at 12:40. According to their web site they closed each day from noon to 1:00 for lunch. Hadley wandered into the town and did not find many dining options. She bought a salad at a supermarket and ate in her car as she watched the county building.

Some small towns in rural areas have grand, old-fashioned courthouses and office buildings as monuments to the by-gone days when things happened there. Hadley would not have been surprised to find a big, marble structure with a wide spiral staircase inside. That is not what Hugo offered, though.

Hugo's county building was a squat, red-brick affair offering all the charm of a strip mall insurance office. It offered plenty of parking. Hadley took a spot in the back of the lot where she could see anyone coming or going.

She finished her lunch as the clock hit 1:00. She waited a couple of minutes and proceeded inside. The outside doors opened into a narrow hallway that extended in either direction. A signboard at the back of the hall contained a directory for the building, the offices listed in two columns, depending on which wing they were located in.

She found the listing for the clerk and recorder on the right-hand side. Room 134. She walked down the hall, her footsteps muffled by industrial carpet squares that had seen better days.

Most of the offices had frosted windows taking up the upper half of the doors, the title and room number stenciled on them. Nearly all of them remained dark and unoccupied.

She found room 134 and was pleased to see the lights were on. She opened the door, which squeaked on its old hinges, and approached the unattended counter. "Be right with you," called a voice from a back room. Hadley waited for five minutes without the person appearing. She looked for a service bell on the counter but found none. She considered opening the door again to let the hinges announce her presence. Instead she called, "Hello! Anyone there?"

A few more minutes later, a man in his 50s came to the counter. What hair he had left was gray and fell in sweaty wisps across his scalp. He had bushy gray eyebrows and a large paunch. He wore blue jeans with a white button-down shirt and a pair of red, white, and blue suspenders.

"Sorry about the wait, young lady," he said. "I had an issue to discuss with my supervisor. What brings you in today?"

Hadley produced the partial incorporation record for TerraPure. "I'm looking for the complete version of this record," she said.

The man withdrew a pair of reading glasses from his shirt pocket, perched them on the end of his nose, and read the form. He flipped it to the blank side and then back to the front.

"Let me see what I can do," he said. He typed something into his computer, hunting and pecking for keys with just his middle fingers. "Hmmm," he said. "Just another minute."

He pushed back from the counter and returned to the back room. Hadley heard snatches of a muffled conversation. The man came back a minute later and rummaged through a drawer in a brown metal filing cabinet.

"Here we go," he said. Hadley didn't know if he was talking to her or to himself. He returned to the counter and slid a piece of paper across to her.

"That was easy," she started to say, but he talked over her.

"Just need you to fill that request out, and then my supervisor will be able to assist you further."

Hadley looked at the paper and saw that it was, indeed, a blank form. "This is a public record," she said. "I'm not sure why I can't just get a copy. I'll pay whatever the normal fee is."

"That goes without saying," the man said, his tone condescending and smarmy. "But, this particular public record"—he emphasized public—"is controlled. It requires supervisor approval for release. Do you need a pen?"

"No." Hadley completed the form, giving her name, address, phone number, and email address. For the reason for the request, she printed "research on the economy of eastern Colorado." She wasn't about to put anything on there about trying to solve a kidnapping.

She passed the form back to the man, who read each word carefully. "Can I see your driver's license?"

She dug her license out of her purse, and he compared it to the information she had provided. "Everything checks out here," he said. "Just a minute."

He disappeared into the back room once again. Hadley wondered what was going on and who his supervisor was going to be. She pictured another figure who looked exactly like him, the Tweedledee and Tweedledum of Lincoln County.

After another lengthy wait, she heard footsteps from the back room. A young woman, probably in her late 20s, approached the counter. She wore a navy blazer with jeans and a white silk blouse. Her brown hair grazed her shoulders. She had dark, serious eyes, and a small, unsmiling mouth. Definitely not Tweedledum.

"Ms. Collins, my name is Jenna. I'm Ray's supervisor. I understand you have requested a copy of a controlled record."

"I requested a copy of a public record..."

"Public, but controlled," Jenna interrupted. "I can get the record for you. Because it's controlled, we need to know who is seeking the information. That's all that means." She offered what might have been a smile. If it was supposed to soothe Hadley, it had the opposite effect. "There's normally a $15 processing fee for in-person record requests. Because this is a controlled record, there's an additional $5 fee, for a total of $20. We take check and money order."

Hadley didn't understand anyone who didn't accept a credit card in the 21st century, but she had prepared for the scenario. She had cash and her checkbook with her. She filled out the check, trying to remember the last time she had done that, and pushed the payment across the counter. Ray took it to the back room.

"We'll just be a few more minutes," Jenna said. Hadley wondered what they could possibly be doing back there.

Jenna was true to her word. After about three minutes, Ray appeared. He offered her a pink carbon-copy receipt and a photocopy of the incorporation document. "Anything else I can do for you?"

"No, thank you," Hadley said. "This has been great." She tried to keep the sarcasm out of her voice but failed.

She waited to look at the document until she was in her car. The business address for TerraPure was a post office box in Limon. That helped narrow the field some, as theoretically, the good people of TerraPure would want their mail delivered somewhere at least moderately convenient. Property three was looking better.

She looked at the listing of business officers for TerraPure. There were only two. The chief financial officer was named Scott Flanagan. The chief executive officer was named Jeremy Costas.

Why would a company owned by Jeremy Costas sell land to a company also owned by Jeremy Costas, Hadley wondered.

She looked at the clock and saw that it was approaching 2:00. She had spent more than 40 minutes in Ray and Jenna's bureaucratic holding cell. Exhaustion weighed her shoulders down, and she had a long drive ahead of her. She stopped back at the supermarket for a diet soda, pointed her Jeep west, and began the trek back to Denver, dreading the 5:00 traffic she'd hit as she got into town.

• • •

Jenna dialed a number she'd never had reason to use before. It had been recorded in the TerraPure file long before she began working for the county. The instructions on file could not be clearer, though. If anyone asked for records on TerraPure, the supervisor was to report it. She was surprised when the number actually rang. She was even more surprised when a gruff voice picked up on the other end.

"What's going on?" a man growled.

"This is Jenna Barkley. I'm with the Lincoln County Clerk and Recorder's Office in Hugo. Someone came in today asking for a record, and I'm supposed to report it to this number."

A long pause. "What record?"

"The incorporation certificate for a company called TerraPure."

Another pause, followed by a series of clicks on the line. "Who asked for it?"

Jenna looked at the file note. It explicitly directed her to give the name and contact information to the person who answered the phone, even though she normally would not release that to an unknown person. She read from the form Hadley had completed. The clicking on the line continued.

"Are you recording this call?" Jenna asked.

"Why did she want the record?"

"Economic research," Jenna said.

"Are you sure?"

"That's what she wrote on the form. I can't verify that, like I can the name and address. Seriously, though, what's all that clicking?"

"Must be a bad connection. Doesn't matter now, though. We're through." The line went dead. Jenna looked up to see Ray watching her from the doorway.

"Whoever said nothing interesting ever happens in Hugo?" she asked.

# CHAPTER 22

*April 20, 2000*

Hadley missed her mom. She missed Heather, too. She missed her house, with her room, her bed, and her stuffed animals. She missed going to school, which surprised her. Maybe she just missed seeing other people.

She'd lost track of how long she had been at the surprise destination. It had been long enough for her mom to get there, and she didn't understand why no one had shown up yet.

She still liked Dan. He was nice to her. He got whatever she wanted to eat and drink. They'd had pancakes and bacon for dinner the night before, with root beer to wash it down. Her mom rarely let her have breakfast for dinner and never let her have soda. Dan never raised his voice at her and hadn't hurt her in any way.

But, he didn't give her good answers about when her mom and Heather were going to show up. He'd say "soon" or "it shouldn't be long," but it had already been a long time.

Dan left the little house each morning after Hadley woke up. He'd give her breakfast, usually cereal, and leave a sandwich for her in the refrigerator. He came back before dinner time, and they'd read a book, play a game, or put a puzzle together until time to eat.

While he was gone, Hadley spent the day drawing pictures and watching cartoons on an old television and VCR he had set up in the living room. The first few days, she explored the house. Not that there was much to explore. There were two bedrooms. Dan's had a double bed and a closet full of his clothes. A warped wooden dresser with a tarnished mirror stood in one corner. The second bedroom was hers. It had a twin bed with pink sheets and a matching comforter. She didn't have a dresser and only had a couple of outfits in the closet.

There was a tiny bathroom across the hall from her bedroom. It had a toilet with a wood-grain seat, a bathtub and shower with a yellowed floor, and a sink without a mirror.

The kitchen was well stocked with snacks and groceries. It had a back door that locked with a keyed deadbolt. Hadley tried to open it every day after Dan left, but it was always locked.

On the other side of the kitchen was the living room with a lumpy sofa in a plaid fabric, a matching chair that leaned to one side, and the television and VCR. A pair of folding TV trays served as their dining table.

The front door locked just like the kitchen door, and it, too, was always locked. The last thing she heard each morning before Dan's truck started was the click of the lock and the jingling of Dan's keys.

On this day, she didn't feel like drawing pictures, and she didn't want to watch any of the videotapes. She went back into Dan's room. She hadn't been in there in a while. Nothing had changed. She looked under his bed. She wasn't sure what she was looking for, but she found nothing there anyway.

She looked in his closet. His clothes were there, just like always. Flannel shirts and jeans. She spied something on the floor. She peered closer and saw that it was a metal ring, about three inches in diameter. She pulled on it and felt it give. She grasped it with both hands, braced her feet and yanked as hard as she could. A trapdoor flipped open, nearly hitting her chin as it flew upward.

She peered into the dark hole that appeared before her. She saw a wooden ladder leading down and descended it. At the bottom of the ladder, she paused. She couldn't see anything in the darkness. She felt around and struck a concrete wall. As she ran her palm over its clammy surface, she found a light switch. She flipped it, and a single bare bulb illuminated the space.

She was standing in the middle of a small room with a low ceiling. It was empty, save for a pair of cardboard boxes in a corner. She opened the first one. It was filled with musty blankets. She shoved them back in the box and tried to make it look unopened. She tried the next box. It held winter boots and a carton of ice melt.

Beyond the boxes, a set of steps led to a nook. She climbed them, and saw another ladder built into the wall, leading to what looked like a door. She climbed the ladder and tried the door. It swung freely, and she stepped out of the cellar and into the sunshine. Dan had either forgotten about this door being unlocked or thought she wouldn't find it.

She hadn't had much fresh air since Dan had brought her to that place. She squinted in the daylight and felt the cold air on her bare arms. Her feet were cold, too. She wondered if she should go back and get her shoes, but the taste of freedom was too great to deny, even for another minute.

She wandered outside the house and saw that it was painted blue. She saw the gravel driveway and the place where Dan always parked. She followed the driveway, pebbles digging painfully into her soles. Trees lined each side of the driveway, so she couldn't tell if there were other houses nearby.

She reached a paved road. The sun-warmed asphalt felt good on her feet. She turned left and followed the road as far as she dared. She didn't see any other driveways. She turned around and followed the road in the other direction. She passed Dan's driveway and continued over a steep hill. As she reached the crest, she could see down the road until it disappeared around a bend hundreds of feet away.

Just before the bend she saw smoke swirling from a chimney. Her heart caught in her throat. A chimney meant a fireplace, and a fireplace meant a house. More people.

She turned and retraced her steps back to Dan's driveway, around the house, into the cellar, and back into his closet. She closed the trapdoor and hoped it looked exactly as Dan had left it.

She missed her mom and Heather. She would give them another chance to meet her at the surprise destination. If they didn't come soon, she would find the house with the chimney and see if the people who lived there could help her get back home.

# CHAPTER 23

*October 25, 2023*

Despite the extra caffeine, Hadley felt exhaustion take over before she was even halfway home. She needed something to take her mind off the miles ahead of her. She called Gary Brice to ask him a question that had been nagging at her.

"What can I do for you?" he asked when she identified herself.

"I know your investigation into the Davidson kidnapping focused on Neil right away, but did you ever look into the woman he was having an affair with?"

"You know about that?"

"From what I can tell, it wasn't exactly a secret."

Gary chuckled, and she pictured him taking a pull on a cigarette before speaking again. "We never considered her a suspect."

"Did you identify her? I haven't been able to get that far."

"We identified her. Interviewed her. Determined she had an alibi."

"I didn't see her interview in the file."

"I didn't give it to Jenny."

"Why not?" Hadley appreciated his candor, but she hated having to pull information question by question. At least it kept her awake.

"Lisa Davidson was convinced her husband kidnapped Jonah. And, she was convinced his mistress had some role in it.

I got to know her well enough during the investigation to know she wouldn't let a little thing like a rock-solid alibi keep her from harassing that woman. So, I kept the identity from the family."

"Would you be willing to share the identity with me?"

"No, ma'am. It won't help with your investigation, and if you gave that information to Jenny, and she shared it with her mother, I'd be responsible for the consequences, and that's not how I want to spend my retirement."

Hadley thanked him and ended the call. She slogged through the rush-hour traffic and arrived home ready to drop. She needed to relax and get her mind off the case. Before she could do that, she needed to assess where they were.

She sat at her kitchen table and wrote her three suspects at the top: Mary Taggert, Neil Davidson, Neil Davidson's girlfriend. She still didn't buy Neil as a suspect, but she couldn't ignore the case Eddie and Gary had made against him.

Interestingly, he had connections to each of the other suspects. If the woman he had an affair with was involved, it was undoubtedly with his knowledge and, probably, encouragement. Mary Taggert had a connection to Neil, and it was quite possible she was involved at his behest. She could have acted independently, but Hadley didn't know how likely that would be.

Eddie may not have been wrong to focus on Neil. Even if he wasn't the perpetrator, or the sole perpetrator, it made sense to give him serious consideration. She had been too harsh on Eddie—even if he had crossed a line during the interview. Vince was right; she owed Eddie an apology. The thought of it made her even more tired.

She circled Mary as her most likely suspect. She was in the neighborhood the day of the kidnapping—*possibly* in the neighborhood that day, she corrected herself. She'd had the weird interaction with Jonah and the camera a few months before. Her work performance tanked after the kidnapping, and she disappeared shortly after.

She circled the name a few more times. Starting in the morning, finding Mary would become her sole priority in the case.

Her phone buzzed with an incoming text. "Just checking in," Vince said. "Probably down here another few days, then back to Denver. Coming back down from Thanksgiving to Christmas. How's the case?"

"A few developments. Update you when you come back. Stay safe."

She poured herself a glass of red wine, ran a bath, grabbed a novel she'd been neglecting, and sank into the hot water. She soaked until the water grew cold, then collapsed into her bed.

The thrumming of a bass and the revving of engines awoke her hours later. She heard doors slam and angry voices. Downstairs, her front door rattled as someone shook the handle.

Heart racing, she grabbed the iPad from her nightstand and opened her security app. The front door camera showed a burly man in a balaclava shaking the front door. She enabled the audio and heard the bass booming from a pair of pickup trucks backed into her driveway, engines running.

"Hadley Collins," the man shouted. "Come out now."

She switched to a tiled view of all her cameras. The man at the front door raised a baseball bat and pounded on the door with it. She watched a second man cross in front of her garage. He held something in his hand, but she couldn't tell what it was. Another baseball bat, she thought.

The man left that frame and got picked up by a camera on the side of the house, where he tried a window. She grabbed for her phone blindly, eyes fixed on the iPad screen. She saw lights come on in the second man's tile, and Roger Flagg, her older next-door neighbor, approached from his house.

"I called the police," she heard him say over the camera. "You need to leave now."

The second man turned, revealing that he, too, had covered his face. He raised the object he carried, and Hadley caught her breath as she saw that it was an AR-15, pointed directly at Roger. She hoped he really had called the police.

She hit the panic button in her app, hoping it would scare the men off but not startle the second guy into pulling the trigger. Strobe lights around the house flashed and a siren wailed. She grabbed her phone and mashed 911.

"I need the police," she panted to the dispatcher. "Possible home invasion." She kept watching her screen. Roger had backed away to his house, and she hoped he was safe inside with Lena, his wife.

Both men returned to their trucks and drove away. She hoped the driveway camera had picked up their license plate numbers. A minute later, red and blue lights came on the scene, and she assured the dispatcher she'd be okay. She turned off the panic system and sent a text to Eddie Fleck.

"Someone tried to break into my house. Don't know if it's case-related. Police here now."

She watched on the app as an officer approached her door. Vince was safe in Texas; she could let him know what happened in the morning. She threw a bathrobe over her pajamas. Clutching her phone and iPad, she ventured down the stairs. She asked the police officer to show his badge to the camera before she'd unlock the door.

Five minutes later, she sat on her overstuffed leather sofa, legs curled up beneath her, and a steaming mug of tea in her hands. Roger Flagg sat on the other end of the sofa; he'd come in with the police and made tea while they searched the perimeter of the property. The two officers joined them in the living room.

"I'm Officer Anderson," the first one, a woman, said. "You can call me Karen if you'd like. This is my partner, Officer Tony Stanford." The male officer nodded at her; he had been the one to come to the door.

"Thanks for coming," Hadley said. "I have video, but I'm afraid it's not helpful." She played the security footage for them, shuddering as she relived the moments of terror, unsure if Baseball Bat was going to break through her door or if AR-15 was going to shoot Roger. She paused the video as the trucks pulled out of the driveway. "They covered their plates. And, with the face coverings, I don't have a good description of either of them, other than that they were huge."

Officer Anderson nodded. "Any idea why they might have come here?"

"The only thing I can think of," Hadley began, "is that they're connected to a case I'm working on. I'm a private detective." The two officers exchanged a glance that Hadley couldn't interpret. She thought it might mean that they thought she was being overly dramatic. "It could have been completely random," she added. "But, I was doing some research today and had to give my name and address to get some information."

"What kind of information?" Stanford asked.

He sat with ramrod-straight posture, his pen poised over his tiny notepad. Hadley knew if she revealed too much about the case, she'd be inviting the police in before she was ready. He could have a buddy in the Park Hill district for all she knew.

"I can't say," Hadley said. "It's an active case."

"We respect that," Anderson said. "But, if your activity led to these men showing up here tonight, you need to tell us everything."

"She's right," Roger said.

Hadley chose her words carefully. "There's a company out past Limon. A business called TerraPure. I'm looking into a potential impropriety about an employee, I guess. It's a weird set up, and I'm not sure if their workers are paid employees or just volunteers. Anyway, I needed information on the company's incorporation. I had to give my name and address to get it. Maybe that got leaked to them."

Stanford took some notes but did not seem impressed with her story. "Did you recognize either of the trucks?"

"No."

"What about their voices?"

"No."

Anderson turned to Roger. "Did you recognize anything about these men? Trucks, voices, clothes, anything?"

He shook his head. "No. I don't think I've ever seen or heard those men before."

The officers asked a few more questions, had Hadley email them her security footage, and walked the property again. She watched their progress on the iPad.

"You should go home, Roger," Hadley said. "But, I appreciate everything you did tonight."

"You can't stay here alone," he said. "You should come next door. I can have Lena make up the guest bed."

"That's kind of you, but I'll be fine."

On the screen, a car tore down the street, screeching to a stop at Hadley's curb. The round silhouette of Eddie Fleck rushed up the driveway and to the front door.

"Looks like I won't be alone after all," Hadley said to Roger. She let Eddie in, and he pulled her into a fatherly embrace. She smelled his tacky cologne but found it strangely comforting. She pressed her head to his chest and tried to hold back the tears.

Anderson and Stanford returned to the front door. Eddie introduced himself, and the officers told her to call them if she remembered any other details. Roger walked out with them.

Eddie took off his jacket, revealing a .357 in a shoulder holster. She recounted the intrusion and showed him the video.

"How sure are you this is connected to your visit to Hugo earlier?" he asked. "You're certain these aren't just some random weirdos?"

"This kind of thing doesn't happen in our neighborhood," Hadley said. "Seems like too big of a coincidence that it happened on the day I got the information on TerraPure. And, they knew my name. A couple random guys who show up to harass someone wouldn't know what to call me."

"I doubt they'll be back tonight," Eddie said. "They made their point. But, if they're stupid enough to show up again, you don't need to worry about calling the police." He pointed his eyes at the handgun, and she understood his meaning. "Get some sleep. I'm on duty for the rest of the night."

Hadley wanted to protest. She wanted to send him home. But, she wanted to sleep even more, and the idea of having a protector sitting in the living room all night offered too much comfort to turn down. "Thanks, Eddie," she said, feeling even worse about the way she had treated him.

It was close to 2:00 a.m. by the time she drifted off to sleep. She awoke at 10:00 a.m. to the smell of coffee and toast. She changed into a pair of sweatpants and a hoodie and followed her nose down the stairs.

"There she is," Eddie said. "Hope you don't mind, but I made a little breakfast." He nodded to his plate, which sat on the couch cushion next to him, she noticed in horror. "I knew it would be too much to hope for some bacon around here, so I made a fried egg sandwich. And, some of that stuff you call coffee. There's more in the pot."

She poured herself a cup and sat in a chair across from him. He took a bite of sandwich and yolk ran down his chin. She retrieved a basket of napkins from the kitchen table and tried to look diplomatic as she handed it to him.

"Eddie," she said. "I was wrong to kick you off the case. You're a good detective, and I want your help. I'm sorry." The words tasted bitter coming from her mouth, but she meant them. He had proven himself loyal and dependable time after time.

He flashed a grin. "I was hoping to get back on the case. Those guys came after my little sister. It's personal now."

Hadley started to say she didn't know he had a little sister, then realized he meant her. She found that even more touching than him showing up the night before. She'd meant her text as a warning for him, but he took it as a cry for help.

"I saw your scribbles at the table," Eddie said. "What are you thinking?"

She walked him through each suspect, making the case for each one. She started with Neil, moved to his girlfriend from 15 years before, and ended with Mary.

"Mary's the one I'm most interested in," she said. "That's not to say there's not a connection to Neil, but the cops looked at him so hard back then, it's hard for me to imagine we'll come up with better evidence against him now. Mary is the new lead, so I want to pursue that as far as we can."

"And, you think she lives in some kind of hippie-dippy farm commune thing?"

"Yes."

"And, the owners of said commune thing are apparently sensitive about being looked into."

She nodded. "If the guys last night are connected to them, they're very sensitive."

"How brave are you feeling?" She didn't answer right away, so he continued. "Seems like they're trying to hide something. And, as I said, it's personal now. I say we take the fight to them."

# CHAPTER 24

*October 27, 2023*

Hadley ended the call and took a deep breath. Not surprisingly, Vince hated the plan. He reminded her how lucky they were during the Batson case and warned her that a much worse outcome was likely. She told him Eddie was on his way to her place and then they'd be off to Limon and that everything would be just fine.

Eddie rang the bell, and she let him in, peering over his shoulder to see the white Toyota 4Runner he'd arrived in. "Did you get a new car?"

"Rental," he said. "Picked it up this morning. They probably got your registration information from your name and address. From there, it's a short journey to find Vince and me. Might as well keep some element of surprise when we arrive."

"Speaking of rentals, I ran the plates on the mystery woman. She rented the car in Ogallala. Probably lives around there somewhere."

Eddie furrowed his brow. "I could probably get the rental agreement and track her down if you think it's worth it."

"How..."

"Don't ask," he interrupted. "It's not completely legal and not exactly cheap."

"Don't worry about it," Hadley said. "She knows more than she's giving me, but I don't know if Mary was in the same place with her. We'll find out more by visiting TerraPure in person."

"Sounds like a plan. Let's see the goodies."

Hadley opened a duffel bag on her kitchen table. Inside, she had placed a collection of electronic devices. She held up a tiny gray circle. Eddie squinted at it. "Wireless mic," she said. "I've got four of these. They transmit to a base station, which can send the audio to the cloud via satellite. If we place these today, we can listen to the audio from wherever we are."

Eddie nodded his approval. Hadley nestled the microphone into its case and pointed out the base station, about the size of his wifi router at home. It resembled a black brick with three antennas. "What kind of power do you need for these things?" he asked.

"They have internal batteries, and the mics and the base station will both last about two weeks, depending on how much transmission we pick up. They go to sleep when they're not actively picking up sound."

"If we get a windy day, will we get a full day of static?"

"No, they're smart devices. They filter background noise. Now, check this out."

She held up a cylinder, slightly larger than the microphones. "Camera?" Eddie asked.

"Yes. I have two of these, and they work with the same base station. They're motion activated. The trick is hiding them. We can put the mics anywhere and they'll pick up audio. Cameras need sight lines."

"Makes sense. What else do you have?"

"That's it for surveillance. I have a taser, binoculars, and my camera."

"I've got my .357," Eddie said. "And, I have a nine millimeter if you want something with more stopping power than a taser."

Hadley made a face. She didn't like guns and normally would prefer Eddie remain unarmed. After the other night, though, she wasn't about to say anything to him about it.

"Suit yourself," he said. "Let's hit the road."

Hadley loaded the duffel into the Toyota's cargo space, and they started their trip. Eddie had the rental's satellite radio tuned to a heavy metal station, and Hadley was reminded of her sister's head-banging phase in high school. Eddie must have sensed that the station wasn't her first choice because he changed it to classic rock.

They started slowly, with the city's morning traffic clogging the highway. Eddie drove aggressively, getting inches from the car in front of him before abruptly swerving into the next lane, inviting honks. He responded with gestures, and Hadley wondered if they'd make it to Limon in one piece. She bit back her cautions and criticisms, not wanting to threaten their newly brokered peace.

They finally passed the Denver airport, with its creepy blue horse and circus tent architecture. The traffic thinned and their surroundings transformed from metropolis to farmland almost instantly.

Eddie set the cruise and stayed in the left-hand lane, whizzing past the slower cars on the right. It was a beautiful fall day, the sky a brilliant blue and the sun shining. Hadley saw frost clinging to the grass in the shadows, a reminder that the seasons were turning and winter would soon arrive.

They passed advertisements for fall festivals and pumpkin patches, and Hadley felt a lump form in her throat as she thought about all the things Jonah's family never got to do with him. She remembered what Jenny said about all of them being held captive, and the words rang true. Even if Jonah himself was waiting to welcome them into TerraPure, bringing him back now would never allow the family to recover the hay rides, corn mazes, and haunted houses that they missed. Still, it beat the alternative of never reuniting him with his family.

"Hey, you there?" Eddie asked.

"Sorry," she said. "Just thinking. What's up?"

"I asked if you'd thought about our approach when we get there."

"Yeah. I think cautious is best. They probably have their guard up." They discussed their options. They had plotted out the section of land belonging to TerraPure. As the mystery woman had said, there were no good images available on Google Earth or any mapping software they tried, so they were going in blind. They decided the best approach was to drive as much of the perimeter as possible and see what entry points they might have.

Hadley had age progression photos from a missing child database. She didn't know how accurate they would be. She thought Mary would be much easier to spot, and that was their goal. Find Mary, figure out how to separate her from the group, and question her about the day Jonah disappeared. If they didn't get a direct sighting of her, the cameras and microphones would give them two weeks to identify her as a resident of TerraPure.

They passed the exit for Hugo, and Hadley tensed, feeling that they had crossed into enemy territory. Eddie took the next exit, and they followed a two-lane highway until they turned onto a narrow, unmarked road.

A series of turns had Hadley disoriented. They ended up on a gravel road far from the highway. They hadn't seen another vehicle or signs of civilization in half an hour. Groups of pine trees and aspens appeared. Eddie pointed at a fence separating the detectives from the trees.

"This is the property," he said. "They've put in the trees to create a visual buffer from the rest of the world."

He slowed the Toyota, and they lumbered down the path, kicking up much less dust at the lower speed. He stopped when they came to a driveway leading away from the path and into a break in the tree line. A thick metal gate blocked the driveway, secured with a heavy chain and padlock. A large no trespassing sign covered the middle of the gate. On each end was a smaller sign with the word trespassing in the middle of a circle with a diagonal line slashing through it. Hadley looked closer and realized the diagonal line was actually an AR-15. The bottom of the sign read, "Property secured by the second amendment."

"I'm going to take a look," Eddie said. Hadley climbed out, too, and they approached the gate. Eddie looked it over from all angles. "I don't see electricity running to it," he said.

Hadley stopped directly in front of the gate, leaning the top of her body over it. She looked as far as she could in each direction. The driveway on the other side of the gate was lined with pines on either side, so there wasn't much she could see.

She didn't see the camera, hidden on a branch of the tree closest to her left side. It recorded their every move from the moment they stepped out of the 4Runner until they returned.

Eddie continued to drive around the perimeter. They turned a corner, and he stopped again. A long-dead tree trunk and a pair of large rocks blocked the path. On the other side of the obstacles, grass and weeds grew over the gravel. "That barricade has been there a while," Eddie said.

He put the Toyota in reverse and executed a three-point turn, driving back the way they came. He passed the driveway and went as far as he could, passing the road where they'd turned onto the path. A couple minutes later, they encountered another barricade like the first.

"One way in, one way out," Hadley remarked.

Eddie scowled, cut the wheel hard to the left and made a U-turn. To Hadley's surprise, he threw the vehicle into reverse and backed into the brush bordering the barricade. The back-up camera beeped incessantly as they crunched into branches and brambles.

Hadley climbed into the back seat and pulled the duffel bag from the cargo bay. Eddie took off his jacket, slipped on his shoulder holster, checked the .357, and put his jacket back on.

"Want me to carry that?" he asked, gesturing toward the duffel.

"I got it."

They continued on foot, going past the barricade and following the fence. Despite the abundant sunshine, the air held a chill and Hadley wished she'd brought a heavier coat.

Eddie stopped at a spot where a stand of aspens bordered the fence. "This looks like a good spot," he said. Hadley agreed, and he gave her a boost over the fence. He struggled to follow, eventually heaving himself over the metal bars. "This was easier when I was younger," he remarked.

The tree growth was not thick, and in just a few seconds they were back in the open. In the distance, they saw a row of greenhouses, with clusters of small buildings beyond. Hadley pulled the binoculars from her bag and peered through them. She passed them to Eddie, who looked for a long moment.

"This matches the mystery woman's description," Hadley said. "They have the indoor gardens in the greenhouses, and a bunch of tiny houses. I'm guessing if we keep going, we'll find the leadership compound, and there should be some kind of livestock out here."

"What's the play?" Eddie asked. "We can go closer, see if we're able to encounter anyone. Maybe we'll get lucky and find Mary right away."

"I think we should go," Hadley said. "Look how open the place is. We're sitting ducks if we go out there. There's nowhere to hide between the trees and the greenhouses. Let's kill some time in Limon, and we'll come back tonight and plant the equipment."

"Good idea," Eddie said. "Take some pictures before we go, we can study the layout while we wait."

She took a few wide-angle shots, capturing their entire view. She zoomed in as far as she could on the greenhouses and the tiny houses. She saw a few people near the greenhouses and a couple more near the houses. She could not zoom in enough to capture their faces or even distinguish if they were male or female. She doubted they could see her and Eddie with their naked eyes, but she still felt like they should exit quickly.

They went back through the trees. Eddie boosted her over the fence again and again had trouble hoisting himself over. "I guess this means more kale," he said, patting his stomach as he tried to regain his breath. They returned to the car, which Hadley was glad to see remained unmolested.

It took them over an hour to wind their way back to Limon. They stopped at a diner for lunch. True to his word, Eddie had a salad, ordering the same one as Hadley. They took their time eating, passing the camera back and forth to look at the pictures.

"I think we target the greenhouses," Eddie said. "If we don't want a run-in with the residents, we can't go any closer to the housing than that."

"Agreed," Hadley said. "With any luck, everyone takes turns working in the gardens, and we'll get some sign of Mary over the next two weeks."

"How close does the base station need to be?"

"They have a pretty good transmission range," Hadley said. "The base station will pick them up from around half a mile away. We can plant the devices first, and carry the base station back with us. I've already paired everything, and it has indicator lights to show us when we're in range."

"With a little luck, we can plant the base station outside the fence," Eddie said. "I'd hate to have a curious hippie find it on the property and ruin this operation."

After lunch, they found a Walmart, where they purchased black sweatshirts, stocking caps, and gloves. They walked the aisles, killing time, and then proceeded to the Limon library.

Eddie settled into the reading room with a stack of magazines. Hadley went to the reference area and found printed archives of the *Limon Gazette*, a weekly newspaper. She selected several random months worth from the previous 15 years and began paging through, looking for any sign of TerraPure or Mary Taggert. She kept an eye out for Jeremy Costas, too; his real estate transaction still puzzled her.

It did not take long for her to realize she was searching for needles inside mountains of haystacks. The *Gazette* did not run much hard news. The papers featured plenty of coverage of local events, farmers markets, and little league games, but there had been hundreds of issues in the past decade and a half; it would take her a year to work through every issue.

Finally, the sun dipped in the sky and the shadows grew longer. They changed into their sweatshirts in the restrooms and started the drive back to the TerraPure property. Eddie had to drive much more slowly than in the morning; the little roads were unlit, and he had to rely on the GPS to announce when a turn was coming.

When they approached the gravel path that skirted the property, Eddie killed the lights completely. Hadley gripped the armrest; Eddie seemed comfortable driving blind, but it made her nervous.

He turned left onto the gravel and found their parking place from the morning. "I should have asked for a black or green car," he said, "but they didn't have many SUVs on short notice."

"We'll be fine," Hadley said.

They donned their caps and gloves. Hadley retrieved the duffel bag, and Eddie adjusted his holster over the sweatshirt. "Do you want me to give you a boost this time?" Hadley asked. Eddie glared at her without answering.

Once in the trees again, Hadley added a night vision attachment to her binoculars and scanned the area. "I don't see anyone out and about," she said. "We'll be quiet and quick."

There were three greenhouses. They wanted to put a camera on the back of the furthest greenhouse from them and another on the front side—facing the houses—of the one closest to them. They'd plant microphones near the front doors of each greenhouse, with the final one on the back of the middle structure.

"There's an adhesive on the back," Hadley said, handing the microphones to Eddie. "You just peel the backing and stick it someplace inconspicuous. We'll do the back side first, then move to the front."

Eddie accepted the devices and they ventured out of the trees. They took a few cautious steps and paused. There was no sign of anyone watching them. They took a few more steps. "We're clear," Eddie said. "Let's go."

They jogged toward the greenhouses. Hadley worried about Eddie, who was already breathing hard, and how he'd do if they had to outrun anyone.

They reached their target without encountering anyone. They stood along the back wall of a greenhouse, catching their breath. Satisfied that they were safe, they went to work. Eddie had it easier with the microphone. The bottom of the greenhouse had a slight overhang above its concrete slab, so he stuck the device underneath.

Hadley did not see a perfect spot for the camera, and finally decided on the eave just above the back door. If she could get to the top, she could point the camera at an angle and capture a wide view of anyone approaching the back doors. She motioned Eddie over to give her a boost.

She had to stand on his shoulders. He wobbled underneath her, and she worried she'd lose her footing. She put the camera gingerly between her lips and used both hands to grab the roof and hoist herself up, using her forearms to support her.

She pulled off a glove, threw it to the ground beneath her, and affixed the microphone in a gap where two shingles met.

Fortunately, the microphone was similar in color to the roof, and she didn't think it would be noticeable. She lowered herself so she was hanging from her fingertips before dropping to the ground.

"Let's do the camera on the front first," she said. Once I get positioned on the roof, you can start doing the microphones."

They slunk from greenhouse to greenhouse and crept around the side of the first one. When they reached the front corner, Hadley held up a hand in a stop motion. She looked through her optics at the housing. She saw movement around a few of them, people walking from the small houses to a larger building. Probably going for dinner in the common kitchen building, she thought.

"There are people out," she said. "But, they aren't looking at the greenhouses. Let's be fast."

They scrambled to the front and repeated the process of boosting Hadley to the roof. As she affixed the camera, Eddie scurried from building to building, planting the microphones. She lowered herself once again, arms extended, then dropped back to the ground, trying to keep her knees unlocked to cushion the landing.

They moved back to the corner of the first greenhouse. Hadley removed the base station from her bag and powered it on. A series of lights flashed in amber. "It's searching for signals," she said. One by one, the indicators turned solid green until there were six dots beaming up at them. "We're good," she said. "I'll watch this as we go back. We'll take it as far as we can with the lights still on."

They crept to the back of the greenhouses and began their return trip. They went at a fast walk, rather than a jog, so Hadley could stare at the indicators. They had almost reached the trees when the world lit up from behind them.

# CHAPTER 25

Hadley looked back and stared into the headlights of a pair of ATVs coming toward them and closing the distance fast. She thought about the sign on the gate: "Property secured by the second amendment."

"We need to get to the trees," she gasped at Eddie. She grabbed his arm and pointed him toward where she wanted to go, a 45-degree angle from their current course. She hoped they could enter the trees, get over the fence, and get to the car without giving away its position.

"Stay where you are," came a voice from behind them. It sounded like the speaker was using a bullhorn. "You're trespassing on private property."

Hadley and Eddie continued to sprint. The trees weren't far, maybe 50 yards. The ATVs separated, one moving above them, the other moving below. The drivers were trying to sandwich them, but Hadley didn't think it would matter if they could lose them in the trees.

They pushed forward, the engines of the ATVs growing louder as the trees grew closer. They reached a group of pines and ducked between them. Eddie took Hadley by the shoulder and pointed her in a diagonal line, going toward the car. She followed him for several yards. They both stopped and leaned against a tree trunk.

"Quiet," Eddie whispered. "Listen for them."

At least one ATV rumbled in the distance, and footsteps rustled through fallen leaves. Hadley looked over her right shoulder and saw a beam of light sweeping through the trees. She nudged Eddie, and he nodded that he saw it, too.

She looked to the left, but did not see additional flashlights. She wondered if the other ATV driver, or drivers, she didn't know how many people it held, stayed at the tree line in case they tried to loop back toward the property.

Eddie elbowed her and pointed in the other direction. The flashlight beam had changed course, and was going further into the trees in the wrong direction. "Now's our chance," he said.

"Wait," Hadley said. She felt her stomach knot and thought she would be sick. "I don't have the base station. I must have dropped it."

"We have to leave it. Let's hope it can transmit from wherever it is."

"No. This is our one shot at doing this."

She heard Eddie sigh. She looked back in the direction they'd come from. She saw tiny green indicator lights on the ground where they'd first stopped.

"I see it," she said. "You go to the fence. I'll grab the base station and come over after you." She handed him the duffel bag and took off before he could say anything. She tried to walk softly, not wanting to give away their position. She heard Eddie's heavier footfalls and hoped the others were too far away to notice.

She reached the base station and checked it. The indicators all held at a solid green. She heard a thud and knew Eddie had just dropped to the other side of the fence. She decided to go directly to the fence in front of her, get over, and find Eddie on the other side. As she stepped forward, a flashlight beam cut through the trees and illuminated her. She stepped back but heard steps running toward her.

She moved back toward the trees where she'd left Eddie, hoping that in the dark and with all the obstacles, her pursuers would not be able to find her. She crouched against a tree trunk, making herself as small as possible and listening for footsteps. She kept a white-knuckled grip on the base station.

"Do you see them?" a man's voice asked. It sounded much closer than Hadley expected.

"No. They must have gone back the other way," a second man said, his voice nasal and whiny.

She heard the static of a radio. The first man said, "Tony, have they come out of the trees yet?"

"Negative," yet another man responded. "They haven't been this way. They're either in the trees or over the fence."

Hadley hoped Eddie could hear this. He needed to get to the car and go. They'd figure out how to rendezvous once she escaped.

The base station had a strap to attach it to a tree branch or other structure. Hadley considered going up the tree she was hiding by, but she didn't want to make noise, and she'd rather get it to the other side of the fence. She strapped it to her shin, turning it so her leg would hide the indicator lights. She tightened it as much as she could and surveyed her surroundings.

She hadn't heard footsteps since the men started talking on the radio. The flashlight beam swept in each direction periodically. She imagined the men having a hushed conversation a dozen yards away, debating what to do.

She crept as quietly as she could to the edge of the trees and turned in the direction where they'd left the car. She'd stay just inside the trees and see if she could sneak past the second ATV. If they were watching for someone to run out of the trees, maybe they wouldn't notice her dash from tree to tree. If she could get past them, she could get to the fence and find Eddie.

Her heart pounded with each step she took. Her pulse pounded in her temples. The crackle of each leaf under her feet amplified by 10,000 times in her mind. Finally, she spotted the second ATV.

They had chosen their position well. They set up next to an area where the trees had thinned out. These were aspens, rather than pines, and they'd lost most of their leaves for autumn. Their trunks were much smaller than the pines, and they were spaced further apart. There was no way Hadley could cross through this group of trees and get past the ATV without being spotted.

She backtracked to the thicker pine trees. She moved through the first row of trees and selected one close to the back side of the growth; she could just make out the fence in the dark. She worried about getting over the fence without getting caught. And, finding Eddie in the dark. If these men got to her before she could hide the base station, the entire trip would be a bust.

She unstrapped the device from her leg. The pine had a branch low enough for her to step on. She held her breath and hoped it wouldn't crack like a gunshot in the quiet night. The branch bounced but held her. She stretched as high as she could reach. Her fingers touched another branch. It was thick and had plenty of pine needles. She strapped the base station to it, turning the indicator lights to face the branch.

Hoping it was high enough to remain hidden, especially since no one knew to look for it, she let go of the branch and let all her body weight rest on the one supporting her feet. The branch swooned downward and snapped. The sound echoed through the countryside.

Without another thought of hiding, she rushed toward the fence. A beam of light from the direction of the second ATV swung her way. "Movement! Over there!" It sounded like the one they called Tony.

As she reached the fence, she saw a flashlight in the other direction. She heard footsteps crashing toward her.

Without Eddie to boost her, she couldn't quite reach the top rail of the fence. She leapt for it, and her left hand caught the smooth iron, cold in the night air. She swung to grab it with her right hand, too, but lost her balance. She hung awkwardly for a second before tumbling down. It wasn't much of a drop, but she landed on the side of her foot and fell. Pain shot through her ankle.

The footsteps grew closer and the lights grew brighter. She scrambled to her feet, stepped on the bottom rail, and used it to boost herself to the top rail. She grasped it with both hands and pulled herself up. She had almost swung her first leg over when a pair of hands caught her waist and flung her to the ground.

She landed on her chest, the wind knocked out of her. The lights trained on her, blinding her. She covered her eyes.

"What'll we do with her?" someone asked. It was the guy who spoke in a whine.

"Get her to the ATV," the first man said. "I'll take her from there."

Someone grabbed her arms and jerked her to her feet. He shoved her roughly in front of him and through the trees. Every few steps, he'd give her another shove, causing her to stumble a few times. Finally, they exited the trees and marched to the ATV.

"Be still," the first man said. "Tony, pat her down. Make sure she's not armed."

She did as she was told as Tony pawed her body. She was glad she hadn't taken Eddie up on his offer of a handgun. She was even more grateful she had left her phone in the Toyota.

"She's clean," Tony said.

The first man wrapped a jacket around her face as a makeshift hood. It stank of sweat, tobacco, and cheap cologne. He tied it tight enough that she could barely breathe. "Keep your hands in your pockets," he said. "Tony, take her to the sheds."

Rough hands shoved her into the ATV, and it soon bounced roughly over the property. She had no idea which direction they were headed in. The cold air whipped past them, and she hoped she wouldn't tumble out of the vehicle.

The ATV stopped, and the man cut the engine. He pulled her to her feet and guided her a few steps until they stopped. She heard a lock click. He guided her through a doorway, then pulled the jacket from her face. She turned to face him. He delivered a haymaker to her stomach, and she doubled over in pain, gasping for air. She heard the door slam and the lock turn. She hadn't gotten a good look at him.

When she could breathe again, she stood and let her eyes grow accustomed to the dark around her. She could make out shapes, but there was nothing to see. As far as she could tell, she was in an empty room, about eight-by-eight feet with a low ceiling. She felt along the walls, corrugated steel. Probably a pre-fab storage shed. She bent down and touched the floor. Concrete. The walls were likely bolted down in the corners.

With the right tools, she could find a seam and work open a hole big enough to climb through. But, she didn't have any tools or anything she could improvise with. She felt the old feelings of being swallowed alive take over her. She'd felt it twice before. Once, with Vince in Virginia. And, once at six years old.

Claustrophobia set in quickly, her heart rate accelerating and her lungs heaving for breath. She wanted to curl up and die in the middle of the floor, anything to make the feeling of being trapped go away. She squeezed her eyes shut and relived years of therapy. She reminded herself that she was bigger than the feelings. She counted to 100 slowly and then back down. By the time she reached zero, her ragged breaths had smoothed and she felt able to stand again.

She made another pass around the structure, feeling the corners for any sign of weakness, trying out bolts to see if any would turn. The situation was hopeless. She curled up in a corner. She wondered if Eddie was still waiting for her in the dark. Surely, he'd heard the commotion and knew they had her.

She hoped he would just go to the police and not try to break back into the property with guns literally blazing.

She drew her knees tighter to her chest and wrapped her arms around them. She closed her eyes and let sleep carry her away.

# CHAPTER 26

*May 1, 2000*

Hadley's stomach growled again. It was past dinner time, and Dan hadn't come back yet. He had lectured her several times about not eating anything other than the lunch he made for her and the snacks he left on the counter each morning. Still, she went to the pantry and looked at the nearly empty shelves. She hoped Dan would be back soon and that he'd gone to the grocery store.

She hadn't gone back into the cellar since she discovered it. If Dan knew she'd been down there, he didn't say anything about it. Each day she thought about going back down there, so she could get outside, but each time, she chickened out. She kept thinking that maybe her mom and Heather would show up that day.

She saw headlights coming up the drive and heard the rumble of Dan's engine and the sound of gravel crunching under his tires. She closed the pantry door and ran to the living room, where she sat on the lumpy sofa.

Dan came in a minute later with a paper sack filled with groceries under each arm. "You're home," Hadley said, smiling at him. He didn't smile back, not at first. When he looked at her, his expression looked fake. Something was off, and she felt that familiar feeling coming back to her stomach.

"Had to work late," he said from the kitchen as he rattled the grocery sacks. He slammed doors and drawers as he put things away. "Get the trays set up. I brought chicken."

Hadley dragged one of the trays from its spot to one end of the sofa and set it up. One leg was shorter than the other, so it leaned precariously. She repeated the action with the second one. Dan set a paper plate with fried chicken and potato salad on her tray, along with a can of root beer. He brought his own plate in with an adult beer.

The chicken was barely warm, and Hadley wondered how far they were from the grocery store. She wanted to ask but had learned not to question Dan on any of the details of their life.

About halfway through the meal, she did ask a question, one that was usually safe. "When are my mom and Heather coming to see us?" The answer was almost always "soon" or "maybe in a few days," and they'd talk about what they'd do when Hadley's family got there.

This time, Dan's eyes grew darker and his mouth turned down at the corners. He put his fork down with potato salad still on it. "I'm sorry, honey," he said. "I talked to your mom today, and they're not coming."

Tears stung Hadley's eyes and threatened to spill down her cheeks. She fought to hold them back. "Why not?"

"Your mom is mad at you," Dan said, looking her straight in the eye. "She wouldn't say why, but she said you did something that made her angry and she wants you to stay here with me."

Years later, Hadley would learn that Dan had deluded himself into thinking he could convince her mom to take him back if he showed her how well he had taken care of Hadley without her. He had called her that afternoon, but as soon as he mentioned Hadley, she'd said there was no chance they'd ever get back together and she was calling the police.

In that moment, though, six-year-old Hadley tried to process what Dan was telling her. She stopped fighting the tears and let them roll freely down her face.

"Don't cry," Dan said. "We can keep having a good time here, just the two of us. You've enjoyed it here, right?"

"I hate it here," Hadley said between sobs. "I want to go back to school. I want you to take me home now."

Dan's face turned from compassionate to angry. He slammed his palm against the tray table, causing his plate to bounce. A piece of fried chicken flipped onto the floor and his beer can fell to its side, the remnants pouring onto the carpet in a small waterfall.

"Look what you made me do," he growled.

Hadley cried even harder, her face turning scarlet and her body shaking.

"I'm sorry," Dan said. He moved toward her and tried to put an arm around her, but she pulled away. "I didn't mean to get angry at you. We'll keep having fun here. You'll see. And, maybe one day, I'll convince your mom to come."

She didn't touch the rest of her dinner. Dan usually had a strict clean plate rule, but he relaxed it that night. She was still crying later when she stood on the step stool in the bathroom to brush her teeth. She went to her bedroom without telling Dan goodnight. She heard him lock the front door and close his own bedroom door. She heard static from his radio followed by some kind of sports game, but she couldn't understand what the announcer said.

She crawled into her bed, hugging the teddy bear Dan had given her. At home, she slept with a stuffed tiger and a pink frog. She missed them. She missed Heather. She missed her mom. She wondered what she had done to make her mom so mad that she wouldn't come and take her home.

As the tears continued to trickle down her cheeks and chin, soaking the front of her pajamas, she thought about the cellar and the door that led outside. She wouldn't spend another night in that house. The next day, she would be brave. She would get outside and find another house and get someone to call her mom. Maybe if she talked to her herself, she could convince her mom to come.

She gripped the bear tighter, whispering her plans in its ear, telling it about the games she and Heather used to play and would play again if she got home. She told it about her school and her friends and how she hated riding the bus.

Eventually, she drifted to sleep. For the first time since Dan had taken her, she felt like she had some control over what happened next.

# CHAPTER 27

*October 27, 2023*

Eddie crouched in the darkness, the .357 in his hand with the safety off. He shouldn't have let Hadley go back for the base station without him. Not staying together was a stupid mistake. He'd known better than that when he walked the beat as a rookie cop.

He strained his ears for any sign of her approaching the fence. He watched the flashlight beams play over the area. They never trained them outside the fence where he hid. They either didn't know he was out there or they didn't care. All their attention was on finding Hadley.

He heard shouting and footsteps. They must have caught sight of Hadley in the trees. He heard something crash into the fence 20 yards away. He rushed that way, hoping he wouldn't step in a hole or trip over a root in the darkness.

The flashlight guys got to the spot before he did, and he saw a guy pull Hadley from the fence. He raised the gun and tried to find a target. The flashlight beams kept moving, and it was hard to pick out any silhouettes against the night sky. He didn't want to risk an errant shot hitting Hadley. He lowered the gun and waited.

After a minute or so, they moved back into the trees and vanished from his sight. He'd missed his chance to take any of them out.

He waited until he heard the ATVs driving away. He unlocked the Toyota, its lights flashing like neon signs in the dark. He cranked the engine and drove away as fast as he dared. He kept one hand on the wheel and one hand on his cell phone, checking for a signal.

He got a single bar before he reached the main road that led back to the interstate. He pulled over and dialed 911. He told the dispatcher he needed to report an abduction. He waited for an agonizing moment until the dispatcher came back on the line and told him he was connected to the Lincoln County Sheriff's Department.

"This is Deputy Morris," a gruff voice answered.

Eddie identified himself and said he needed to report the abduction of an adult.

"Wait a minute," Morris said. "An abduction, like a kidnapping? I need you to calm down and tell me the details. Who, what, where, when."

"I'm a private detective from Denver," Eddie said. "My partner and I were doing some research on a property owned by a group called TerraPure. Some men from that property took her into their custody, against her will."

"They took her but not you?"

"That's right, Deputy. I was on the other side of the fence."

"So, your partner was on TerraPure property at the time?"

"Yes."

"How old is she?"

"Thirty or so, I guess. Why's that important?"

"I assume you're both aware that the TerraPure land is private property. That fence clearly marks it, and I think their signs plainly state there's no trespassing."

Eddie couldn't believe it. His blood boiled, and he tried to keep from shouting. "That doesn't justify a kidnapping."

"Sir, I'm going to contact the people at TerraPure and see if they can tell me what they know about your partner. I'll take your number and call you back."

Eddie gave him his cell number and waited. He sat in the dark car, watching the road in front of him. He hoped he'd see a cruiser tear by with lights flashing, but nothing happened. Fifteen minutes later, his cell phone rang.

"This is Deputy Morris," the same gruff voice said. "I spoke with a resident at TerraPure, who confirmed that two people were trespassing tonight. They located one, a female around 30 years old, but couldn't find the other one. I told them we'd spoken and you claimed to be off the property. I hope that's true."

"Yes, I'm in my car right now."

"Good. They've agreed not to press charges. You should consider yourself lucky."

"What do you mean not press charges?" Eddie's voice raised to a thundering yell. "They kidnapped Hadley, and you need to get out from behind your desk, get out here, and get her back."

"Calm down," Morris said. "They escorted your partner off the property. You can probably find her by the main gate. Listen. I've never had trouble with TerraPure before. They're being gracious to not press charges. If I hear any more reports of you or your partner going over the fence, I will ensure you're prosecuted. And, I speak for Sheriff Gonzales, too."

They ended the call, and Eddie sat fuming in the car. He put it in gear and made his way back toward TerraPure while imagining moving to Lincoln County, running for sheriff, and firing all the deputies.

He found the gate to the property, but Hadley was not there. He kept the Toyota pointed toward it, engine running and headlights on. He holstered his gun and stepped out of the vehicle. The air had grown colder, and he felt a chill through the sweatshirt.

"Hadley," he called in his normal speaking voice. No answer. "Hadley," he called again, louder. He walked the fenceline in each direction, calling her name. She never answered.

He got back in the car, muttering about the cops being in TerraPure's pocket. He didn't have many options. His first choice was to drive through the gate and onto the property and search every building until he found Hadley. The second option was to find a place to sleep and come back in the morning.

Every fiber in his body screamed for him to take option one. He gritted his teeth and revved the engine before throwing the rental back in park. They'd be watching for him. They knew the terrain, and he didn't. He'd be vastly outnumbered. They had AR-15s; he had a pistol.

Grudgingly, he turned around toward Limon, listing out the ways he'd inflict pain on every TerraPure resident if they harmed Hadley.

Back at the Walmart, he purchased a sleeping bag, a pillow, the biggest thermos he could find, a bag of powdered donuts, and a box of granola bars. His promise to eat more kale would wait. He found a gas station and filled the thermos with steaming coffee.

He made his way back toward TerraPure, stopping at the final turnoff before the path that led to the gate. He ate two granola bars, folded the backseat down, and settled into the sleeping bag for the night, keeping his gun under the pillow. He promised himself that first thing in the morning, he was going back and not leaving without Hadley.

# CHAPTER 28

*October 28, 2023*

Hadley awoke while it was still dark. She stood to stretch, wobbling on jellied knees. She felt weak from not eating or drinking and from all the adrenaline she expended the night before. She reached upward in an almost sun salutation, and her muscles screamed in protest. Her arms, shoulders, and back ached from a night on the concrete floor. Her abdomen hurt where the guy had punched her.

She put her hand under the sweatshirt and traced the painful area on her skin. She still couldn't see, but she was certain she'd have a fist-shaped bruise on her stomach. She tried to remember if she'd ever been punched before. She'd had fights with Heather growing up, mostly pushing and hair pulling, with the occasional headlock. She and Vince had been roughed up before, but the punch was more vicious and seemed more personal than any previous altercation.

Gradually, a gray light invaded the structure through gaps in the seams. She had guessed correctly; it was a corrugated metal building, probably meant to store lawn mowers and other tools. She wished something had been left inside. She surveyed her surroundings once more and found nothing.

She assessed her situation. Not good, obviously, but maybe not as dire as it had appeared the night before. They had let her live through the night. She had not heard any gunshots, so a firefight with Eddie had not occurred. Having Eddie on the outside was a major advantage. He could get the authorities involved and rescue her.

She had a harder time pinning down the intentions of the TerraPure group. Aside from the punch, they hadn't attempted to hurt her. There had been no interrogation. She wondered if they knew who she was and why she was there. She doubted they had seen her and Eddie plant the devices. They would have intervened much sooner. They'd probably been spotted on their way back to the tree line, so maybe she could play the whole thing off as some kind of innocent misunderstanding.

Footsteps interrupted her thoughts. She looked around frantically, trying to decide what to do. Her only defense was to hide behind the door and try to overpower whoever came through. That had little chance of success, so she stood where she was and waited.

She heard the jingling of keys. The door swung inward, morning light flooding the hut and temporarily blinding her. She squinted and recognized Tony from the night before. He didn't have a gun, but that didn't mean there wasn't someone outside who did.

He approached her and shoved a piece of fabric at her. A sleep mask. "Put this on," he ordered. She did what he said. He shoved her forward and led her outside, where she was pushed onto a vinyl seat. She recognized it as the ATV. The coughing of the engine a moment later confirmed she was right.

They only drove for two minutes before they stopped. "Get out," Tony commanded. Hadley gingerly swung her legs to the side and stepped out, just in time for Tony to shove her again. She heard a door open and sensed a change in the light and the air. They must have gone inside. They walked a few feet, and Tony turned her 90 degrees.

"We're going down some stairs," he said. He took her arm and led her down. They went slowly, Hadley feeling for each step with her toes before descending. They turned on a landing and continued downward, Tony's hand clamped on her bicep like a vise.

Finally, they reached the bottom and she was led through a series of turns until Tony pushed her into a hard chair. "You can take the blindfold off," he said.

She did and looked around. She was sitting in a kitchen. It could have been in any neighborhood in Denver. Granite countertops, stainless steel appliances. She turned her head as far as she dared, and she spied a connected dining room with a large oak table and paintings on the walls. Just beyond, she could make out the beginnings of a living room.

"Sorry about your accommodations last night," a voice said, appearing from around a corner and crossing the kitchen to stand in front of her. The voice belonged to a man in his late 40s or early 50s. He had sandy blond hair that was thinning at the top. He stood at least six and a half feet tall, but couldn't have weighed much more than 170 pounds. He was not intimidating in the least. "We're not used to having guests here," he continued, a wry smile on his face, "and you showed up unannounced."

He paused. Hadley assumed he wanted her to say something, to acknowledge her trespassing or explain why she had climbed the fence. She sat in silence. He turned his back to her and walked toward the refrigerator. When he was almost there, he wheeled around and glared at her.

"Please don't make this difficult, Ms. Collins," he growled.

• • •

The sun poured through the windows of the 4Runner, waking Eddie from his fitful sleep. He sat up, the sleeping bag a sweaty, tangled mess around him. He reached into the front seat and found his shoulder holster. With it in place, he took the .357 from under the pillow and stepped outside.

A chill hung in the morning air. He wondered where Hadley had slept and how she was doing. Gritting his teeth, he climbed into the front seat and poured coffee into the thermos lid. It was still warm, and he gulped the bitter liquid. He wiped his mouth with his sleeve, started the car, and made his way back to the TerraPure gate.

He had company this time. A pickup truck sat in the driveway on the other side of the gate, its bed toward him. Two young guys, probably in their 20s, sat on the tailgate, legs dangling. They wore black tactical pants and camouflage coats. Each held an AR-15 across his lap. One of them had bright red hair, the other had dark black hair the color of a raven.

When he put the Toyota in park, they picked up their weapons. Red hopped off the tailgate and approached the fence. Eddie didn't like the look on his face. He reminded him of recruits they'd have come through the police force from time to time, crazy eyes and itchy trigger fingers, a deadly combination of ignorance and bravado. Those guys never lasted long, but they were always dangerous to have around.

Eddie opened the door and stepped out, keeping the door between him and the two men. "I'm here for a friend of mine," Eddie said. "She was last seen on this property last night."

Red propped his gun on the gate, not exactly aiming but ready to. Raven scowled and lifted his weapon, pointing it directly at Eddie. "This is private property," Red said. "No trespassing."

"I realize that," Eddie said. "Just the same, I'd like to find my friend and leave. We won't give you any trouble."

Red grinned and licked his upper lip twice, a maniacal look in his eyes. Eddie tried to stare him down, but the kid made him uncomfortable.

A radio in the truck bed crackled. "Garber, you there?" a static-filled voice said. "Garber, come in."

Red lowered his weapon and backed up to the truck. Raven took a step forward, keeping Eddie in his sights. He creeped Eddie out even more than Red.

"I'm here. What's up?" Red said into the radio.

"Tell that guy to get back in his car and wait. And make sure he knows the sheriff is ready to lock him up if he takes another step closer to this property."

Red waved the radio toward Eddie. "You heard that, right? Better do what he says."

Eddie closed himself in the Toyota and watched the two guys. After a minute they returned to the tailgate, guns back in their laps. Eddie breathed slowly, willing his blood pressure back into a normal range and wondering what they were doing to Hadley.

•   •   •

The skinny man stepped back toward Hadley and crossed his arms across his chest. He looked like a scarecrow, but he had a fire in his eyes that made Hadley nervous. "Your friend called the police last night. One of the sheriff's deputies explained to him how this works. The two of you trespassed, so you forfeited your legal protections."

Hadley pursed her lips but didn't correct him. He clearly wasn't an expert in the law, but she had a feeling the law as she understood it didn't count for much within the bounds of the fence.

The man's eyes flitted nervously around the room before landing on her once again. "He gave the police your name. We know you requested records on us from the county, and now you've shown up on our property. I'd like nothing more than to get you out of here and send you back home, but first, I need to know what's going on."

The room felt heavy with silence as Hadley debated how to proceed and how much to tell him. To buy some time, she said,

"I assume those were friends of yours who paid a visit to my house the other night?"

The man smirked and continued to stare at her, arms still across his chest. She knew from photos that this man was not Jeremy Costas. She wondered if he was Scott Flanagan, listed as the CFO of TerraPure, or if he was someone else who had not been named in the incorporation documents.

To avoid his smirk, she focused her eyes on his arms and chest. He didn't look like he had a muscle anywhere in his upper body, just a skeleton with skin stretched over it. She wondered how heavy the chair she sat in was and if she could swing it fast enough to take him down before he could react. She heard movement behind her and remembered Tony, who definitely had muscles. She wondered how many other people might be in the house or waiting outside if she escaped.

The skinny man broke the silence. "I need you to tell me what your interest is in this place," he said. He stepped forward until he was mere inches from her, towering above her. "And, I need assurances that we'll never see you here again, Ms. Collins."

She heard footsteps behind her and felt Tony getting closer. He cast a shadow over her, and she could smell the scent from the jacket she'd been blindfolded with.

"I've been doing some research," she said. "I'm interested in communes in Colorado." She took care not to say anything about cults.

"Now we're getting somewhere," the man said. "What kind of interest?"

"Just what the lifestyle is like. How many people are here. How you live. How you interact with the surrounding communities, that kind of thing. I couldn't find much online about you, so I thought I'd pay a visit in person."

"And how much of this has to do with you being a private detective?"

"Not much," Hadley said, hoping he wouldn't see through her deception. "A recent case stirred up my interest, but you're not suspects in a crime or anything." That was closer to the truth; she would not add that TerraPure might be harboring a suspect.

The man unfolded his arms and leaned back against a counter. She felt Tony move back, as well. "We saw you and your partner look at the front gate yesterday, but you didn't try to climb it or come onto the property. That appears to have happened later. How long were you on the property, and what did you do?"

Hadley processed the information as quickly as she could. They had some kind of surveillance set up, at least at their entrance. That meant they could have more. He was either asking to see how truthful she would be, or they didn't have additional cameras and he wanted to see how much she would give away. She played it down the middle.

"We weren't here long," she said. "I mean, I've been here all night, but that wasn't my choice." The man's smirk returned. "We looked at your greenhouses and saw the housing from there. We didn't interact with anyone. Other than Tony and his buddies."

The man threw his head back and cackled with hollow laughter. "You have spunk, Ms. Collins," he said. "Did you attempt to enter any of our greenhouses?"

She shook her head.

"I'm still not sure what you were hoping to accomplish."

"Like I said, just to get a feel for what the community is like." She paused, then cast her bait. "I have a particular interest in single mothers and how they end up in communities like this."

She watched the man closely. He furrowed his brow, just for a second, maybe less, and seemed to search for words for the first time that morning. "Ms. Collins," he finally said, "none of that is your business. If you didn't find anything about us online, there was a reason for that. And, if we have a big gate at our entrance with no trespassing signs, there's a reason for that, too."

He covered the space between them in a single stride and viciously kicked the chair out from underneath her, his work boot thudding against the wood with a resounding thwack. Hadley fell to the floor in a heap. Tony rushed in behind her, and she felt small and powerless, surrounded by the two men.

The skinny man raised his foot and put it on her shoulder. He lowered his foot, forcing her to lie down. His boot heel dug into her as he exerted more pressure. She wanted to cry out in pain but wouldn't give him that satisfaction.

"People come here for a lot of reasons," he said, still not raising his voice. "One reason is to avoid people like you. We're a private community, and we like it that way." He dragged his boot from her shoulder to her neck. He leaned forward, pressing down on her windpipe. Her eyes watered as her breathing turned into gasps. "Keep your research off our property and you won't get hurt. Come here again, and I can guarantee it won't have a happy ending."

He stood motionless, keeping the pressure on her neck. Hadley's breathing became more labored by the second, and she feared he would crush her throat and leave her there to suffocate on the kitchen floor. She looked up his long leg, past his long torso, and into his smirking face. His eyes showed no emotion at all, just cold, calculated cruelty.

He stepped off her throat and she gulped for air, not daring to sit up or move. He put his foot right next to her head. With a slight flick of his ankle, he delivered a mini-kick to her temple. Her vision exploded with stars and she felt a wave of nausea rise in her stomach. When the man turned away and strode out of the kitchen, she sat up and put her hands to her face. It was only then that she realized she was crying.

Tony's rough hands took her under the arms and yanked her to her feet. "Come on," he said, shoving the blindfold over her face again. "Your friend's waiting for you."

It was the best thing she'd heard all day.

# CHAPTER 29

They bounced over the uneven terrain. Blindfolded, Hadley couldn't anticipate what was coming and flopped around the front seat of a pickup truck with each new bump; she was glad it wasn't the ATV this time until she slid sideways and hit the window with her temple in the exact spot where the skinny guy had kicked her. She yelped in pain and felt bile rise from her stomach into her throat. An unfriendly chuckle issued from the driver.

The truck skidded to a stop and she heard the driver's door open, followed seconds later by her own. Tony ripped the blindfold from her, bumping her temple as he did. She gritted her teeth as pain stabbed through her once again.

"Get out," he said, stepping aside.

She stood on unsteady legs and blinked in the sunlight. As her vision cleared, she saw they had parked next to another truck, where two younger guys held rifles. Eddie's rental sat on the other side of the gate. She squinted in the glare on the windshield and saw Eddie.

He opened his door and hopped out, rushing toward the gate. Both of the younger guys jumped from their tailgate and trained their guns on him.

"Relax, everyone," Tony said. "Boys, put your weapons down. You, over there, step back to your vehicle." The red-haired guy obediently swung his rifle back to his side. The one with dark hair took a few extra seconds but grudgingly did as instructed. Eddie stood rooted to his spot, his legs spread to shoulder width. He stood in a sort of bow-legged hunch-crouch that made Hadley think of a sheriff preparing for a shootout in a western. No one moved or made a sound. Eddie finally straightened up and took a few tentative steps backward toward the Toyota.

"I don't feel like going through the trouble of undoing the lock and chain just to let your friend out," Tony said. "So, here's what we're going to do. You, get back in your vehicle. She's going to climb over the gate, then she's going to get in your car, and we'll never see or hear from the two of you again. If you make any move I don't like, Garber here is going to shoot you."

The redhead started laughing and bounced gleefully on the balls of his feet. Eddie looked disgusted but returned to his seat. When he closed the door and started the engine, Tony took Hadley's arm and guided her toward the gate. She found her strength again, stepped onto the bottom slat of the gate and started the short climb. She leaned her body over the top and winced when she put pressure on the bruise on her stomach. She gritted her teeth and swung her legs around. Before she could drop to freedom on the other side, Tony stepped forward and put a hand on her shoulder.

"We know where you live and where you work," he said, his voice low and menacing. "We can get to you anytime. Whatever you're up to out here, you need to let it go."

With that, he stepped back. "Come on, boys," he said to the others. "Let's get back home."

Hadley remained balanced on top of the gate for a moment as she watched the others get into their trucks. They started their engines, and Hadley dropped to the ground. She half-ran to the Toyota and jumped in.

"What happened?" Eddie said, his voice full of concern. Hadley assumed she looked awful.

"Just drive," she said. As he bumped along the road, Hadley pulled down her visor and opened the mirror. She had a purple and yellow knot on the side of her head. The rest of her skin was pale, deathlike. Even her lips lacked color. Heavy bags drooped under her eyes. She needed water. She looked around the vehicle and spotted Eddie's new thermos. It wasn't water, but it would at least be wet. "May I?"

"Be my guest."

She poured the lid half full and drank, the liquid reaching down her throat and into her stomach, spreading warmth everywhere it touched. As they neared the interstate, she told Eddie about her night in the shed and being questioned in the kitchen. When she mentioned the skinny guy stepping on her throat and kicking her, Eddie's hands shook on the steering wheel.

"I oughta go back there right now and take care of that guy," he said.

"Forget it, Eddie," she said. "I'm not a damsel in distress. Don't act any different than you would if it had been Vince."

"I think you're forgetting what I did to Nick Batson," Eddie said, with a slight grin.

He pulled into a diner just off the interstate. The clientele was mostly truckers. Country music played over the speakers. Hadley started to protest that they weren't that far from Denver and they should just go home, but the thought of hot food and a cold glass of water beckoned her to stay.

Eddie ordered biscuits and gravy with more coffee. She decided on a Denver omelet with toast, water, and orange juice. While they waited, she excused herself to clean up in the restroom.

Some of the color had returned to her face, but the lump looked nastier. She tried to arrange her hair to cover it but gave up and returned to their booth. As she slid into her seat, her phone chirped with an alert from her security cameras at home.

She took the device from her pocket and watched a video of a large man in a pickup truck pull into her driveway. The man wore long-sleeves and a balaclava. He did something at her front door then left. She shoved the phone at Eddie, so he could watch, too.

"Looks like one of our buddies from the other night," he said. Hadley nodded, thinking about Tony's last words to her.

The waitress brought their order, and they ate in silence. Hadley drained her water glass immediately and started feeling better. She didn't realize how dehydrated she had become. They finished, Eddie paid the bill, and they took the Toyota back to her place.

Eddie drove past her house slowly when they reached her street. "There's a paper or something on the front door," Hadley said. Eddie went all the way down the street, made a block, and took another slow pass by the house. He turned at the end of the street again, repeating his route.

"I didn't see anyone watching the house, and it doesn't look like anyone is following us," he said. Hadley agreed, and he pulled into her driveway. "Hand me my gun from the glovebox," he said. "Probably don't need it, but we're not taking any chances."

They approached the front door, where a sheet of plain white paper was taped. Hadley pulled it from the door and flipped it over. "We're watching you. Leave us alone, and we won't have any more trouble."

Eddie looked around in all directions but didn't see anyone. "The video didn't show anyone breaching the house?"

Hadley shook her head. She opened the door, and they looked around inside. No one had been in the house; nothing had been touched. Eddie stayed by the front door while Hadley packed a bag. She put a week's worth of clothes and essentials in a suitcase and took it to her car, which sat undisturbed in the garage. Eddie insisted on looking for tracking devices under the bumpers and fenders.

"You're sure you don't want to stay with me?" Eddie asked.

"I'm sure," Hadley said. "They know where I work, so I'm sure they know you're involved. It wouldn't surprise me if there's a note on your door, too."

"I doubt it. They probably think I'm just the muscle and you're the real brains of the operation. Not too far off on that, either. But, there's no point in trying to intimidate me."

Hadley gave him a weary smile. For as much as Eddie frustrated her, she could always count on him to be available in a crisis. She gave him a quick hug and locked the house, arming her alarm. "Probably best to stay away from the office for a while. They could be watching. I'll arrange a work space for us over the weekend," she said. "We can meet there Monday morning. Vince should be back in town by then, too."

She took a long, zig-zagging tour of Denver, getting on the interstate, then exiting, backtracking, and re-entering. She did several loops around downtown, where there were numerous one-way streets that made it easier to see if anyone was tailing her. She imagined Eddie did the same thing on his way to return the rental.

When she was finally convinced no one was following her, she parked in an underground lot and walked the stairs to the 16th Street Mall exit. She found the free Mall Ride, a trolley-like train that ran from one end of the shopping district to the other. While she rode, she booked a hotel room nearby.

She rode the train all the way to the end, then made her way back to the parking garage to retrieve her car. Once checked into her room, she locked the deadbolt and secured the chain, then hauled a nightstand in front of the door, just to be safe.

The bed was soft and called to her, but she needed to get clean first. While the water warmed up, she undressed and looked at herself in the mirror. A deep purple bruise, fading to a sickly yellow on the edges, had formed on her stomach where Tony had punched her. It hurt to take a deep breath or to laugh. She wondered if he had done any damage to her ribs or a lung.

The knot on her head had stopped growing but matched the stomach bruise in color. It remained tender to the touch, and she tried to wash it carefully in the shower, drawing a deep breath when she touched it too hard and immediately felt the pain in her abdomen.

She dried off and reminded herself things could have turned out a lot worse. She sank into the bed and remembered that she hadn't checked the device feed yet. She reached for her phone and navigated to the app that connected to the base station. It still showed six indicators, four microphones and two cameras.

Her eyes closed against her wishes; she needed to rest. She'd spend the rest of the weekend monitoring the feeds and getting the agency a place to work. With a little luck, the risks she and Eddie had taken would pay off.

There was something going on at TerraPure, something beyond a mistrust of outsiders. She hoped when they got to the bottom of it, they'd unlock the secret of where Jonah Davidson had been for the past 15 years.

# CHAPTER 30

*October 30, 2023*

Hadley rented a temporary office at a downtown space called Work Together. It was within easy walking distance of her hotel, and as a bonus, it had a coffee shop on the ground floor. She'd be meeting Vince and Eddie in a third-floor office/conference room combo that morning, but first, she had a meeting with Jenny Davidson at the coffee shop.

The place buzzed with energy. Commuters stopped in for their morning coffee before reporting to work. Entrepreneurs held cell phone conversations with investors on the East Coast, unaware that they grew steadily louder as they became more excited talking about their once-in-a-lifetime opportunity.

Hadley ordered a coffee and found an empty table in a semi-quiet corner. She inhaled the rich aroma of the brew while she surveyed the space. Fall had officially arrived; a few patrons still wore T-shirts, clinging to the hope of another warm up, but most of the customers wore sweaters, sweatshirts, or jackets. One woman came in wearing a ski jacket and beanie.

Jenny walked through the door wearing a smart business suit and carrying a briefcase. Despite the wind blowing outside, not a hair was out of place, and Hadley couldn't help feeling shabby in her jeans and sweater when she saw how well put together Jenny was.

Jenny declined Hadley's offer to buy her a coffee. She was ready to get down to business. "What are the latest developments?" she asked.

Hadley explained that they had still been unable to identify her father's girlfriend but they felt like Mary Taggert was a key person of interest and, perhaps, a prime suspect.

"We've been making progress locating Mary," Hadley said, feeling a pang of guilt for stretching the truth. She talked Jenny through the process of identifying the TerraPure property as a potential site for Mary's commune and said they were monitoring the location for any signs of her. She did not go into detail about how they were monitoring, and she definitely did not share that she had been held captive overnight. She also did not mention that the microphones and cameras had picked up almost no activity over the weekend, and that the camera on the backside of the greenhouse had blown loose and changed position, so it was pointing straight down, giving a narrow view of the back door instead of the wider angle she had planned for.

"With a little luck, we'll get a bead on Mary this week and we'll either question her ourselves or get the authorities involved."

Jenny sat impassive, not moving through the entire update and showing no emotion. When Hadley finished, she took a deep breath and then let it out in a slow sigh, allowing her shoulders to slump and her chin to sink down toward her chest.

When she still didn't speak, Hadley ventured in. "I take it this isn't the update you were hoping for. I understand that, but you build an investigation brick by brick, and locating Mary Taggert is a significant brick."

"But you haven't located her," Jenny said.

"No, not yet."

"There's a chance she's not there at all. She could be anywhere for all we know. The entire case hinges on finding this woman, and we don't even know that we're looking in the right state."

"An investigation like this is not quick or easy," Hadley said, hating the defensive tone that had crept into her voice. "There is trial and error. I can't go into everything right now, but I can tell you that the people at TerraPure really don't like us snooping around, which makes me think they have something to hide."

"But you have no idea if that thing is Jonah," Jenny said.

"We'll know soon," Hadley said, raising her voice enough that the people at the next table looked over. She took a deep breath before continuing. "I think this is a good lead. I really do. If it turns out to be a bust, we'll move on to the next lead. As I told you when you hired us, this may take some time, but we'll do everything we can to find Jonah."

"Unfortunately, we're out of time," Jenny said. A tear trickled its way down her cheek, carving a streak in her makeup. "My mom is sick. I told you that when I hired you, but I didn't tell you how sick. The cancer isn't responding to treatment. We found out Friday that it's getting worse. Spreading. She asked me to call this off. Said we could use the money I'd be spending on this case to take a last trip together."

With that, she broke down fully and fled to the restroom. Hadley sat uncomfortably, aware that people were watching the table and unsure of what the protocol was in situations like that. She had just decided to gather their things and find Jenny in the bathroom, when Jenny reappeared at the table. She still had tear streaks on her face, but she had composed herself and looked every bit the confident businesswoman who had walked through the door 15 minutes earlier.

"I'm so sorry," Hadley said when Jenny sat back down. "I had no idea your family is going through this. When I met with your mom, she seemed healthy. I never would have guessed..." Her voice trailed off.

"That's part of what makes cancer so nasty," Jenny said. "There are days where I swear there's nothing wrong with her and she seems like she'll be with us forever. Then, there are other days." She swallowed hard. "At any rate, I thought getting someone new to look at the case would bring her some hope, maybe offer some comfort. But, I think it's time to admit that we're never going to find Jonah."

"Jenny, we've found things the police and other detectives didn't find. This is not the time to give up hope."

"I appreciate what you've done, but my mom is right. You can invoice me for the hours you've put in, and I'll pay you the rate we agreed to."

"I hate to give up now," Hadley said. "If Jonah is out there, we need to find him. And not just for you and your mom. We need to do it for Jonah. Who knows what lies he's been told over the years. He deserves to know the truth."

Jenny drew her lips into a straight line across her face, once again showing no expression. "Sorry, Hadley."

"One more week?" Hadley asked. "Can you give us one more week? We'll charge our normal rate, so less than what you've been paying, and we'll give you a comprehensive report you can share with the police. If there's something in there worth pursuing, they can take over, and it won't cost you another penny." Hadley tried not to beg, but she heard a bit of a whine in her voice.

"Why is this so important to you?" Jenny asked.

"Because I was Jonah once," Hadley said, and she told Jenny the story of her own kidnapping, a story she had never told anyone before. By the end, both women were a mess of tears and tissue.

Jenny wrapped her arms around Hadley and pulled her into a tight embrace. "I never knew that about you," she said.

"I've tried to not let it define my life," Hadley said, "When I was in the middle of it, I thought I'd escape and that would be it. It's been over 20 years, and I still have to escape almost every day."

"One more week," Jenny said. "Let's meet back here at this time next Monday, and you can hand over your complete report then."

They bid one another farewell, Jenny exiting to the street, and Hadley going into the building to take the elevator upstairs. The office had a long conference table facing a screen. A complicated speaker phone sat in the middle of the table. The wall facing the hallway was entirely glass and had a bar running its length with numerous stools. Vince and Eddie were seated at the table when Hadley came in.

"Did you get the wifi instructions I sent you?" Hadley asked. Both men nodded. "Good. The network here is a little sketchy, so I thought it would be better to use our own hotspots with some encryption. How was Texas?"

Vince turned his chair to face her. He looked tired. "It was okay, under the circumstances. My cousin is staying with my parents until Thanksgiving, when I'll go back down. He's there at night, and there's a home care worker coming during the day. We're hoping that by Christmas, my dad will have full mobility again, and I'll be able to come back here. The one positive to being down there was that I had a lot of down time, so I did some research into Jeremy Costas."

He opened a notebook and shared what he had found. For a billionaire, Costas had little information online. It was almost all about his business and being a pioneer in alternative energy. "Interestingly, though," Vince said, "he decided to take Costas Energy public a while back. According to some media reports, he needed the accountability of a board and shareholders to be taken seriously by regulators and get in on big dollar government contracts. He sold the land to TerraPure right before that happened."

Hadley took a moment to digest that information. "It seems like whatever is going on at TerraPure was some kind of side project for him, and he didn't want it on the books when he went public?"

"Exactly. Out of sight of the board of directors and the regulators. He probably sold to a company to put an extra layer of paperwork between himself and people digging into his finances. I suspect he paid off someone in Lincoln County to make the records harder to get. Now, let me show you the most interesting thing I found. Some blessed soul made a digital archive of CU's yearbooks. Check this out."

He opened his laptop and messed with some cables at the end of the conference table. "The TerraPure incorporation paperwork identified Jeremy Costas and Scott Flanagan as the two principals. We suspect Mary Taggert is a resident there." The big screen lit up and he pulled up a photo of two men and a woman, all college aged. Hadley recognized all three right away but let Vince go on with his show.

He pulled up two photos side-by-side. On the left side of the screen, he displayed a version of the yearbook photo with the two men cropped out. The woman was a younger version of Mary Taggert, Hadley's photo of her displayed on the right. "We all agree this is Mary in both photos, right?"

"Absolutely," Hadley said. "I saw photos of her from her college years. That's definitely her."

Next, he pulled up a side-by-side of the first man, wearing a CU sweatshirt in the college photo, with a press clipping photo of Jeremy Costas. "So, that's young Jeremy," Eddie said. "He hasn't changed much over the years. Who's the second guy?"

"Scott Flanagan," Vince and Hadley said simultaneously. Vince advanced to his next slide, a side-by-side of the second man from the yearbook photo, tall and gangly, wearing wire-rimmed glasses, with a more current photo.

"It was harder to find a recent photo of Flanagan, but I came across this one in a *Denver Post* article about a fundraiser Costas Energy sponsored a couple years ago. Apparently, Flanagan is part of his accounting team there—not the CFO like he is for TerraPure but still involved in the company's finances."

"He's the guy who kicked me," Hadley said.

Eddie seethed, and Vince pushed back from the table. "Whoa...wait a minute. You told me they were watching us and that you weren't staying at home to play it safe. When did it get violent?"

Hadley had given him the quick version of their trip to TerraPure over the phone. She had left out the details of being caught and interrogated. She repeated the story now, filling in the gaps she'd left before. As she talked, Vince crossed his arms. The further she got into the story, the deeper his scowl grew. When she finished the story, he stood and paced between the table and the wall of glass.

"This agency is a mess," he said. "I know I wasn't here to help, so I blame myself as much as anyone. But, look at us. We're hiding out in a rented office because we can't risk going to our actual building. Hadley, you're sleeping in a hotel, and before I left for Texas, you'd actually thrown Eddie off the case. And, this is the only case we have because it's taking all of us to make any progress. The only good thing we have going for us right now is that Jenny Davidson is the dream client who will pay us unlimited amounts without questioning what we've done."

He stopped, out of breath, and flopped back into his chair. Eddie looked from Vince to Hadley and then looked down at his notes. Hadley felt a stab of guilt. Everything Vince said was true. They had been mismanaging the firm, and she'd let this case overwhelm them, just like Eddie and Vince had warned her when she brought it to them.

"This probably isn't the best news to share right now," she ventured, "but Jenny's no longer a dream client." Eddie and Vince both snapped to attention in their seats, giving Hadley their full focus. "I just met with her. She's giving us a week to wrap up and get her a final report."

"That's not much time," Eddie said.

"It's all I could talk her into. I told her we'd take our normal rate for the final week." She looked away, afraid of how Vince might react. To his credit, he didn't have another outburst. He pulled his chair closer to the table and rolled up the sleeves on his shirt.

"That's certainly not the best news," he said. "We need to full-court press this, get as far as we can, and then pivot to find more clients next week, or this might be our last case. Now, where were we? We've established that Mary knew Jeremy and Scott in college, which is around the time she was radicalized, for lack of a better term. That makes TerraPure the most likely commune for her to disappear to."

"Which makes those cameras and microphones even more valuable," Eddie said.

They sketched out a plan for Hadley to continue monitoring the devices, for Eddie to track down an identification on the mystery woman, and for Vince to reread everything from Jenny's files to make sure they weren't overlooking something important.

"I hate to say this," Vince said. "But, all our eggs are in the TerraPure basket at this point. If that turns out to be a dead end, we'll never solve this case. Not in a week."

"We have more problems," Hadley said, staring at her laptop screen. Vince and Eddie came around to her side of the table to see what she was looking at. She pointed at the interface for the devices. "We lost one of the cameras. The rear side of the greenhouses. It had already fallen out of place. Someone must have noticed it." She called up the archive footage from the camera and showed how it was pointing straight down.

"There's a lead wire running from the adhesive disc, where the battery is, to the actual camera. It's only an inch or so long. The camera came loose from the disc, and it looks like it was hanging by the leader from the way the image is swaying."

She skipped ahead to the last transmitted signal from early that morning. A stout guy wearing jeans and a flannel stood under the camera and looked straight up at it, giving them a perfect view of his heavy brow and thick goatee.

"It's our buddy, Tony," Eddie said.

Tony disappeared from view. He came back a few minutes later with an A-frame ladder. He opened it and climbed until his chest was at the same height as the lens. The image wobbled as he pulled the adhesive disc from the roof and stared at the device. He studied it for more than a minute, chewing his lower lip as he looked at it from all angles. The image spun and showed the greenhouse wall, then spun again and showed Tony still chewing. The image went completely dark.

"He must have pulled out the wire," Hadley said. "Disconnected it from its power source. We're down to the one camera out front and the microphones." She went back to the interface and pointed at the lights. "They're all still functioning, but if they found one of our devices, they'll find the others."

"We need Mary to walk past the other camera," Vince said. "Like, today."

They went back to their tasks. Vince read the police interviews carefully, breaking the silence with the scratching of his pen against notepad.

Eddie concentrated on his computer screen, trying to access a back door into Friendly Rental's system, where the mystery woman's car was registered. He kept hitting a firewall that prevented his access.

Hadley watched her laptop screen, headphones over her ears. Her eyes grew wide as she watched a scene play out in front of her. She found the microphone that had the best audio and synced the two feeds, so she could get the full picture of what was happening at the greenhouse.

"Eddie, any luck finding mystery woman?"

"No," he growled. "It might be quicker to go to Nebraska and squeeze it out of an employee at the rental agency."

"No worries," she said. "We might not need her after all. I think we just caught our break."

# CHAPTER 31

Hadley connected her laptop to the big screen and the conference room speakers. The footage looked grainier on the large display, but Hadley was still impressed with how good a picture the tiny camera captured.

They watched a young woman approach the greenhouse. She looked like she was in her late teens, but Hadley thought she might be 20 or 21; she wore her blond hair in pigtails, which made her look young. She wore jeans and a gray sweatshirt and moved with a cautious gait. She looked around her, checking over each shoulder several times before she looked up.

"My name is Danielle," she said, her voice not quite a whisper. She gave a nervous laugh. "This is silly. I don't know for sure that there's even a camera up there. But, my dad found one on the back of one unit earlier today. He said to be on the lookout for others. Jeremy's going to send some equipment to scan the whole place for them, so I need to take my chance now."

She walked closer to the greenhouse and disappeared from view. Vince and Eddie exchanged puzzled looks. "Just wait," Hadley said.

On cue, Danielle reappeared, looking over her shoulders once more. "I assume the woman who broke into the property last week planted the camera. So, you're probably looking for some kind of information about us. I can tell you everything."

She stopped talking and spun around, looking in each direction before returning to face the greenhouse again.

"I go into town on Wednesday mornings. There's a Shop and Save grocery store on 287, just outside Limon. Meet me there at 8:30. I'll tell you whatever you need to know."

With that, she disappeared into the greenhouse. Eddie and Vince looked at each other once again, and then they both stared at Hadley. "When was this captured?" Eddie asked.

"About half an hour ago," Hadley said. "What do you think?"

"I think we're going to Limon on Wednesday morning," Vince said.

"Interesting that she mentioned Jeremy," Eddie said. "I was under the impression that he was hands off. At least, living on a commune doesn't seem to be his thing, since he's running a major business in Denver and always making commercials."

"She said he's sending equipment," Vince said. "That doesn't mean he lives there."

"True," Eddie said. "The other thing that interested me is that she said her father found the mic."

"And, we know Tony found it," Hadley said.

"Wonder how she'd feel about knowing her dad punches women," Eddie said.

"Wait...what?" Vince looked from one to the other.

"We had a minor scuffle the other night," Hadley said.

Vince rolled his eyes. "It's a miracle no one was seriously hurt," he scolded. "You should have gotten the police involved."

"I tried," Eddie said. "The cops aren't lifting a finger against TerraPure."

"Why that is will be on my list of questions for Danielle," Hadley said. They all agreed and sketched out their plan for the interview.

•   •   •

Early Wednesday morning, Hadley joined Vince and Eddie in Vince's Subaru for the drive to Limon. They rode in silence for the first half, sipping coffee and squinting into the morning sun. As they drew closer, they became more talkative, going over their plan.

"We'll all go in," Hadley said. "If she seems spooked or overwhelmed, Eddie, you'll come back to the car, and Vince and I will run the interview. I'll be the primary. She may be more comfortable talking to another woman and someone closer to her age."

"It's not like we're ancient here," Vince said. Hadley smirked but did not respond.

They exited the interstate for Highway 287 and a few minutes later pulled into the parking lot for the Shop and Save. The supermarket, painted a bright yellow, was a lot smaller than the grocery stores in Denver. The lot's asphalt was potholed with a fair number of weeds growing.

Vince parked at the back of the lot, and they waited. He pulled out of the spot and took a slow loop around the entire lot before returning to his original space. "What do you think?" he asked.

"Looks clean to me," Eddie said.

"Me, too," Hadley concurred.

Eddie left the car first and walked to the entrance. When Hadley and Vince still didn't see any suspicious movement, they followed him.

Inside, a huge display screamed for shoppers to order their Thanksgiving turkeys. A bin of unsold Halloween candy occupied a table near the checkout. They walked the aisles, drawing wary glances from the handful of shoppers and employees out that morning, an unknown group in a town where most people would be familiar.

They reached the last aisle with no sign of Danielle. "She seemed pretty serious about wanting to meet us," Vince said. "But, maybe it was a prank."

"Or maybe she was drawing us away from the city for some reason," Eddie said.

Hadley remained silent. They had talked about the possibility of the meeting request being a hoax or a trap, but she'd gotten her hopes up for it being the real thing.

They started toward the front door. Eddie nudged Hadley and gave a subtle point with a half-raised hand. She followed his finger and saw Danielle walk into the store alone. They held back and waited for her to see them. She smiled and walked in their direction.

"I'm guessing you're here to see me," she said. She wore jeans and another gray sweatshirt, her hair still in pigtails.

"I'm glad you came," Hadley said. She introduced the three of them. Danielle suggested they meet over coffee and directed them to a coffee bar tucked into a corner of the store. Eddie paid for four drip coffees, and they huddled around a table meant for three.

Danielle did not seem intimidated in the slightest. On the contrary, she came across as confident and in control. Hadley stuck to the script they'd developed and eased into the interview. "I guess the first thing we're wondering," she said, "is why you want to talk to us?"

"I'm just tired of the bullying, you know," she said. "Jeremy and Scott try to control everything we do, and it's all kind of pointless in the end."

Hadley made a mental note to come back to that before they were finished. She moved to the next question. "What's life like at TerraPure? What do you do on a day-to-day basis?"

"It's a lot of work," Danielle said. "Mostly gardening. We're supposed to be this self-sufficient community. That's what the leadership sells it as. But, we're not. I'm here today to buy meat, dairy products, and medicine. We grow a lot of produce, but they gave up on livestock a couple years ago. We used to have cows and sheep. They tried pigs once, but that was a disaster, not that the cows and sheep were any better. Now, we just have chickens and the gardens."

"And, everyone lives in the houses facing the greenhouses?"

"Not everyone. The leadership crew lives on the other side of the compound. They say they have tiny houses like ours, but my friend Colin told me they only look that way from the outside. Once you go inside, they have these huge basements. They're like modern houses you'd find in a city."

"I think I've been in one of those basements," Hadley mused. "Who's Colin?"

"He's Scott's son. Scott is in charge of the compound, unless Jeremy is around."

"And, that's Scott Flanagan and Jeremy Costas?" Vince asked.

"You've done your homework. That's right."

"What are the people like?" Hadley asked. "Are there a lot of single people, or is it mostly families?"

"Mostly families," Danielle said. "It makes assigning housing easier."

"What about you? Are you there with your family?"

"It's just me and my dad now," Danielle said. "My mom left a few years ago. She tried to get me to go with her, but I was still too brain-washed by the place to think that a life outside might be worth pursuing. It makes me sad to think about my mom leaving, though. I wish she could have stayed. For me." For the first time, Danielle didn't look excited to be talking to the detectives. Hadley changed gears.

"Your dad found our camera, huh?"

That brought the smile back to Danielle's face. "Yeah, and he was pissed about it. I can't imagine how Jeremy and Scott reacted. Supposedly, Jeremy will be at the compound himself today or tomorrow to sweep for bugs."

"I have a couple specific questions for you," Hadley said. "And, it would help us a lot if you could answer. But, first, I have to ask. Why are you talking to us now? You said you were too brain-washed to want to leave when your mom did. What's changed?"

"I see more of the inner workings of the place now," Danielle said. "My dad has worked his way up to a sort of semi-leadership position, and I hear things from him about decisions that the leaders make. It seems like they view the rest of us as objects. Like the compound is an experiment or game for them, and we're all pawns. We're just part of their hobby, not real people. Since I've gotten older, they've started letting me come into town on supply runs. Seeing more of the outside world makes me wonder what I've been missing. We have movie nights on the compound. That's how I know about spy stuff like hidden cameras and things like cell phones. But, I've never actually seen a cell phone in real life. So, I decided to take a chance and talk to you all. Other than small talk with cashiers, you're the first people outside the compound I've ever talked to."

Hadley took her cell phone from her purse. "Here's your chance to see what a real life smart phone is like. I'm going to show you a couple of pictures, and I'd like to know if you've ever seen the people before and if they live on the compound with you." She thumbed through her pictures and stopped on her photo of Mary Taggert. She slid the phone across the table to Danielle, who picked it up with a kind of reverence. She seemed scared of dropping it, but she also grinned widely, running her fingers along its sides and back.

"Yeah, I know her. That's Cara."

"Cara? Are you sure that's her name?"

"Yeah. I mean, it could be a made-up name. I've heard some people make up names when they come to TerraPure."

"Any idea how long she's lived there?"

"A long time. She's probably been there almost as long as I have."

"Do you know if she has a son?"

"Yeah, she does. Why?"

Hadley ignored the question and gently took the phone back and switched to the next photo, the age progression of Jonah Davidson. "Is this her son?"

Danielle took the phone back and furrowed her brow in confusion. She squinted at the picture and put the phone down. "That kind of looks like him, but not completely. There are definitely some similarities, but that's not Colin."

"Colin?" Vince asked. "Didn't you say that's Scott's son?"

"Yeah," Danielle said. "Scott and Cara have a son named Colin."

"How old is he?"

"A little younger than me. Seventeen or 18."

"Were Cara and Scott married when she came to TerraPure?" Hadley asked.

"No idea. My mom would know for sure; she and Cara were friends. But, I have no idea how to find Mom anymore. I could ask Colin about his parents. But, you never told me why you're interested."

Hadley looked at Eddie and then at Vince. They each nodded their approval to go ahead. "Fifteen years ago, a child named Jonah Davidson was kidnapped in Denver and hasn't been seen since. We have reason to believe that Mary, Cara, as you know her, had contact with him before he was taken, and then she disappeared a short time later. There's a chance that your friend, Colin, is actually Jonah Davidson."

Danielle looked around the table, studying their faces, as if she expected one of them to laugh and tell her it was all a joke. When nothing happened, she spoke again. "It wouldn't surprise me. If you wanted to hide somewhere, TerraPure would be the perfect place for it. Nobody can visit, and the cops stay away."

"Do the leaders pay off the cops?" Hadley asked.

"No idea."

They all sat in silence. Danielle tapped her coffee cup against the table. She glanced at her watch. "I have to get going. I'll be expected back before long."

"It would help if we could talk to Colin," Eddie said. "There's a test we can do to determine if he's really Jonah Davidson. Could you help us set that up?"

Danielle inhaled for several seconds and blew out the breath slowly. "It's risky," she said. "But, I think I could get him to meet you tomorrow night. It'll have to be later. Let's say 9:00 p.m. You know where the property is, right?" Eddie nodded. "The last paved road before you get to the gravel path. If you meet us where you first turn on to that road, we can talk to you for a few minutes."

"I have a cell phone I can give you," Hadley said. She retrieved a burner from her purse. "It's fully charged and it has my number preprogrammed into it. I'll show you." She did a quick demonstration of the phone, showing Danielle how to power it on and how to access the contacts before powering it off. "You won't get a signal from the compound, but if you can't meet us for some reason, you can call me the first chance you get to leave. But, no one can know you have this."

Danielle chuckled. "You don't have to tell me that." She picked the phone up from the table and handed it back to Hadley. "I can't take that. Too risky. I'm already taking a big chance getting Colin to sneak out with me. Now, I have to go."

With that, she fled the table, claimed a shopping cart, and began shopping frantically. Hadley, Vince, and Eddie left the store, looking for any observers as they returned to the car.

They waited until they were back on the interstate to debrief. "What do you think?" Eddie asked.

"I think she's telling the truth," Hadley said. "And, it all fits together in a weird way." She had formed a new theory of the kidnapping, where the price of Mary's entry to the community was to bring Scott a son. Perhaps she had shared photos from the birthday party with him and gotten his approval for Jonah. Then, she bided her time until the perfect moment came. The thought chilled Hadley, thinking of two people being so calculating.

"I hope they show tomorrow," Vince said. "In the meantime, I'm thinking that our mystery woman is Danielle's mother. It might be a good idea to track her down."

"My thoughts exactly," Eddie said. "And, Hadley, I'd recommend talking to Mary's sister again, see if she has any information on a romantic interest between Scott Flanagan and Mary."

Hadley agreed. She scribbled down the to-do list before the next night's rendezvous. She'd been dreading the next meeting with Jenny Davidson. Though she cautioned herself against getting her hopes up, she looked forward to it; she couldn't wait to see the look on Jenny's face when she shared that they'd cracked the case.

# CHAPTER 32

They worked independently for the rest of the day and met back at the office that evening to compare notes on their progress. Hadley had gotten in touch with Esther Morton to ask more questions about her sister.

"She confirmed that Mary had never married and never had any kids," Hadley said. "So, if we can find someone who said that Mary showed up at TerraPure with a kid, that reinforces our case to make her the number one suspect."

"I don't think we need much reinforcement," Eddie said. "Did she know anything about Scott Flanagan?"

"Yes, she remembered Mary's college friends including Scott and Jeremy. But, she didn't know anything about any kind of romantic relationship between Mary and either of them. She said she couldn't remember Mary ever dating anyone."

"Well, it's more than we had before," Vince said. "But, it's still not enough to get the FBI involved."

"Your contact doesn't buy the story?" Eddie asked.

"I reached out to Agent Trotter," Vince said. "We met during the Batson case, and he said he knows we do good detective work, so, he's not dismissing us outright."

"What's the hesitation then?" Hadley asked. "This is a kidnapping. Isn't that FBI jurisdiction?"

"He said there are a lot of variables involved," Vince said. "Mostly, he said his superiors don't want another Waco, not on their watch. So, he won't even bring the case to them until we give him evidence that would give them probable cause to go in."

"Did you tell him they have the local cops in their pocket?" Eddie asked. "That should get their suspicion up."

"He said that's just another reason for the FBI to stay away unless they get probable cause. I tried to convince him to have someone come along with us tomorrow in case we can confirm that Colin is really Jonah. He won't do it, and he was skeptical that we'd be able to get anything from a conversation that would convince his supervisors."

"We need a DNA test," Hadley said. "Let's put that on the to-do list for tomorrow. I know a guy who works in a lab. I bet he'd process it for us right away. I'll call him when we wrap up here."

"We'll need comparison DNA, too," Eddie said.

"I'm sure they have Neil and Lisa's on file from before," Hadley said.

"Yeah, but that's a law enforcement lab. Will your guy be able to access their data?"

"Let's add a visit to both Neil and Lisa to our list for tomorrow," Hadley said. "Good thing we're not meeting until late. Eddie, how did you do?"

"I hit the jackpot," he said, grinning. "I finally got past the firewall for the rental agency and identified Mystery Woman's car as being rented by Donna Turner. Did some searching on Donna Turner and found that she's most likely Donna Knowles, who married an Anthony Knowles 22 years ago. They have a daughter named Danielle. No recent car registrations, voter registration, taxes, property, or anything else. It's like they vanished."

"That has to be our mystery woman," Hadley said. "Good work. Did you get contact information?"

Eddie nodded. "Phone number and physical address. Lives in Ogallala. Do you want to contact her? Ask about Mary's arrival at TerraPure?"

"Let's wait on that," Hadley said. "I'd like to talk to Danielle again first."

•   •   •

They split up the next day with a list of errands. Vince drove to Monument, Colorado, a town just north of Colorado Springs, to meet Brad Cummings. Brad ran a commercial laboratory testing facility in a strip mall, wedged between an insurance office and a credit union. Vince entered through the glass door and found himself in a small waiting room with a counter separating it from the rest of the facility. A wall behind the counter blocked the lab from view.

A man in his late 20s emerged from the lab. When Vince told him who he was, he introduced himself as Brad. He didn't wear scrubs or a white coat; he had on jeans and a cable-knit sweater that hugged his athletic body. He had dark black hair and each of his eyebrows was pierced. When he shook Vince's hand, Vince saw that Brad also had tattoos on his fingers.

"Thanks for helping us out," Vince said. "We appreciate it."

"Well, Hadley helped me out of a few jams in college," he said. "I probably wouldn't have graduated without her help, and then I wouldn't own all this." He gestured at the room around them.

"You're the owner?"

"Yes indeed."

"Do you do a lot of business?"

"Yeah. I'd like to move to the Springs or go north to Denver eventually. More people equals more business, right? But, we do pretty well for Monument."

"What kind of testing do you do?"

"Paternity, allergies, food sensitivities, blood sugar, different genetic markers. If it can be read from a bodily fluid, we can process it."

"That's a catchy marketing slogan," Vince said. Brad laughed and handed over a paper bag.

"Your test kit is in there," he said. "Hadley said you need to test one subject against two controls. She said you're already getting the control samples, so the kit includes a swab for your test subject and instructions and bar codes for labeling each sample. Get all three back to me tomorrow, and I'll get you a same-day reading. Tell Hadley I'll email her the full report and that this gets us closer to even." He winked and clapped Vince on the shoulder.

While Vince retrieved the kit from Brad, Eddie headed north to Fort Collins to meet Neil Davidson. They had spoken briefly on the phone that morning, and Neil agreed to meet Eddie outside his office.

"Do you really think you found Jonah?" Neil asked when Eddie approached him.

"I didn't say that," Eddie said. "Remember, don't get your hopes up."

"Well, what's this about then?"

"We've identified a potential candidate, and the test will tell us if he's a good candidate or not. I'm just going to dab the inside of your cheek with this cotton swab." Neil opened his mouth and stuck out his tongue as if he were in a doctor's office. Eddie swabbed his cheek several times in each direction, then placed the swab in a long vial with a solution in the bottom and sealed it.

"What happens if you get a match?" Neil asked.

"We'll let you know the results either way," Eddie said. "If there's a match, we'll have to get the authorities involved. This test will not hold up in court. We would need a certified chain of custody and testing by a state agency. The next steps would probably be for the police to take the child we've identified and reaccomplish the testing. It won't be a quick process, but we'll know if we have a match or not by tomorrow evening."

At the same time Eddie was swabbing Neil Davidson's cheek, Hadley was doing the same thing with Lisa. She didn't look as healthy this time. She seemed tired, her skin sallow. Hadley wondered how much time she had left.

Jenny had taken Hadley's call the night before and tried to come up with any solution that would keep Hadley from interacting with her mother. "You're working off a hunch, and you could be totally wrong," Jenny said. "I don't want to get her hopes up. Test me instead."

Hadley eventually prevailed, and Jenny had passed the phone to Lisa, who enthusiastically agreed to meet with her. Hadley finished taking the swab and gave Lisa a speech similar to the one Eddie had given Neil.

"Will you be able to take a picture of him?" Lisa asked. "I think I'd recognize my baby if I saw him, no matter how long it's been."

"I'll do what I can," Hadley said. "I just don't want you to be too disappointed if this doesn't work out."

"I can handle disappointment," Lisa said. "After this many years, it's worth the disappointment if it means feeling hope again."

# CHAPTER 33

*May 2, 2000*

Hadley watched two episodes of a cartoon about time-traveling kids and talking dinosaurs after Dan left for work. Then she went to her room and pulled her pillow out of its case. She stuffed her second outfit and her pajamas into it, followed by her toothbrush and the bear Dan had given her.

She went to his room and looked in the ancient dresser. It rocked on uneven legs as she pulled the top drawer open. He had a pack of cigarettes and a lighter inside, a car magazine, and a medicine bottle. At the back of the drawer, she found what she was looking for. She picked up Dan's flashlight and flipped the switch. A beam of light shot out from it.

She left the flashlight and pillowcase by Dan's closet and went back to the living room. She peered out the window. When she saw no sign of Dan, she found her shoes near the door, ran back to his room, and heaved open the trapdoor in the closet.

The flashlight made her feel better about going back into the cellar. She climbed down the steps and shined the light into each corner. It didn't look like Dan had been down there since she had discovered it.

She worked her way to the back corner and up the steps to the outside door. Fear gripped her as she wondered if Dan had discovered the door was unlocked. She tried it, and it stuck. Her eyes welled with tears, but she gave it another shove and it flew open. She stepped outside and gulped in the fresh, springtime air. She turned in a slow circle, arms outstretched, and let the sun warm her skin.

She turned off the flashlight and dropped it into the pillowcase. Slinging the pink case over her shoulder, she crept around the cabin to the driveway. It was easier to walk on the gravel this time with her shoes on. She made her way to the road and turned in the direction where she remembered the smoke coming from.

The weather had warmed, and people stopped using their fireplaces. With no smoke to guide her, Hadley told herself to be brave and followed the road, climbing the hill to its crest. She turned and looked back. Dan's cabin was hidden in the trees from there. She turned and looked down in the other direction. The other cabins were hidden as well. She started down the hill, planning to turn in at the first driveway she found.

The downhill side dropped steeply, and she had to lean backward to keep from falling head over heels. She dragged her feet as she went, keeping her eyes trained on the side of the road for an opening in the trees.

After a few minutes, she found one. This driveway was longer than Dan's. It twisted and wound its way to a cabin that looked a lot like his. And, like his, there was a beat-up pickup parked in front. There were no toys outside, no swingset, no sign of children. The truck scared her. She didn't want to knock on the door of anyone who might be like Dan. She sprinted back to the road, not daring to look back.

She walked for several more minutes, reaching the bottom of the hill before she found another driveway. She turned into it and followed it to yet another cabin. This one was larger than Dan's or the last one and had a deck built around three sides of it. A station wagon was parked out front. Three wide steps led to the front door, and pots of flowers decorated their edges. Hadley felt a lot better about that place.

She reached the steps and looked up at the door. She tentatively took the first step, hoping whoever was on the other side of the door could help her find her mom. She ascended the last two steps and knocked on the door.

She heard no sounds from inside. No dog barking, no people coming to answer the door. She wondered if she had knocked too softly. She tried again, pounding as hard as she could with the fleshy underside of her fist.

She heard a noise this time. Coming from behind her, not from inside the house. She turned, expecting to see Dan there, ready to fetch her home.

Instead, it was a man and a woman. Each wore jeans and a long-sleeve T-shirt, the man in navy blue and the woman in yellow. A bulldog bounded down the driveway behind them, overtaking them and running toward Hadley, its tail wagging and its mouth open, strings of drool running down its massive jowls.

"Evie, wait," the man called. The dog obediently stopped. The couple caught up to Evie and stared at Hadley. "What do we have here?" the man asked.

Hadley took a step back, her back touching the door. The tears returned to her eyes, this time spilling down her cheeks. She didn't know why she was crying.

"Arthur, she's trembling," the woman said, stepping forward. She knelt in front of Hadley and opened her arms. Hadley rushed into them, burying her face in the woman's shoulder. The woman wrapped her arms around her, and Hadley held her tight. She felt cared for and comforted in that embrace. It had been a long time since she'd felt that way. "Let's get you inside," the woman said, "and figure out where you're supposed to be."

# CHAPTER 34

*November 2, 2023*

They took Vince's car; he drove, with Eddie navigating from the backseat. There were few cars out once they left the city, and by the time they exited the interstate, the only light came from the stars, moon, and Vince's headlights.

"I hope they both show," Hadley said for the 10th time since they left.

"Relax," Vince said. "They'll be there."

"Unless it's a trap," Eddie said from the back. He had his gun holstered under the jacket he wore.

"That won't help Hadley relax," Vince said.

Hadley offered a weak smile, but she felt her stomach tighten as they got closer to their destination. The memories of being blindfolded and tossed in the shed for the night—and of Scott Flanagan kicking her head—made it difficult to keep calm.

She checked her phone while they still had a signal. "Uh-oh," she said, looking at the app for their hidden devices. "We lost the other camera and the microphones. Jeremy must have come through with the bug sweeper."

"We need to be extra careful, then," Eddie said. "They may be watching for us. Vince, the gravel road is right up ahead." Vince slowed and pulled off the road. He turned off the headlights, and they waited. They heard crickets chirping in the night and a crow cawing in the distance. Their meeting time passed.

"How long do we give them?" Eddie asked.

"As long as it takes," Hadley said. "This is our last play."

Just before 9:30 they heard a crunching over gravel and the murmur of voices. Vince put the key in the ignition, ready to bolt if needed. Then they saw the outline of two bicycles appear at the turn off. The two riders passed them on the road. The one closest to them was Danielle; she waved as they rode by.

Hadley craned her neck to watch them go down the road and pull off into a field. Danielle came back to the road and motioned for them to come that way. Hadley collected her backpack and the three exited the car. Eddie gave a wary glance around the entire area, keeping his hand near his holster.

They met Danielle at the edge of the road, and she led them a few yards into the field where a tall, thin boy spread a blanket over the ground.

"This is Colin," Danielle said. The three detectives introduced themselves. Colin was much taller than Hadley had anticipated and moved with an awkward, teenage lankiness. Colin muttered a greeting to them, then flopped to the blanket.

They all sat, Eddie groaning as he lowered himself to the ground. Hadley zipped her coat to keep the night chill at bay. "Thanks for meeting with us," she said. She took a battery-powered camping lantern from her backpack and turned it on. It cast a ring of light that reached the edges of the blanket and allowed her to get a better look at Colin's and Danielle's faces. "We have some questions for you about life at the compound and about some people. Colin, how long have you lived here?"

"Basically my entire life," he said. "I don't remember anything from before we moved here."

"Do your parents ever talk about how they met or when they got married?"

"Not really. I know they met before my mom and I came here. My dad came early to help get the place set up, and then my mom and I moved in."

"So, they were already married when you and your mom came?"

"I guess."

"We don't have traditional weddings or anything like that here," Danielle offered. "There's no marriage license or state recognition. It's what TerraPure recognizes that counts."

"I see," Hadley said. "Colin, you must be a senior in high school now?"

He looked puzzled, then shook his head. "Our schools don't work like yours do. I finished school a couple years ago. Now, I work in the greenhouses and with the summer crops."

"Do you still live with your parents?"

"Yeah, I'm still counted as part of their household, until I marry. Then I become head of a house." He cast a sideways look at Danielle and grinned.

Hadley took her phone from her backpack and opened it to the photos. "I'd like to show you some pictures. Do you recognize any of these people?" She flipped through photos of the Davidsons—Neil, Sara, Jenny, and Lisa. Colin shook his head at each one. She showed him a picture of Mary Taggert from her college years.

"That's my mom," he said. "When she was younger."

"Danielle, I have a few questions for you, too," Hadley said, squinting at the young woman through the lantern light. "Is your father Tony?"

"Yes," Danielle said. "And, I'm sorry if he was rough with you before. He's just like all the other brain-washed men around here." She rolled her eyes and looked at Colin, who drew his knees up to his chest and scowled at her.

"Is your mom named Donna?"

"Yes," Danielle said, breaking the word into two syllables. "How did you know that?"

"I think I met her," Hadley said. She gave a brief recap of her rest stop meeting with the woman in disguised. "She was terrified of what would happen if anyone here found her."

Colin scoffed. "That's ridiculous. If they found her, they'd bring her back where she belongs. That's it."

"Sounds like she doesn't want to come back," Vince offered.

"She never should have left," Colin said. "She abandoned Tony and Dani, and she put all of us at risk. The fact that you're here right now proves that. We don't need outsiders poking around and ruining our community."

"If you feel that strongly, why are you meeting with us now?" Eddie asked.

"I'm only doing it for Dani."

Turning back to Danielle, Hadley said, "I think your mom would love to see you again and to be with you. Just not here."

A tear ran down Danielle's cheek. "I had a chance to leave with her," she said, "but I didn't want to leave my dad, and I still thought there was something special about this place, that we would live a better life here than we could on the outside."

"But, you don't think that any more?"

Danielle looked at Colin, who stared daggers at her. She looked back at Hadley and didn't answer, but the look in her eyes told Hadley everything she needed to know.

"Colin," Hadley began. "This next part will be hard to hear, but I want you to listen to me. We don't think Scott and Mary are your real parents. We believe you were taken from another family when you were two years old."

Colin sat still for a moment, staring intently at her. He looked as if he anticipated a punchline. When none came, he leapt to his feet. "Come on, Danielle," he said. "This is ridiculous."

"Colin, wait," Danielle said, but he had already stormed off in the direction of the bikes. Danielle followed him. They had a hushed, but animated, conversation by the bicycles. Colin waved his arms frequently and shook free of Danielle when she put a hand on his shoulder.

"There's no way he'll agree to the test," Vince whispered.

"I'm not against holding him down and forcing the swab in his mouth," Eddie said. "What does he weigh? Fifty pounds?"

"Be quiet, you two," Hadley said. Colin and Danielle appeared to reach a settlement, and Colin lay his bike on the ground and trudged back to the blanket, dragging his feet along the way. He slumped to the ground. Hadley nodded to Vince to take over the questioning.

"Colin, have you ever seen any pictures of yourself as an infant? Do your parents have a baby book or anything like that?"

He shook his head. "No, but, again, that's not a thing we do here. I know our life probably seems strange to an outsider, but it's good here, and it can only stay good if we keep to ourselves and reject outside influence."

"Any influences in particular?" Vince asked. "Or, just outsiders in general?"

"Any outsider can bring information with them that can poison our members." He glared at Danielle. "Like you did to Dani."

"We have to take extra care to keep the government from coming in," Danielle offered. "And, businesses. A lot of capitalists would love to come to a place like this and try to turn it into something they can monetize, but that's not what our lifestyle is about." Hadley thought it sounded like they were reading from a pamphlet.

"How involved is Jeremy Costas here?" Vince asked. "Does he run the place, or is it mostly your dad, Colin?"

"My dad's in charge when Jeremy isn't here," Colin said.

"Which is a lot," Danielle added. Colin gave her another harsh look, and Hadley felt like they were eavesdropping on an argument the two had had before. "He spends most of his time with his businesses, which, by the way, are all about monetization and making a profit." She glanced at Colin, who opened his mouth to speak, but she rushed forward. "That's why I decided to talk to you all. I probably shouldn't have, but it just seems wrong that we have all these people who are completely bought into what Jeremy teaches, but he doesn't follow his own principles."

"None of this has anything to do with me or my parents," Colin said. "Who are my real parents. I wasn't kidnapped or anything. I look just like my dad, for crying out loud."

That comment took Hadley aback. He had a point. His height and build, hair color, voice—all of it was like a copy of Scott Flanagan. She put the thought aside and broached the next difficult topic.

"There's a way for us to prove it," Hadley said. "Or disprove it. There's a simple test that will tell us if you're a genetic match with the family we think you were taken from."

"What kind of test?"

"We just rub a cotton swab inside your cheek, and a lab will test your DNA."

"No way," Colin said. He braced himself on his hands like he was about to jump up again. "There's no way I'm trusting the government with my DNA."

"We're not the government," Hadley said. "In fact, the authorities we've talked to have refused to help us."

"Then why are you here?"

"This other family has been looking for their son for 15 years," Hadley said. "They want him back, and they hired us to help them." Colin didn't respond, but he leaned back and crossed his arms. Hadley forged ahead. "Look at it this way. If you're someone else's son, you have a right to know that. And, if you're not a match for them, we won't come back. You'll never hear from us again." He still didn't look convinced. "I don't tell people this," Hadley said. "But, when I was a little girl, I was kidnapped. I didn't know it at the time because the person who took me knew my family. He convinced me my mom was mad at me and that's why I had to go away. I can't imagine how painful it would be for me to have never found out the truth."

She looked at Vince and Eddie who both stared at her with mouths slightly open. She looked back to Colin, who uncrossed his arms but still hadn't said anything. "Just take the test," Danielle said, rubbing his arm. "It's better to know than not to know."

"Fine," he said after a lengthy silence. "I'll do it. But, you better keep your word. When it comes back negative, and it will, I never see you again."

Vince removed the testing kit from Hadley's backpack and approached Colin. He explained what he needed to do for the test, and Colin opened his mouth wide. Vince wiped the swab against the inside of Colin's cheek and stored the swab in its vial.

"Last thing," Hadley said. "We need a photo of you to go along with the test."

"Why?" Colin asked.

"It's just part of the testing protocol," Hadley said. "It helps for identification purposes with the samples." It sounded ridiculous to her, but Colin didn't protest. She quickly lifted her phone and snapped a photo. The flash lit up the night, and Colin blinked ferociously.

"Well, thanks again for meeting with us," Hadley said. "Danielle, could I have a private word with you."

Danielle looked at Colin as if seeking permission. He shook his head and reached for her arm, but she stepped aside. "It'll just be a minute," she said. She and Hadley walked to the edge of the road, while Colin gathered the blanket and stood up their bicycles.

Hadley dug into her backpack and produced the burner phone Danielle had previously rejected. Hadley thrust it forward toward her. "Take this," she said. "I will send a message to that number with your mother's phone number. You can call her the next time you go into town." Danielle reached forward and tentatively cradled the phone in her hands. "I'd also like to get a picture of you," Hadley said. "I need to talk to your mom again, and I think she'll be more likely to listen if she knows I've been in touch with you."

Hadley raised her phone to take the photo, but Danielle turned around and looked in the direction of Colin. He waved for her to come over. She turned back toward Hadley and bit at her fingernails.

"I can do better than a picture," she said. She looked over her shoulder once more. "I want to come with you. As I said, my dad is completely brain-washed. I want to see my mom again."

"You're an adult," Hadley said. "You're free to make your own choices. We'll take you with us, but make sure that's what you want to do. You seem nervous."

"Of course, I'm nervous," Danielle said. "I'm leaving everything I know. I'll go back with Colin now, so he doesn't alert the leadership that I've gone. I'm going to pack up some of my clothes and take the bike back out here in about an hour. Can you pretend to leave and then double back and wait for me?"

"Sure," Hadley said.

Danielle gave the phone back to her. "I'll be back in an hour, 90 minutes tops. If it's longer than two hours, assume I can't get out or changed my mind and leave me behind."

Hadley joined the others in the car. Colin and Danielle biked down the road just past them and then turned and watched the car. Vince pulled onto the road and turned around, driving in the opposite direction. He drove slowly, keeping his eyes on the rearview mirror.

Eddie turned around in the backseat and watched. "It's hard to see, but it looks like they're headed home," he said.

Vince drove to the next turn and doubled back, retracing their tracks. When he reached the spot where they had parked before, Eddie told him to turn the car around yet again.

"We want to be facing the direction of our escape in case Danielle isn't coming back alone," he said.

They waited. Eddie grumbled about how he would have brought food if he'd known they were on a stakeout. Vince told him that he had recently spent most of the day in that very car at a light rail station waiting for a guy to return, and that the reward for his diligence was that he got to see that the guy had bought a guitar as part of a surprise for his wife. They all got a laugh out of that. A quiet settled back over the car while they waited.

"Hadley," Vince said after a while. "Are you going to fill us in on that bombshell you dropped to Colin? You were kidnapped once?"

Hadley looked at her watch and sighed. They had left Danielle at 9:30. It was 10:15, which meant they could wait for another an hour or more. "Eddie," she said. "Switch places with me. I can turn around in the backseat and watch for signs of Danielle."

Once they resettled themselves, Hadley dove into the story. "I was six," she said. "My sister was nine. There was one day a week when I had to go home by myself. It wasn't far from the bus, maybe two blocks, and I usually walked with a friend. But, she was sick that day, and it was raining. My mom's boyfriend—ex-boyfriend, as it turns out, but I didn't know that at the time—showed up at the bus stop and offered me a ride. And, it would be months before I'd see my family again."

She continued the story, telling them about being locked in Dan's cabin every day and her eventual escape. She didn't like telling the story, and her voice broke a few times as she recounted it for her partners. She reached the end; neither Vince nor Eddie spoke right away.

"I didn't know about any of that," Vince finally said. "No wonder you're so dedicated to this case."

"I thought you had a personal connection to Jenny," Eddie said. "But, this goes a lot deeper than that."

Hadley nodded in the dark. "The worst part about the whole experience is that I didn't even know I was a prisoner. I believed the lies Dan told me. I don't know what his end game was once my mom rejected him again. But, if I hadn't gotten away, there's a chance my life would look nothing like it does today." After a long moment, she continued, "That's why I want to find Jonah. He's spent his whole life believing something that isn't true."

"I want to find him, too," Vince said. "But, I wonder if we're too late. If Colin really is Jonah, finding out now complicates his life, and there's no way to undo the last 15 years."

"He still deserves to know," Hadley said. "Stepping into the light after being in the dark for so long isn't easy. It's painful. But, it's worth knowing the truth. I see movement."

The two men in the front of the car turned as far as they could. Hadley watched out the window of the hatchback as a form took shape. Danielle biked along the edge of the road, alone. She balanced a burlap sack on the handle bars. Hadley jumped out.

"I'm glad you came," she said. "Let's put your stuff in the back here," she opened the rear hatch and reached for Danielle's bag, but the young woman clutched it tighter and pulled away. Hadley closed the door and said, "You can sit in the backseat with me. We don't have room for the bike, so let's hide it over there."

Vince drove slowly through the many turns to get back to the state highway that led to the interstate. They stopped at a gas station, where Eddie and Vince purchased drinks and snacks. Danielle turned them all down. She sat on the far edge of the seat, scrunched up against the door, her face an odd mixture of fear, regret, and determination.

"We're going back to Denver tonight," Hadley said. "I'm staying in a hotel; you can stay there with me. We can book your own room or you can stay in mine, whatever's more comfortable. Tomorrow, Eddie will take the DNA tests down to the lab, and Vince and I will take you to see your mother. We need to talk to her, anyway." Danielle nodded her agreement but kept her eyes focused out the window.

As Vince approached the interstate, Hadley realized this was probably the furthest Danielle could remember being from TerraPure. Hadley could empathize with her and the emotions that were probably swirling through her at the moment. The next day would be even tougher, but, Hadley hoped, rewarding.

# CHAPTER 35

*November 3, 2023*

Danielle had asked to stay in Hadley's room, and Hadley had gotten a miserable sleep. Danielle stirred every time a door in the hotel hallway closed, the elevator dinged, or a noise came up from the street below. Hadley took the sounds for granted, just part of living in a city, but when an ambulance drove by before dawn with sirens blaring, Danielle had bolted upright in the bed, clutching the comforter to her chest.

Hadley got a laugh out of how much the size of the bathroom impressed Danielle. Her shower at TerraPure had been a tiny cubby tucked away in the corner of the closet-sized bathroom. She marveled at the size of the bathtub.

Vince volunteered to drive, and Hadley was grateful. She sipped coffee from her to-go cup and leaned her head against the passenger window, her eyelids heavy. The monotony of the plains of eastern Colorado did nothing to rouse her spirits, and she dozed a few times while Danielle peppered Vince with questions about living in the city and being a detective. About half an hour before they reached Ogallala, Hadley's cell phone chimed with a text message from Eddie. He had delivered the DNA samples to the lab.

A few miles before the town, Vince exited at the rest stop where Hadley had previously met with Donna. Hadley dialed

Donna's number before they started driving again. A voice on the other end answered with a tentative "Hello."

"Hi, Ms. Turner," Hadley began. "My name is Hadley Collins. We met at a rest stop a couple weeks ago." The line went dead, and Hadley redialed. Voicemail picked up. "Ms. Turner, this is Hadley Collins. I'm with your daughter, Danielle, right now, and it's urgent that we speak with you. We're not far from Ogallala. Please call me back when you receive this message." She left her phone number and clicked off.

"Now what?" Vince asked.

"Let's start toward her house," Hadley said. "She's going to call back."

True to Hadley's prediction, her phone rang a moment later. "I'd like to speak to Danielle," Donna said tersely. Hadley passed the phone to the backseat.

"Mom," Danielle said. There was a long pause on that end of the conversation, and Danielle began crying. "We're close to your house," she said. "We can be there in a few minutes." She shoved the phone back toward the front seat.

"Ms. Turner?" Hadley said, relieved that Donna was still there. "I need to ask you a few questions when we get to your place. Would that be okay?"

"Yes, I suppose so, but I've told you everything I'm willing to already."

"I'd still like to ask. We'll be there in about five minutes." Hadley ended the call.

Vince exited and drove through the town. The GPS took them to the southeast side of town and a small trailer park. The park consisted of a green space bordered by three streets with stalls for trailers. A variety of RVs, travel trailers, and single and double wides filled the space. Donna's stall held a single wide with a vinyl lawn chair on a patch of astroturf outside the front door.

They let Danielle go to the door. Before she could knock, the door burst open, and a woman who looked like an older, heavier version of Danielle stepped outside and wrapped her daughter in a tight hug. They both talked at the same time, and when they turned to face Vince's Subaru, tears were streaming down both their faces.

"Come on in," Donna said. She didn't sound pleased to be welcoming the two detectives.

Inside, the trailer had a kitchenette at one end, a living room with a single sofa facing a television stand, and a bed at the far end. A door that Hadley assumed led to the bathroom stood between the living room and bedroom. Donna motioned for the three of them to sit on the couch. She stepped outside and came back with the lawn chair, which she set down in front of them. Once she was seated, her knees and Hadley's were only an inch apart.

"Does anyone know you're here?" she asked.

"No," Danielle answered. "I spent last night in Denver, and we came straight here this morning."

"You weren't followed?"

"No, Mom. It's fine."

"I'd like to know how you ended up here," she said.

Danielle told the story about Hadley planting cameras at the compound, which raised Donna's eyebrows. She explained how she left them a message and ended up meeting with them.

"How did you know you could talk to them through the camera?"

"I didn't. It was a shot in the dark." Danielle told her mom how she started thinking more and more about leaving, so when she met with the detectives again, she ran away.

"How did you find my phone number and address?" Donna asked Hadley. "I was careful to keep from being identified when we met."

"I followed you from the rest stop," Hadley admitted. "I was able to get your license plate, which led us to the rental agency. An associate of ours obtained your contact information from there."

"They just gave you my personal information?" Donna sounded indignant.

"It wasn't exactly that simple," Hadley said. "And, we weren't going to track you down, but once we talked to Danielle and realized she was your daughter, I thought it would be good to find out how to reach you again." Donna nodded but said nothing else. She kept looking at Danielle, and new tears would leak out. Hadley pressed on. "We'll give you and your daughter some time alone, but we really need your help. We believe a boy who lives at TerraPure was kidnapped as a toddler and brought there by Mary Taggert."

"I gathered as much when we met at the rest stop. You didn't come right out and say it, but you were accusing Cara, who you call Mary, of kidnapping Colin."

"Do you remember when Mary arrived at the commune?"

Donna took a deep breath. She looked at the ceiling and then at her hands. Hadley worried she would retreat into her shell again, overcome by fear of being discovered by TerraPure. Having her daughter with her seemed to embolden her.

"She came after we had been there about a year."

"Did she arrive with anyone else?"

"Yes, her son, Colin."

Hadley established that Colin would have been around two at the time and that Mary arrived without a husband or anyone else in their party.

"Were she and Scott married when she arrived?"

"Hard to say," Donna answered. "Marriages at TerraPure aren't like on the outside. I don't know if they were married before she arrived or not, but she moved into his place right away and they lived as a family."

Hadley found a picture of young Jonah Davidson on her phone. She held it up for Donna to see. "Is this what Colin looked like when they arrived?"

Donna took the phone and studied the photo carefully, squinting at it. "It's been a long time," she said. "But, he definitely looks familiar."

Hadley flipped to a picture of Mary Taggert. "And, just to confirm we're talking about the same person, this is Mary, who you know as Cara?" Donna nodded. "Danielle said you and Mary became close. Did she ever say anything to you about her life before TerraPure? How she met Scott?"

"No. Talking about the outside was strictly forbidden."

"Did she ever tell any stories about Colin as a baby? His birth, first steps, first words? Anything like that?" Again, Donna shook her head. "Last question," Hadley said. "I have a laptop and printer in the car. If I typed up a statement of what you've told us today, would you be willing to sign it?"

"I can't do that," Donna said. "I'm already way more involved than I should be."

"We're getting some DNA processed," Hadley said. "It might prove that Colin is really Jonah Davidson. It would be helpful for the next steps to have a witness to Mary and Jonah arriving at TerraPure 15 years ago as Cara and Colin."

"I'm sorry. I don't want my name connected to this. These people—they have unlimited resources, and they're vindictive. TerraPure is their toy, and they don't want anyone to interfere with it."

Hadley wanted to press her further, but Danielle said, "Hadley, can you give us a few minutes alone?" Hadley and Vince stepped outside. Hadley returned to the car and slumped on the hood. She was physically and emotionally exhausted. They could present the case to the FBI with just the DNA, but Donna's statement would increase the chances of getting help.

Vince joined her, and they watched the trailer door. A flock of Canada geese flew overhead in a V, honking as they passed. "You did good," Vince said. "We've taken this case further than anyone else has in 15 years, and it's because of you."

"Thanks," Hadley said. "I'll feel more accomplished if the DNA actually pans out."

The trailer door opened, and Danielle bounded out, followed by Donna. "Mom will sign the statement," Danielle said. "And, I'm going to stay with her for a while."

While Danielle gathered her things from the car and went inside to unpack, Hadley quickly typed a statement for Donna. She connected the battery-operated printer and soon had two paragraphs with Donna's name at the bottom.

Donna came to the car and read the statement several times. She accepted a pen from Hadley and with the statement on the hood of the car, signed off. Danielle offered Vince a handshake and gave Hadley a warm hug.

"Thanks again for doing this," Hadley said to Donna.

"I'm the one who should be thanking you."

Hadley and Vince got back in the car and started toward Denver. Hadley conceded that they were unlikely to find any healthy options on the road, so they stopped at a fast food place for lunch. Back in the car and on the interstate, Hadley's phone chimed. She looked down at the text message: "The results are in."

# CHAPTER 36

Hadley opened the email from Brad Cummings and tapped the link to the report. She peered intently at the screen, enlarging the image, turning the device, and resizing the image once more. She read through it and said, "This is hopeless. It's all gibberish." She swiped to her contacts and located Brad. She hit call, pushed the icon for speakerphone, and held the device between her and Vince.

"Hello," Brad answered almost immediately. "I thought you'd be calling."

"I'm not a geneticist," Hadley said without giving any greeting.

"Wait, what are you saying?" Brad asked, his voice playful. "There's something that Hadley Collins doesn't know how to do?"

"I could figure it out, but there aren't a lot of resources where we are right now," she retorted. "Can you give me a simple explanation of what I'm looking at?"

"Sure. I'm actually typing up a summary for you now. The forensics person with the police or FBI will know exactly what that report means. Without getting into too many mind-numbing details, the numbers are codes for different genetic markers. There's a column for the main test subject. In this case, that's the youth. Jonah, I think? Anyway, there's a second column for paternity testing and a third for maternity."

Hadley kept the call in the background and went back to the report Brad had sent. She identified the three columns. "Okay," she said. "I'm with you."

"Cool. Now, what you'll notice is that we have a strong correlation between the subject and the maternity test. Actually, I wouldn't say correlation. We have a match. Lisa Davidson is definitely his mother."

"How sure are you?" Vince asked.

"One hundred percent," Brad said. "No equivocation. My lab is certified by the same guys who certify the state crime labs, so if the authorities run the test again, they're going to get the same results. I'd bet my business on it."

Hadley's heart soared. She felt a lightness she hadn't experienced since the case began. She couldn't wait to share this information with the Davidsons. "Lisa and Neil are going to be thrilled," she said. "Thank you so much for getting this done so fast."

"Hang on," Brad said. "We haven't talked about Neil yet. This is where it gets interesting."

Something in his voice made Hadley look back at the report. She still couldn't quite follow all the numbers, especially on the tiny screen.

"You still with me?" Brad asked.

"We're here."

"We don't have nearly as strong of a correlation on the paternal side," Brad said. "Again, I wouldn't call it a correlation at all. I'd say that this test disproves paternity for Neil Davidson."

"Say that again," Vince said, glancing from the road to the phone screen and back.

"There is a zero percent chance Neil Davidson is this boy's biological father."

Hadley sat back in the seat, her mouth open. She let the reality of what Brad told her sink in. "Brad, this is going to be unwelcome news for our clients," she said. "You have to be sure on this."

"I know, and I am. You can take this to the feds, local police, whoever. Lisa is the mother, but Neil is not the father."

Hadley thanked him again, promised that she owed him big time, and ended the call. "I was not expecting that," she said.

"It doesn't affect our case, though," Vince said. "If Lisa's the biological mother, then Mary Taggert can't be."

"True," Hadley said. She saw the outline of the mountains forming in the west as they drew closer to Denver. They would be back in the office in another hour, and could start putting the final case package together. "Who do you think we tell first? The Davidsons or the authorities?"

"I'll call Agent Trotter as soon as we get back to the office," Vince said. "I think I can convince him to give the case a second look. If we don't have probable cause for them to go in now, we never will. Let's see what he says about notifying the family."

"Sounds good to me," Hadley said. "Part of me wants to let the authorities do the notification, but part of me wants to see if I can get Neil and Lisa to tell us the rest of the story and make sure it doesn't impact the case."

"I'd be surprised if the FBI will discuss our test results with anyone," Vince said. "If it had been an FBI lab, that's one thing, but this is a totally civilian outfit. They're going to leave the door open to blame us and Brad if this whole thing falls apart." He continued driving in silence for a few minutes, then added, "If Neil's not the father, I wonder who is?"

"I could make an educated guess," Hadley said. "He used to be an accountant for Jeremy Costas, and now he runs TerraPure."

•   •   •

Will Trotter buzzed with energy. He paced around the rented office taking jaunty steps, while Vince, Hadley, and Eddie gathered their presentation for him.

"Thanks for hosting me," he said. "I had to be downtown anyway, and sometimes it's easier for me to stop in somewhere than bring you all to me."

Hadley turned the projector on and brought up their slideshow. "Have a seat, Agent Trotter," she said, hoping to corral some of his restlessness.

"It's just Will," he said, smiling broadly. He took a seat and immediately started drumming his fingers on the table. Hadley wondered how much caffeine he had in a day.

She flipped to the first slide, displaying a picture of Jonah at two years old. "Jenny Davidson retained our services to locate her brother, who disappeared without a trace 15 years ago," Hadley said. She explained how there had been no helpful leads during the time he'd been missing. "No witnesses, no evidence left behind, no suspects, and no motive."

The next photo showed Mary Taggert at Sara's birthday party. "No suspects until we came across a video of Mary Taggert at the Davidson house." She recounted how Mary came to be at the birthday party and seeing her take a picture of Jonah. "We would later find out she had been hired to clean a neighbor's house and may have been in the neighborhood on the day Jonah was taken."

From there, she transitioned to a photo from TerraPure. "We traced Mary to a community in eastern Colorado. It's not exactly a religious cult and not exactly a political compound, but it feels like a mashup of the two," she said. She skipped the part about being taken prisoner and held overnight. She wanted to stick to the facts of Jonah's case. She displayed the picture she took of Colin when they met with him.

"This young man has been living at that commune for 15 years as Mary Taggert's son. He consented to a DNA collection. The test results show a match with Lisa Davidson. He is her son.

A friend of Mary's from the compound signed a statement saying that Mary arrived at the compound within a few months of Jonah's disappearance, and she had a toddler who resembled the first photo of Jonah that we have."

She took a deep breath, calmed her nerves, and gave her closing statement. "In short, we have probable cause for you to take Jonah, also known as Colin, into custody. His mother is Lisa Davidson, and he was taken from his parents and brought to TerraPure 15 years ago."

Trotter drummed his fingers on the table again. "You all do good work," he said. "You've buttoned this one up, maybe even tighter than the Batson case. Kidnapping can be within FBI jurisdiction, so I'm going to call my supervisor and see what our next steps are. First, a couple questions. Have you had any contact with the local law enforcement? And, have you had any contact with the TerraPure people? If this is as simple as walking in and asking the young man to come in for questioning and another DNA test, it makes my life a whole lot easier."

"Nothing's ever easy," Eddie said. Trotter's eyebrows shot up.

"Yes, on both counts," Vince said. "Eddie and Hadley had an unpleasant encounter with the TerraPure leaders, which led to an unpleasant encounter with the Lincoln County sheriff's office." He walked Will through what had happened. "Actually, now that I think about it," Vince added, "we don't know where they got the guns they have. Maybe that's another reason for you all to go in."

Trotter wrinkled his nose and shook his head vigorously. "Remember, I told you we don't want another Waco. Guns would be ATF, not FBI. That brings us closer to Waco territory. And, we have no reason to believe they didn't purchase their weaponry legally. Nope, we're out on weapons charges. We only care about the kidnapping. Be right back."

With that, Trotter bounded out of the office to call his boss. "Assuming they take the case," Vince said, "and I think that's a good assumption, let's find out at what point he wants to notify the Davidsons."

"Agreed," Hadley said. She leaned back in her chair and hoped Trotter wouldn't take long. No matter how many cases she worked, she'd always find the long waits, biding time to see if some action would materialize, were the hardest.

It took Trotter half an hour to come back. He had a to go cup from the coffee shop when he came in. Hadley worried about his heart.

He sat and gave an overly dramatic pause. Then he flashed an enormous grin. "We're in," he said. "Given what you told us about the weapons, it's going to be a complex operation. We need more agents, and we're going to have to coordinate with the state troopers and sheriff's office. Which means, this isn't happening today, and probably not tomorrow. But, we're going to put together an operation as quickly as we can."

"What can we do in the meantime?" Vince asked.

"Nada," Trotter answered. "Sit back and relax. We cannot tip off anyone that we're going in."

"What about the family?" Hadley asked. "When can we tell Lisa that we had a match for her DNA?"

"And tell Neil that we didn't on his," Eddie said.

Trotter gave them a puzzled gaze. "You're going to need to explain that one to me. But, I think the best thing to do is to tell them there's a delay with the results, and I'll call you tomorrow with more details. I'd like the three of you to be on site during the operation, so you can identify the key parties. And, I think it's only fair for the family to be nearby, too. But, I'll find out what my supervisor says."

Vince walked the agent to his car, explaining Neil's DNA test results on the way. Hadley packed up her computer. Eddie pushed back from the table and put his hands behind his head, elbows pointed out to the sides.

"This was good work, Hadley," Eddie said. "I know we had some rough patches during this case, but your instincts and decision making have been top notch."

"Thanks, Eddie," Hadley said. She tried not to act too impressed by his compliment, but she realized she'd been waiting for his approval for a long time.

# CHAPTER 37

*November 5, 2023*

The morning started gray and grew drearier. An occasional flurry fell from the overcast sky, breaking up the monotony of the drive into the plains. Vince, Hadley, and Eddie rode in Agent Trotter's black SUV. When they reached TerraPure, they would transfer into the matching Suburban carrying Jenny Davidson and her parents. Hadley was grateful for the separation during the two-hour drive. She couldn't imagine how awkward and tense the Davidsons' trip was.

They had met with them at the rented office the night before. Neil drove from Fort Collins, straight from work, dressed in khaki pants and a blue blazer. Lisa looked tired and pale. Jenny sat next to her, holding her hand, anxious to hear what the detectives could reveal. Sara listened in on the conference phone.

"As you know, we took some DNA samples from both of you," Eddie said, nodding toward Neil and Lisa. "We tested it against a sample from a youth we located east of Limon. We maintained a chain of custody of the samples from the time they were taken until they were delivered to the lab." Hadley was impressed with Eddie's stoic, no-nonsense demeanor. He could be a pain at times, but in situations like that, he oozed credibility and confidence.

Eddie picked up an envelope. "I will share the test results with both of you," he said. "I have copies right here. But, the bottom line is, we believe the boy we tested is Jonah."

Neil and Lisa both jumped from their chairs and embraced. Jenny pushed back from the table, stood, and collapsed again into her chair. A moment later, Neil pulled her to her feet, and the family shared a group hug.

They eventually took their seats, Lisa and Jenny both a mess of tears and runny makeup. Neil wore a broad smile and seemed a decade younger than when he'd walked in. "What happens next?" he asked.

"We can't talk about that over the phone," Eddie said. "Sara, we're going to have to let you go now."

They heard what might have been a sigh, but could have been a growl, from the other end of the line, followed by a click and a dial tone. Eddie disconnected from their end. He explained that the FBI would be leading a team to bring Jonah into their custody the next morning. The family could accompany them if they wished.

"There is one other matter we need to address with you," Eddie said. "But, Jenny, I'm going to need to ask you to step outside for this part."

"What?" Jenny asked, indignant. "I'm the client, remember?"

"Trust me," Hadley said. "It will be better if you wait in the hall."

Jenny looked at her mother, who gave a reassuring nod. Jenny stomped out the door.

"What's this about?" Neil asked.

Eddie passed copies of the test results to them. "The lab matched Colin, the boy we believe is Jonah, to Lisa. She is his mother. No doubt about it. The paternity test did not yield the same results."

"What does that mean?" Neil asked.

Hadley looked at Lisa, who looked at the ground. "It means you're not the father," Hadley said. She watched as Neil deflated, like a balloon slowly losing its air. "We can leave the room if you need to talk things over." Neither Davidson responded. The tension thickened in the room. The exuberance of a few minutes earlier had vanished with the news.

Neil stepped toward the door. "You knew," he said, hand on the doorknob. "All these years the police have suspected me, believed that the kidnapping had something to do with my affair. You knew there was another father, someone else they could have been looking at instead. And you said nothing."

Lisa sobbed, and Neil stormed out of the room. Jenny replaced him a moment later, looking bewildered until Lisa shoved the test results envelope at her. They left, holding each other, their world different in so many ways since they had walked through the doors.

Despite the family drama, all three Davidsons had shown up at the FBI building for the trip to TerraPure. Only Sara would sit it out.

"Look at that," Will said, pointing out the window of the Suburban. Hadley saw a red Ford Ranger in a field, pointed toward the road. "Did you see the guy inside with binoculars? They're expecting us."

The convoy pulled off the road before they reached the gravel drive. About 20 agents suited up in black body armor with "FBI" emblazoned on the front and back in tall, yellow letters. The detectives waited for Will to take them to the family SUV. Instead, he held up a spare body armor unit. "Hadley," he said. "Since you're the most familiar with the property and the people, would you be willing to ride along with me? We may need your help to make a positive identification on Jonah Davidson."

"Can't you identify him from the picture?"

"Sure, but it's always better if we can do it in person. I can't promise that there's no danger, but the Suburban has bulletproof panels and glass, and this is Class IV body armor. We won't bring you out until we need you."

She accepted the body armor, and he helped her put it on. Her shoulders immediately sank under the weight, and she had a newfound respect for anyone who could wear that gear for hours at a time.

Vince and Eddie bid her good luck and followed an agent to the rear vehicle to join the Davidsons. She climbed into the backseat of Agent Trotter's vehicle, behind Special Agent Trevin Boyd, Trotter's supervisor. Boyd had a slender frame and wore round, wire-rimmed glasses with thick lenses. He looked like he would be more at home teaching at a university than in the field.

They were second in a convoy of six SUVs. Another half dozen state trooper cruisers had joined them. Hadley remembered Vince's stories about being in military convoys and felt like she understood him a little better. She reminded herself that this was a law enforcement operation—not going into battle.

They turned onto the gravel road. One hundred yards from the gate, the bullets started flying.

# CHAPTER 38

The first volley of bullets hit the dirt in front of them, either a warning or the TerraPure gang were all terrible shots, Hadley thought. Still, her heart pounded and she found it hard to breathe as she tried to make herself small in the back seat.

"Fall back," Special Agent Boyd commanded into his radio as Trotter hit the brakes. The road gradually narrowed as it approached the driveway, and the law enforcement convoy was in the wrong end of a funnel for a quick escape.

More bullets flew, most hitting the dirt, but a few struck the SUV. Hadley heard them plunk into the Suburban's armored panels. One hit the glass in front of Boyd, leaving a ding in the bulletproof material. Hadley scrunched lower in the seat.

Trotter maneuvered the big vehicle into a 180 and followed the other cars. The SUV in front of them executed the same turn. More shots rang out. Hadley heard a whoosh of air, and the Suburban listed to one side. Trotter muttered profanities under his breath. "They got a tire," he said.

Boyd now had a bulky satellite phone and engaged in a tense conversation. Hadley couldn't tell if he was talking to the FBI or the sheriff's office, but he was determined to get a helicopter to fly over.

The convoy cleared TerraPure's sightline as a final volley of bullets rained down toward them. Bullets clanged against the

SUV behind them and one or two hit the roof above Hadley. She squealed and immediately felt silly. Neither Trotter nor Boyd said anything about it.

They pulled off the road again, and Boyd jumped out of the Chevy to join a group of FBI agents forming up nearby. "Stay here," Trotter barked, and Hadley gladly obeyed. She turned in her seat so she could watch the conversation from the safety of the vehicle.

While she watched, a pair of agents from another SUV opened the back of the Suburban to retrieve the spare tire. With her still in the vehicle, they jacked it up and changed the tire.

Boyd did most of the talking. The top officer from the state trooper contingent appeared to argue with him a couple of times, but Boyd dismissed him with a shake of his head and a wave of his hands. At one point, Boyd mimed the movement of an aircraft flying overhead. Hadley checked her phone for a signal. She wanted to check in with Vince and see how he was holding up. She still had no service.

A few minutes later, Trotter and Boyd returned to the vehicle. "Here's the plan," Trotter said. "The troopers are going to have a chopper fly over. We have an FBI one en route, too. Once we get both passes done, they'll give us an assessment of the threat. If it's clear, we're going to cut the chain on the gate and drive in, with the choppers flying ahead of us. We arrest anyone holding a gun."

"I don't think they're up for a gunfight with trained professionals," Boyd added. "I suspect that was just a show of force to buy them some time."

Hadley thought about Scott and Mary fleeing the property with Jonah, using some secret back road only they knew about, while the FBI waited, and the thought made her sick.

* * *

Tony Knowles dialed a satellite phone. "Hey, boss," he said to the man who answered. "The boys did what you said. The feds turned away, but they haven't gone back out to the highway yet. They're somewhere between the property and our spotter."

"Any chance they're going to come back on foot and try to breach the property that way?"

"There's always a chance, but we haven't seen any signs of that. We're watching the perimeter as best we can, but it's tough with the tree line."

"Are you watching the camera on the front gate? Any sign of them coming back yet?"

"I'm watching, boss, but I don't see anything yet."

"Have the men at the gate retreat into the compound. If they haven't engaged yet, it means they're bringing reinforcements. We don't need a massacre. Can any of the shooters be identified?"

"No, they were disguised well. It may have affected their shooting. I'll have them hide the guns, just like we talked about, and I'll wait at the gate to see if they have a warrant."

"Tony, you're ready for a promotion into the inner circle."

Tony disconnected the call and thought about the boss's last comment. It was about time.

•   •   •

A helicopter flew low overhead, the rotors kicking up dust and sending tumbleweeds flying in all directions. A trooper came over the radio, his voice staticky over the tinny speaker. "Agent Boyd, the chopper doesn't see any sign of gunmen at the gate. There's one truck there now, and it looks like just one guy."

"Let us know what else they see," Boyd answered. To Trotter, he said, "What'd I tell you? Show of force. What do you bet we don't find any weapons on the premises?"

"Sweep one is complete," the trooper said. "No one is out and about, other than the guy at the gate. We're going to do another sweep to confirm."

"Acknowledged," Boyd said.

A few minutes later, the FBI helicopter flew over. The state chopper stayed in the area, flying in a wide circle over the property, while the FBI aircraft completed its sweeps. The pilot reported in to Boyd. "Sir, nothing significant to report. We don't see any signs of weapons or aggressors."

"Pierson," Boyd said into his radio. "We're moving back in. When we get to the gate, announce the warrant and demand the gate be opened."

"Yes, sir," Agent Pierson answered from the first SUV. Trotter put their vehicle into gear and followed Pierson back to the gate. Hadley's heart rate quickened, and beads of sweat formed on her brow and neck.

"This is the Federal Bureau of Investigation," Pierson announced via the loudspeaker on his vehicle. "We have a warrant to search this property. Open this gate immediately and stand down."

Hadley watched as Tony Knowles swaggered from his pickup to the gate. "I want to see the warrant," he yelled.

"What a piece of work," Trotter said. He and Boyd stepped out of the SUV and approached the gate. Boyd shoved the warrant in Tony's face. Tony took it and read slowly. Hadley could see Trotter lose patience as he waited, shifting from foot to foot and looking at the sky frequently. Finally, Tony handed the paper back to him and said something.

Boyd and Trotter returned to the vehicle while Tony unlocked the chain on the gate. "What do you think?" Trotter asked his boss.

"He has a point. The warrant is for us to search the property for Colin and Cara Flanagan. It does not give us wide leverage to impound other property or arrest people. If we have probable cause in the performance of the warrant, we can take action. Since we can't identify anyone who fired at us, I don't know how we'd go about bringing them in. We'll focus on the kid and the woman."

"Understood," Trotter said. Tony swung the gate open, and Pierson drove through. Trotter followed him, with the rest of the convoy behind him. They would search the housing area first, then fan out and search the rest of TerraPure.

They reached the greenhouses, and Pierson stopped. A parade of agents from the rear SUVs leapt from their vehicles and ran forward. They teamed up and took a squad of four into each greenhouse. Hadley watched their movements through the glass walls. The search did not take long, and they exited through the back doors and returned to their vehicles. Each squad leader reported back on the radio no signs of the persons of interest.

Next, they arrived at the tiny houses. Again, the agents teamed up into squads of four, and quickly went from house to house. At each house, they had the occupants come outside. Boyd and Trotter walked Hadley past each family, the men glaring at her, women and children avoiding eye contact. At each house, she confirmed that none of the individuals were Jonah or Mary.

The common areas were empty, except for one man who had been in a restroom. Hadley remembered that the leaders lived in a different location, and she assumed that Jonah would live in one of those houses.

The convoy drove past the houses to the perimeter opposite of where they had entered. They fanned out and drove slowly through the rest of the property. They stopped at chicken coops, abandoned goat pens, and several fenced in gardens. At each location, there was no sign of people.

In a far corner, they spotted three additional houses. They looked like slightly larger versions of the tiny houses the rest of the families lived in, but spread out more and with no common areas in between. Hadley knew that was because underground the houses had sprawling basements with modern amenities. She mentioned that to Boyd.

"We're going to search each of these houses now," he said into his radio. "But, be aware of the basements. Keep your eyes out for hostiles."

At the first house, the agents brought out a man and woman with their young daughter. Hadley confirmed none of them had a known connection to the case.

No one answered the doors at the other two houses. After trying the doors and windows, the agents popped the doors open with crow bars. The team that searched the first house reported back that the house was empty. Moments later, the team from the second house reported the same.

Hadley accompanied Trotter and Boyd into the first house. The upstairs comprised a small sitting area and a bedroom to one side. A miniature bathroom rounded out the level.

They found a staircase and descended. They walked through a large living room with a big screen television and leather sofas. To one side of the living room was a large bedroom with a master bathroom. On the other side was another bedroom, but instead of furniture, it was outfitted with a bank of monitors. One monitor showed the front gate.

They walked through the living room to a kitchen and dining area. Hadley's stomach twisted as she recognized it as the place where Scott Flanagan questioned her.

"I think this is Flanagan's house," she said. Boyd nodded and told the accompanying FBI team to take anything that might have DNA on it.

An agent exited the bathroom with evidence bags holding toothbrushes and hairbrushes. "Looks like the adults were down here, and the kid was upstairs. We'll nab his toothbrush up there."

"No can do," another agent shouted down the stairs. "His bathroom is cleaned out. Lot of empty hangers in the closet, too. We may have a runner."

Boyd went to the master bedroom closet and revealed that it was only half full and had plenty of empty hangers. "We may have a whole family of runners," he said. "At least the grownups were kind enough to leave their toothbrushes behind."

The agents at the next house reported that it was similarly empty and that it did not appear to have been lived in much. Unlike the two other houses in that area, the kitchen had only meager stocks of canned goods in the pantry; no perishables of any kind. The bathroom had travel-sized toiletries.

"That's probably Costas," Hadley said. "Our theory is that he handed the place off to Flanagan and seldom visited."

They returned to the vehicles and made a slow circuit around the entire property, finally exiting through the gate. The helicopters each did an additional pass over the property before returning to their home bases.

"Well, this was a dud," Boyd said. "Unless the evidence produces some DNA. Now comes the hard part."

"What's that?" Hadley asked.

"Telling the family we came up empty."

•　　•　　•

Vince and Eddie joined Hadley in Trotter's vehicle for the ride back to Denver. Boyd went with the Davidsons. "How did they take the news?" Hadley asked.

"Not great," Vince said. "There are a lot of emotions in that vehicle right now. The history between Neil and Lisa doesn't help."

"Did they say anything about who the biological father might be?" Hadley asked.

"No," Vince answered. "To me, there's little doubt that it's Scott Flanagan, but I don't know how Lisa met him or if Neil knows about him."

"It's going to be a long ride to Denver," Hadley mused.

They rode most of the way in silence, making occasional small talk about the scenery or a car they passed. As Trotter pulled into the visitor lot at the FBI building, Hadley asked him, "What happens now?"

"We'll test the samples the team brought back from the property," he said. "It would be better if we had something of the kid's to test, but based on what you've presented, we will continue a search for Scott Flanagan, Colin or Jonah, I don't know what to call him at this point, and Mary Taggert." When Hadley didn't respond, he continued, "You all did phenomenal work on this case. You should be proud. But, it's an FBI matter now. You understand that, right?"

The three muttered that they did and exited the vehicle. He turned around to exit and reenter through the gate for cleared personnel. Before he left, he rolled down his window and called out, "I'm serious. This is FBI business now."

They watched him drive out of the lot and then turned toward their own cars. "What time do you want to meet tomorrow?" Eddie asked.

"What do you mean?" Hadley said.

"I mean, we have a missing person we need to find."

"Didn't you hear what Agent Trotter just said?" Hadley asked.

"Sure did. What time do you want to meet?"

# CHAPTER 39

*May 2, 2000*

The woman, she told Hadley her name was Janet, made Hadley a cup of cocoa, while her husband, Arthur, brewed a pot of coffee. "Are you hungry?" Janet asked.

Hadley shook her head and drew her knees up to her chest. She shrank into a corner of the leather sofa. She felt safe there, with Arthur and Janet and their bulldog. She also felt scared—scared that Dan would show up any moment and take her away, scared that Arthur and Janet wouldn't be able to help her, and, most of all, scared that her mom really was mad at her and wouldn't come get her. Janet beckoned her to the table. Hadley stood on nervous feet, and the tears began again. Arthur brought her a handful of tissue, and she dabbed at her eyes.

Janet sat across from her, steaming mugs in front of both of them. Hadley took a deep breath, inhaling the aroma of chocolate wafting from her cup, mingling with coffee from the other cups. The cabin smelled like dog, too, but the steaming mugs overpowered Evie's scent.

"Honey," Janet said, "can you tell us what's brought you here? Do you live around here?" Hadley shook her head. She took a sip of the cocoa but put the mug down right away as the liquid burned her lips. "Where do you live?"

"Denver."

Janet and Arthur exchanged a look, and Hadley saw concern in their eyes. It was the same look her mother had when she or Heather had a fever.

"Denver, as in Colorado?" Arthur asked. Hadley nodded.

"What are you doing here? Is your family here on vacation?"

"It's just me," Hadley said. "Me and Dan. He said my mom and sister would come, but they never did."

"I know it's hard," Janet said, "but can you start at the beginning? Tell us who Dan is and how he brought you here."

Hadley blew on her cocoa and took another tentative sip before beginning. She started into the story and found herself in a verbal gush, the words cascading like she was a waterfall. She told them about the bus ride, about Dan's truck, and about being in his house until she found the trapdoor in the closet and the cellar door outside.

She reached the end of the story. Arthur leaned close to Janet and whispered in her ear. Janet nodded, and Arthur left the room. "Let me show you some tricks that Evie can do," Janet said.

"Can you help me find my mom?" Hadley asked.

"We'll try," Janet said. "Watch this." She went to a cabinet and produced a canister of dog treats and had Evie sit, lay down, and roll over. "Do you want to try?"

Hadley got the dog to sit and shake. A moment later, Arthur came back in the room.

"The police are on their way," he said.

Hadley was confused. She didn't understand why the police were coming instead of her mom and Heather. "I want to go home," she said, and her eyes flooded yet again.

Janet wrapped her in another embrace. The woman smelled like coffee, bacon, and Evie. She had a soft shoulder, and for the second time that morning, Hadley burrowed into the hug and let a feeling of security envelop her.

# CHAPTER 40

*November 6, 2023*

"If Scott Flanagan is the father, then this definitely wasn't some random kidnapping," Hadley said. "And, Neil definitely wasn't involved." She looked at Eddie and let her words sink in. He lifted his hands in an "I'm innocent" gesture.

"I get it," he said. "No need to twist the knife anymore. Just explain your theory for where we're going to find them now."

Hadley smiled, letting him off the hook but savoring her victory. "For starters, I think they were gone by Saturday night. While we were scrambling to get ready for the trip the next morning, the sheriff's office tipped Flanagan off, and they went on the run. And, if Scott is Jonah's biological father, there's a strong motivation for them to stay together."

Eddie crossed his arms across his belly and nodded. "Not bad. What do you think, Vince?"

"Makes sense to me. Think Jonah knows what's up?"

"Who knows," Hadley said. "He's been lied to for his whole life. It would be easy for them to tell him we're part of a conspiracy against TerraPure, and I think he'd buy it."

"They head for the hills Saturday night," Eddie said. "Probably can't fly anywhere, unless Flanagan got a fake ID for Jonah, since the kid doesn't have a driver's license or anything."

"He has the means," Vince said.

"But, that's Costas's money," Hadley said. "He could've cut Flanagan loose by now."

"Let's figure they fled by car," Eddie said. "It's been what, 36 to 40 hours? Leaving from near the center of the country, with easy access to an interstate."

"They could be anywhere," Hadley said. She slumped into a chair. She had to admit the office chairs at the rental office were a lot more comfortable than their furniture at the agency, but she missed being in their own space. They had decided to lie low for a few more days and see if anyone surfaced at Hadley's place or the agency. If not, they could get back to normal.

"What leads do we have?" Vince asked. "Who could help us track down a potential hiding spot for Flanagan?"

"Well, there's Costas," Hadley said. "I don't know if he'd talk to us, but he probably knows Scott as well as anyone."

"Don't forget Danielle," Eddie said. "If they had some kind of contingency plan, Jonah may have told her about it."

"Unless they figure she's a traitor and avoid places she'd know about," Vince said.

"It's still worth asking," Hadley said. "I can call her. Eddie, do you want to try Costas?"

"Sure, but what's Vince going to do?" Eddie asked. "I hope it involves donuts."

"Your eating habits have turned to crap again," Hadley said.

"Mason," Vince said, seemingly oblivious to their conversation. "He gave us the leads on properties where we might find a cult."

"Yeah, and we hit the jackpot with one of them," Hadley said. "Do you think he can help us again?"

"He might have already helped," Vince said. "Remember the other property that Costas owned? Could that be a potential landing spot for three fugitives?"

"That's not a bad thought," Hadley said.

"Thanks. I aspire to being not bad."

Hadley rolled her eyes at him. "Why don't you do a deeper dive on that property while Eddie hunts down a phone number for Costas. I'll call Danielle."

• • •

An hour later, they walked to another downtown high-rise. Hadley smelled tacos from a nearby brunch spot, and a group of 20-somethings sat at a round table on the patio, laughing and clinking their mimosa glasses together.

"Doesn't anyone have real jobs anymore?" Eddie grumbled. "Shouldn't they be somewhere, doing something?"

The doorman let them into the building, accompanied them to the elevator and selected their floor from a panel on the wall between elevators. The doors opened, and a computerized voice announced they'd be going to the ninth floor. Inside the elevator, there were no controls, just cold, sleek stainless steel.

The elevator opened into a large suite with a "Costas Energies" sign on the far wall. They heard footsteps echo across the terrazzo floor. Hadley recognized Jeremy Costas immediately from his billboard near her exit.

He didn't bother showing them to his office or even a conference room. He motioned for them to sit in the fake leather sofas in the waiting area in front of the empty reception desk. He wore jeans and a flannel shirt, along with a pair of brown loafers that looked brand new—and expensive.

"I should ask how you found my cell phone number," he said, "but, I suppose in your line of work, you have certain resources." He smirked and winked. Hadley decided she didn't like him. He continued, "I don't know why you don't just talk to your friends at the FBI about this. I've already told them what I know, and it's not much."

Hadley let the comment pass unanswered and jumped in with their first question. "We're curious about how involved you were with the operations at TerraPure."

He threw his head back and laughed. He slid back in his chair and crossed his legs. "I wouldn't use the term operations. It's a community, where people can live off the land and their own work. That's what the American dream was 120 years ago, and we're trying to recover that."

"But, how involved were you?" Hadley pressed. "How often were you there?"

"Not as often as I'd like to be," he answered. "I go when I can, but I have other obligations here. The alternative energy technology that allows TerraPure to stay off the grid is developed by Costas Energies."

"Is Scott Flanagan in charge of TerraPure?"

He laughed again. "I don't know why this is hard. No one is in charge. It's a community living the American dream. Scott is part of that."

Hadley had witnesses that contradicted his statements, but they weren't trying to get Costas to confirm what they already knew. These questions were just to soften him up, and she didn't want to further antagonize him. "Do you know where Scott is now?"

"No idea."

Vince opened a folder and removed a map showing the property near Sterling, Colorado. "Do you know what this map is showing?"

Jeremy took a pair of reading glasses from his shirt pocket and peered at the printout. He nodded. "That's private property," he said, the hint of a menace in his otherwise inflectionless voice. "My company's property."

"Did Scott Flanagan ever go there?"

"No." Hadley noticed Eddie scribble a note for the first time during the interview.

"You knew him for a long time, right?"

"Yes. We went to college together. When I started Costas Energies, he was one of my first employees."

"Why didn't he become your CFO? My understanding is he's an accountant. With his background in the company and your relationship with him, I would've thought he'd be a natural fit for that position."

"People have different career goals," Costas said. "I'm conquering board rooms and regulators, and Scott's living off the land. You tell me who has the better deal. Now, I have some business to attend to, so I'll show you out."

He rose and motioned them toward the elevator, flicking his hands in a "shoo" gesture. When they reached the street, Hadley said, "What did you think?"

"He was lying about Flanagan and the Sterling property," Eddie said. "He looked up and to the right when he said it. It was the only time in the interview that he broke eye contact. And, he gave a one-word answer. With the other questions, he was more verbose. If you're going to lie, keep it simple. That's what he did."

"Danielle didn't know anything about that property, and Colin had never said anything to her about it. She did say there were times when he disappeared for an entire day and wouldn't say where he'd been. She always assumed he was off property somewhere."

"We need to decide what to call this kid," Vince said. "Colin or Jonah."

"Let's just worry about finding him first," Eddie said. "And, I'll bet you we do that in Sterling."

# CHAPTER 41

*November 6, 2023*

The road to Sterling looked remarkably similar to the road to Limon. Once they left Denver limits, traffic thinned and the landscape opened up. Hadley drove this time, with Vince in the passenger seat. Eddie rode in the back grumbling about how he'd made more trips to eastern Colorado lately than he had ever made in his life.

Vince tried unsuccessfully to reach Agent Trotter, eventually leaving a voicemail for him. "Will, it's Vince Marcotte. We believe Scott Flanagan may have fled to Sterling, Colorado. Just wanted to give you a heads up."

Hadley followed the GPS to their exit. A few turns later, they found themselves on an old farm road. A rusty barbed wire fence ran alongside it. On the other side of the fence, they saw rows of solar panels, the autumn sun shimmering off their silvery surface. Beyond the solar panels, a group of wind turbines turned slowly.

In contrast to the TerraPure property, Hadley still had a cell phone signal at the solar farm. Hadley slowed her Jeep, and they crept along the fenceline. They passed the solar panels and turbines. A field of fescue and rye grass filled the treeless space. The property stretched as far as they could see. Hadley did not see any security or monitoring devices.

As the solar panels receded behind them, buildings dotted the field in front of them. Hadley pulled off the road next to the fence, and they surveyed the area.

The biggest building, in the center, was a two-story wooden barn. From her vantage point, it looked in need of repair. The roof sagged on one side, and one of the enormous doors sat crooked on its hinges.

On either side of the barn were a pair of narrow brick buildings. Hadley didn't know what they were used for, but suspected they were storage sheds, perhaps for feed for animals from when it was farmland or tractors or other equipment.

Behind the barn, she saw two red brick buildings that looked like cottages. They appeared to be in better condition than the barn.

Hadley pulled back onto the road and continued driving. "There was probably a farmhouse at the end of the property where the solar panels are now," Eddie said. "Costas tore that down and let the rest of the property go to seed."

They reached the end of the property, and Hadley maneuvered the Jeep into a three-point turn. She drove back slowly, taking in the buildings from a different angle. She and Vince must have seen it at the same time, because she hit the brake as Vince yelled, "Look at that."

He pointed exactly where she stared. A pickup truck was parked along the far side of the barn. It had been hidden from view from their original angle.

"Eddie," Hadley said. "Does that look like one of the trucks from TerraPure?"

"Hard to say," he answered. "Definitely looks similar, but I don't want to jump to a conclusion."

"Do we agree that if Flanagan and company came here, one of these buildings would be the most likely place to find them?"

"Yeah," Vince said. "The cottages would be the most comfortable. The little brick buildings probably offer the most security."

"The barn would be my last choice," Eddie said. "Doesn't give protection from the elements, multiple points of entry, and it's the first thing you see as you approach."

"Where do we want to start, then?" Hadley asked. "The cottages?"

"I think we start with the brick buildings closest to us," Vince said. "Two people clear a building. One of us stays outside in case someone comes out of another building. Then we move to the next one, the cottages, and then the brick on the other side of the barn. If we still haven't found anyone, we finish in the barn."

Eddie nominated himself the lookout, and Vince and Hadley retrieved their gear from the back of the Jeep. They each donned a headlamp. Hadley put on a small backpack that contained a first aid kit, a lock pick set, and a camera. Vince put on a nylon web belt with his jeans and clipped on a multi-tool that included pliers, blades in two sizes, and flat head and Phillips screwdriver bits. On the other side, he clipped a holster that held a can of pepper spray. Hadley clipped an identical holster to her jeans pocket.

Eddie had a pair of binoculars and his .357. He scanned the area with the optics and then with his naked eyes and declared it safe. They threw a horse blanket over the barbed wire fence and carefully lifted themselves over.

They reached the first brick building. It had an aluminum sliding door with no lock. Vince motioned for Hadley and Eddie to both stand aside. He crept to the door and pulled it open, moving with the door to keep a barrier between him and whatever was inside. The door shrieked, cutting through the silence of the fields.

They stood still, watching the world around them. No one came out of the buildings. They didn't notice movement anywhere. Vince and Hadley turned on their headlamps and stepped inside the structure.

It was around 15 by 20 feet and completely empty. Cobwebs hung in the corners, and the place stank of motor oil and fertilizer. With the big sliding door on it, Hadley guessed the building had housed a tractor or two and maybe some other farm implements. It had a concrete floor covered with a thick layer of dust. There were no footprints and no sign that anyone had been in there recently.

They left the door open and moved to the next building. This one was about the same size as the previous one, also brick with an aluminum roof, but it had a standard door. They circled the building, and seeing no signs of anyone else, returned to the door. It was also unlocked, and once again Vince pulled it open. It swung outward, and he kept it between him and the inside.

When nothing happened, Vince and Hadley went inside. Hadley peered into the far back corner, her headlamp cutting through the darkness. Unlike the previous building, this one still had contents: rusty metal buckets, bags of quick-set concrete, rakes, shovels, hoes, and a wheelbarrow without a tire. A rustling in the other back corner drew their attention, and they trained their lights on it just in time to see a skinny tail escape through a small hole at the base of the wall. Hadley grabbed Vince's arm, her fingernails digging into his flesh even through his sleeve.

They stepped outside, and Hadley caught her breath. She put her hand to her chest and gulped in air as she stifled a laugh. Eddie sidled over, still keeping a watch around him. "What happened in there?"

"Just a rat," Vince whispered.

They moved to the nearest cottage next. As they got closer, they saw that it wasn't a permanent building and the brick exterior was not really brick. The building was actually a trailer covered with a vinyl veneer painted to look like red brick.

They walked around the trailer, inspecting it carefully. There was a front door, again vinyl with a wood-grained veneer, and a matching back door. There were curtains on the windows, so they weren't able to look inside. They did not notice any footprints or other signs of life, no smells of food or sounds of any kind.

Eddie set up by the back door while Vince tried the front door. It was locked. They switched places, and Vince tried the back door. It, too, held fast. They regrouped by the front door. "We'll come back to this one," Vince whispered. "Let's check the other buildings first, and if we're still empty, we'll pick the lock."

They moved to the next cottage, another trailer with the same decorative features as the first. Vince pointed at the base of the front door. There was a concrete stoop covered in dirt, but an arc had been swept away in the shape a door would make when opened. He mouthed the words "someone has been here."

They walked toward the barn for a conference, all eyes trained on the second trailer. "Eddie, keep watch on that trailer," Hadley said. "Let's look at the other sheds first and the barn, then we'll come back here. If someone is in there, I'd rather rule out any surprises coming from the other buildings before we go in."

"Agreed," Eddie said. He unholstered his gun and flicked off the safety.

The other two brick buildings were identical to the first two. The one closest to the trailers had a standard door, which opened easily. Again, they saw no signs of footprints or other disturbances. This one was lined with shelves but otherwise empty. Hadley stepped closer to the shelves and found a packet of snow pea seeds.

The last shed had a sliding door like the first one. This one opened easily. It rumbled in its track as Vince pulled it open, but it didn't make the noise that the first door had.

This one had a toolbox in it, along with an old-fashioned school desk with a built-in chair, a bicycle with flat tires, and a rusty bumper that looked like it once belonged on a truck of some sort. Hadley crept around it gingerly, on the lookout for rats. Nothing seemed to have been disturbed. Like the other storage buildings, it did not seem like anyone had been there recently.

That left the barn. They surveyed it from the outside first. It had the giant doors, no longer hung properly, as well as a second-floor window and doors on each end. They examined the truck parked outside. Unsurprisingly, the hood was cool. It hadn't been driven that morning. There were fresh tracks under the tires, though.

Hadley peeked through the windows. A crumpled bag of chips lay on the passenger seat, along with an empty plastic Coke bottle. The bed was empty.

"I'll go in first," Vince whispered to her. "Watch to make sure no one runs outside. If it's still clear after about a minute, come in and look with me."

Hadley nodded and they walked around to the big front doors. Vince was able to shimmy his way in through the crack between the door and the barn frame. She waited, anxiety building inside her as she silently counted to 60. When no one came out, she followed Vince through the same crack.

The place smelled terrible, like mold and decomposing plants. Bales of rotting hay filled the lower level, the source of the stench. Vince picked up a stick and prodded at the hay, ensuring nothing lurked beneath. Hadley couldn't fathom how anyone could stand to hide in there.

Other than hay, the lower level was empty. Vince pointed toward a ladder leading to a hayloft. Hadley waited at the bottom while he climbed it. Once he swung over the top into the loft, Hadley ascended the rungs to join him.

They found the tattered remnants of a blanket in a corner, along with some empty beer and soda bottles and ancient candy bar wrappers. "I don't think this is recent," Vince whispered. Hadley nodded, the lights of her headlamp bouncing up and down in the dark. They descended the ladder and reunited with Eddie outside.

Hadley took off her backpack and found the lock pick set. She had practiced on some basic locks and was getting the hang of it. More complex locks still mystified her. The trailer doors appeared to be on the simple side.

"Let's start with the first trailer," Hadley said, gesturing toward the one without any signs of entry. She wanted to practice on one before getting to the one where people might be lurking on the other side. "I'll do the lock. Eddie will back me up. Vince, you watch the other trailer."

The two men nodded their heads in assent to her plan. Hadley took a deep breath and steeled her nerves. She entered the first tool into the lock, feeling for a groove where it might catch. With it in place, she inserted a second tool and felt until it, too, caught. She twisted lightly and felt the lock tumble. She removed the tools, put them back in the set, then swung the door outward, keeping it between her and the inside, just like Vince had done earlier.

When no one ran out, Vince and Eddie switched places, and Vince accompanied Hadley inside. The trailer looked a lot like the single-wide Donna Knowles/Turner lived in. The door opened into a small living area with a kitchenette immediately to the left. A bathroom and bedroom were to the right. Unlike Donna's, this trailer's bedroom was separated by a door. They searched the trailer quickly. The refrigerator and cabinets were empty of food, but they found a set of plastic dishes. Tarnished silverware and a can opener occupied one drawer. There was no furniture in the living room. The bathroom was empty. That just left the bedroom.

The trailer was equipped with a space-saving pocket door. That meant they'd be exposed as soon as one of them slid it aside. Vince motioned Hadley to step back and take cover by the wall.

He slid the pocket door aside, and they both rushed into the room.

The room had a small wardrobe in one corner, which was empty. A large armoire occupied the widest wall. Hadley tried to open it and it swung away from the wall. She stepped to the side as the panel came down. It was a façade hiding a Murphy bed. The double mattress still had sheets on it that smelled like body odor and were discolored in patches. She flipped her discovery upward and secured the bed back into place.

They made their way back through the trailer and out to Eddie. Hadley shook her head to let him know they hadn't found anything. "Any movement?" she asked, her voice barely audible. He shook his head.

Hadley withdrew her lock picks from the backpack once again and went back to work on the second trailer. Eddie stood behind her, ready to train his gun on anyone who opened the door. Vince stood outside the back door, keeping a hand on the pepper spray.

It took her a couple tries, and Hadley started getting frustrated with herself. She focused on keeping her hands steady and tried to operate by feel rather than sight. On her third try, she felt the lock give. She breathed a silent sigh of relief and took her position. She motioned for Eddie to follow her in, leaving Vince to watch the back door.

The trailer had the same layout as the first one. A gas station cup and sandwich wrapper sat on a kitchen counter. Two bottles of water and a Coke were in the refrigerator. Like the first trailer, there was no furniture in the living room. The bathroom had a roll of toilet paper sitting on the back of the commode.

Hadley motioned Eddie to the pocket door leading to the bedroom. He slid the door open, and they both rushed inside. If Hadley had surveyed the entire room, she would have noticed that the wardrobe in this one was in the opposite corner, and rather than a Murphy bed, this one had a free-standing twin bed pushed against one wall.

She didn't notice any of that, however, because her eyes were focused on the young man cowering in the corner. He was alone, wearing gray sweatpants and a navy blue hoodie. He had blond hair and a lanky frame. Hadley's heart soared at finding him, but she wondered where Scott and Mary were. He avoided eye contact, almost as if he were hoping they'd walk away if he didn't acknowledge them. Hadley disabused him of that notion right away.

"Hello, Colin," she said. "Or would you rather be called Jonah now? Either way, we should talk. And, you should know, there are a lot of people looking for you."

# CHAPTER 42

*May 2, 2000*

Two police officers came to Janet and Arthur's cabin. They were both men and both had short hair. They each wore an identical green uniform, with long sleeves and a golden star pinned above the left breast pocket. Above the right pocket, one had a nametag reading "Colson;" the other's read "Allen." Each had a radio attached to his shirt front and wore a gun along his right hip.

Officer Colson did most of the talking. He asked a lot of questions about where Hadley was from and about her mom and sister. Officer Allen chimed in with questions about Dan. He seemed frustrated that Hadley couldn't tell them more about where he worked or what he did all day. He was happy, though, that she could describe Dan and his truck and that she knew he usually arrived home between 5:00 and 6:00.

The officers left Hadley with Janet and Arthur, promising that they'd be back later. Hadley waited anxiously, watching the wall clock in the living room. She and Janet played with Evie, and Arthur helped her put together a puzzle while Janet made sandwiches for lunch.

After lunch, Arthur turned on the television, and they watched a series of game shows that Hadley didn't understand but Arthur seemed to enjoy. He kept blurting the answers out before the contestants, and at the end of each show, he'd mutter, "I could beat any of them." When it became clear that Hadley was bored, Janet found a cartoon, and she and Arthur had a hushed conversation in the kitchen.

At 5:15, a firm knock on the door got their attention. Arthur opened the door and invited Officer Colson back inside. He asked Hadley to get her things and go for a ride in his car.

"Are you taking me to my mom?"

He smiled and nodded, and Hadley felt as though she could walk on air. She gave Janet a hug, and Arthur patted her back. She gave Evie a hug, too, and walked outside with the officer. His partner, Officer Allen, waited outside with a woman wearing a navy blue pinstripe skirt with a matching blazer over a silk blouse. She said her name was Tabitha, and she'd be riding with them.

Hadley got into the big backseat and buckled her seatbelt. She was fascinated by the grate between the backseat and the front seats. She noticed there were no controls on the rear passenger door—no handle, no way to lock or unlock the door, and no way to roll down the window.

They drove up the giant hill she had hiked down that morning. They were only on the road for a minute when they pulled into a driveway. It seemed familiar to Hadley. When Dan's truck came into view, she realized with a sinking sensation where they were going.

"Why are we here?" Hadley asked. "Is my mom here?" She thought she might throw up.

"We're going to see your mom soon," Tabitha answered. "There's one thing we have to do first."

Two more officers brought Dan out of the house. They had him handcuffed, and each officer held one of his arms. He glowered at Hadley, and she shrank back, trying to hide behind the seat in front of her. Tabitha slid across the backseat and took Hadley by the hand.

"Hadley," Officer Colson said, his voice loud and gruff. "Do you know who that man is?"

"Yes," Hadley said, her voice tiny compared to the policeman's. "That's Dan."

"He brought you here from Denver?"

"Yes."

"And, he's kept you in that cabin ever since."

"Yes."

Officer Colson got out of the car and approached Dan and the other officers. Hadley watched Dan's face. As Colson spoke, Dan grew angrier, and then his face turned ashen. The officers pushed him into the back of a second police car that Hadley hadn't noticed. Officer Colson returned to the car, and they pulled onto the road. The police radio squawked with excited voices.

"Pete, can you turn that off?" Tabitha asked. Officer Allen flipped a switch and the noise stopped. Hadley stared outside, watching the trees and the roads pass by.

They drove for a long time before they passed a sign reading "Welcome to Colorful Colorado." Hadley wondered where she had been if not in Colorado. She couldn't remember ever being out of the state before. Officer Colson took the next exit, and they pulled into a rest stop, where several police cars were parked. The lead car had its lights on, flashing red and blue in the dying embers of the daylight.

Tabitha came around to Hadley's side of the car and opened the door. "Hadley," she said, "you've been very brave. I want you to keep being brave. You're going to have to answer a lot of the same questions you've already answered, but with a new set of police officers. Just tell them the truth, and you'll be back with your mom soon."

Tabitha took her by the hand and led her to another officer that Colson was speaking with. He looked just like Colson, except his uniform featured a light blue shirt instead of the dark green. He introduced himself as Officer Rodriguez and led Hadley inside, where a female officer, who said her name was Lucy and her nametag read "O'Connor," sat in a greasy booth. They ordered Hadley some chicken nuggets from the rest station grill, and both officers asked her questions as she ate. Just like Tabitha had promised, they were the questions she'd already answered for Arthur and Janet and for Colson and Allen.

They stopped asking questions, and she finished eating while Officer Rodriguez went outside. A few minutes later, another police car arrived, followed by a white Volvo station wagon. Hadley sprinted from the rest station to meet her mom as she exited the Volvo.

She leapt into her mother's arms. Her mom cried harder than Hadley could remember ever seeing her cry. She held Hadley tight and kept saying, "My baby. My baby." Hadley felt a tug at her arm and looked to see Heather there, too, tears running down her cheeks.

Hadley and Heather climbed into the backseat together while their mom talked to the police officers. Finally, she took her spot behind the wheel and began the drive home. Heather kept asking questions about the past two months until their mom interrupted. "Heather," she said, "remember, not so many questions. She'll talk to us about it when she's ready."

They rode in silence. Hadley pressed her cheek against the cool glass of the back window and watched the world around them. The lights of Denver emerged in the distance, and her mom said, "There's the city. We're almost home."

They drove for another hour, finally taking the exit into the city and winding their way through turns into their neighborhood. They pulled up alongside the curb outside the front of their house. Hadley unbuckled her seatbelt before the car was in park. She wanted to run in through the front door, to see the house and her room and make sure everything that was happening was real. Before she did, she needed to say something.

"Mom," Hadley said, her voice still small and thin. "I'm sorry."

"What do you mean, honey?"

"I'm sorry I made you mad."

Her mom looked back in the rearview mirror and Hadley saw her eyes. They looked tired and puffy from all the tears. "Baby, I could never be mad at you."

"Dan said I made you really mad, and that's why I had to go with him and why you wouldn't come live with us."

Her mom exited the car, opened the back door, and picked Hadley up. She held her so tight Hadley could barely breathe. "That's not true," she said, her voice a breathless whisper. "You could never do anything that would keep me away from you."

Hadley hugged her back, not aware of the porch lights coming on up and down the street. She heard a neighbor call out, "Welcome home!" More people yelled it out, and soon the street was lined with onlookers. Someone began clapping, and the applause spread until they were receiving a standing ovation from the entire block. Hadley's mom put her down. Hadley clung to her hand as they walked up their sidewalk and front steps amid the cheers and applause of their friends and neighbors.

# CHAPTER 43

*November 6, 2023.*

"I'm not an idiot," Colin said. He hadn't moved from the corner. He drew his knees to his chest and wrapped his arms around them. "When my dad told me the cops were raiding TerraPure, I knew it had to be related to you guys. And, if it was, that meant that you got the results of the test back." He looked up and made eye contact with each of them, appraising them with a careful once-over. "I don't care what the tests say, they're still my parents."

Hadley looked at Eddie and then Vince, not sure how much to tell him. Neither offered much help, so Hadley put the problem off. "Where are they now?"

He shook his head and a shock of hair flipped down over his eyes. He pushed it back and said, "I knew they were planning on all three of us leaving yesterday morning before the cops got there, so I took off the night before. I figured they'd come looking for me here. Maybe they're on their way now. I needed to think things out. If those test results say they're not actually my parents..." His voice trailed off. "I know I just said they're my parents no matter what. And, I mean that. But, the tests could complicate things, you know?"

"You have no idea where they were going?" Hadley asked. He shook his head. She thought about asking if he wanted to step outside, get away from the stuffiness of the trailer, but decided keeping him contained was more important than making him comfortable. She forged ahead. "We got the test results back," she said. "And, you're right, that was why the FBI and the police came to TerraPure."

He stared at her hard, as though trying to see through her. The look reached enough of an intensity to make Hadley uncomfortable. Finally, he said, "So, what were the results?"

"I'd call them mixed results," she said. "The tests showed that a woman who lives in Denver is your biological mother, but her husband is not your father."

"Maybe I was adopted," he said.

"Your biological mother's only male child was abducted when he was two years old. You have to be that child. There are media reports and police reports that confirm the abduction. You weren't adopted."

Colin rubbed at his eyes with the back of his hand. His face flushed a deep red. He jutted his jaw out. "What does that part about her husband mean?"

"We had been working on the assumption that he was the biological father, and whoever matched the woman's DNA would also match his. Since that didn't happen, it means someone else is your biological father. My working theory is that it's Scott Flanagan."

"If he's my father, how could he be guilty of kidnapping me?"

"I don't have all the answers, and it's a complicated situation," Hadley said. "What I want you to know, though, is there is another family that loves you very much, that has been looking for you for 15 years. I think it would be best if you came back to Denver with us. You could talk to the FBI, and they could arrange for you to meet this other family."

"This other family, they're the ones you showed me pictures of?"

"Yes."

"If I go with you now, I still want to go back to my parents. Scott and Cara."

"I can't make any promises," Hadley said. "Remember, it's complicated."

"You're telling me," he said. He pushed himself to his feet. He stood taller than any of the detectives. He brushed past Vince and Eddie on his way through the living room to the kitchen. He retrieved the water bottles and the Coke from the refrigerator. He opened the soda and drank half of it. He took a set of keys out of his pocket.

"It's probably best if you ride with us," Hadley said. "You don't have a driver's license, do you?"

Colin smirked, as if the idea of needing a license to operate a motor vehicle was well beneath his station. "I want to bring the truck."

"I'll drive you," Eddie said to Hadley's surprise. "You can ride shotgun, and Hadley and Vince will follow us into town."

Colin didn't answer. He slapped the keys onto the kitchen counter and left the trailer.

"Why not make him ride in the Jeep with us?" Hadley asked. "Keep us all together?"

"This will give Vince a chance to call his buddy at the FBI while we drive. Besides, it seemed like he was getting spooked. Don't want to push him too hard."

He had a point, even if Hadley didn't want to admit it. They filed out of the trailer. Hadley locked it from the inside on their way out. Her heart skipped a beat as she realized they no longer had sight of Colin. Her panic subsided a moment later, when she saw him standing next to the pickup truck.

"I'll go first," Eddie said. "That way if he bails out or anything like that, you can keep an eye on him. We're not stopping unless it's an emergency. I hope he has enough gas to get to Denver."

"Let's go straight to the FBI building," Vince said. "I'll try to get Trotter on the line while we drive. He's going to freak."

• • •

Agent Trotter did not look happy to see them pull into the visitor lot. He stood, wearing jeans and an FBI windbreaker, his arms crossed and a deep scowl creasing his face. Special Agent Boyd stood next to him, dressed the same, with an angrier expression. Vince was the first one out of the vehicles, and Hadley watched as he approached and offered a handshake to each of the agents. Neither moved.

Hadley joined him, and Eddie and Colin completed the group. Hadley gave the two agents high marks for their poker faces; both remained impassive as they looked the young man up and down.

"Follow me," Trotter said. The group fell into a single-file line behind him, with Boyd bringing up the rear. They stopped at the guard shack to the main entrance. Trotter had a quick conversation with the security officer and waved them all in.

Vince had described the inside of the FBI building to Hadley. Based on what he told her, she expected to take an elevator to a floor that would look like any other office building, with cubicles and anonymous offices occupying most of the space. Instead, they took the elevator down to a windowless basement. They wound through the catacombs, bare concrete under their feet and the walls painted a flat white. They passed through various corridors, with doors marked as evidence lock-ups, until they reached a plain room with a round Formica-topped table in the middle. Four faux-leather chairs stood around it.

Boyd motioned for Colin to come inside. The youth obeyed, but Hadley could tell from his wide eyes and dragging feet that he was having second thoughts about the arrangement. She stepped forward to follow him, but Trotter cut her off. "You three are coming with me," he said. "We'll debrief separately."

He led them further down the hall, scanned his badge on a reader at the door, and brought them into a slightly larger room with an identical table and chairs. Before entering, Hadley looked over her shoulder and saw another agent slip into the room with Boyd and Colin.

"They're not interrogating him, are they?" she asked as she took a seat between Eddie and Vince.

"Not an interrogation," Trotter said. "An interview. We're trying to confirm everything you told us is accurate and see if we can figure out where to find our two suspects."

"What do you need from us?" Eddie asked.

"Officially, I'm here to take statements from you about how you found him and see what else you know."

"And, unofficially?" Vince asked.

Trotter popped up from his seat and slammed his palms onto the table. "I want to know how it is that when I tell you to stop investigating this case, you think it means to drive across the state and pick up a person of interest."

His eyes had a fire in them that Hadley hadn't seen before. She wondered if he was angry that they hadn't followed orders or that they'd cracked a case the FBI hadn't even shown interest in until a few days earlier.

With notepad and pen in hand, he peppered them with questions about how they knew to look in Sterling, if they'd seen any signs of anyone else being there, if anyone had followed them, and what Colin had told them when they found him. He did not have a list of questions in front of him, and Hadley was impressed with how efficiently he moved from one subject to another, making sure he'd gotten everything out of them that he wanted on one thread before pulling on another.

After 30 minutes, he flipped his notepad closed and looked at each of them in turn. "I'm still not happy," he said. "You were supposed to leave this case alone. Things could have turned out badly, and I'd be trying to solve murders in addition to a kidnapping."

Hadley didn't feel the slightest bit shamed by his speech. She had run into that mentality with other law enforcement officers and had long ago decided that she could make her own decisions and be responsible for her own actions. Dire consequences came with the territory of being a detective.

"But, since you've actually saved me some work, I'll give you a little insight. This is totally off the record, mind you. Based on our testing, the DNA from one of the toothbrushes we bagged at TerraPure is a match with the sample you had tested."

"Which means..." Eddie said.

"Which means, one of his parents used a toothbrush at TerraPure. And, since you've already confirmed who the mother is, and we have a short list of people at TerraPure, you can probably use your detective skills to reach a conclusion on the father."

"Will you retest Colin?" Hadley asked.

He nodded. "They should be getting the sample from him during the interview. And, we're getting a new sample from Lisa Davidson as we speak."

"Is she here?" Hadley asked.

Trotter nodded. "The whole family is. We've cleared it with them. They want you to be in the room when they're reunited with Colin."

"Don't you need to complete your own testing before you reunite them?" Eddie asked.

Trotter pursed his lips and gave his head a slight shake. "Again, this is totally off the record," he said. "The test results you gave us are solid. We need to do our own to establish a chain of custody and make sure the prosecution sticks. But, this reunion isn't a law enforcement operation. It's just facilitating an introduction of some people who should meet. Personally, I think it would be cruel to make the family wait any longer based on what we already know. Speaking of which, we should take you up there now."

With that, Trotter led them back through the maze of halls to the elevator and took them to the top floor. This floor had spacious offices and few cubicles. They entered a room labeled "Executive Conference Room" and saw the Davidson family seated in leather swivel chairs at an enormous oak table.

Jenny rushed forward to hug Hadley and greet the others. Neil and Lisa thanked them over and over again. A woman in her early 20s stayed rooted to her chair, looking at her fingernails. She had short blond hair with jagged edges. Hadley wondered if she cut it herself without using a mirror. Her blue eyes were hidden behind circles of dark makeup, and her lips were colored a deep maroon, contrasting with her pale skin.

"You must be Sara," Hadley said. The woman looked at her and nodded. Hadley remembered how strange things were between her and Heather when she first came home and imagined how much more difficult it was for Sara, since she blamed herself for what happened to Jonah.

She noticed that Neil and Lisa positioned themselves on opposite sides of the room. Lisa looked better than the last time Hadley had seen her. She seemed more alert and healthier. Neil looked relieved but not exactly happy.

They waited for 20 awkward minutes. Neil attempted to make small talk with Eddie and Vince. Jenny looked like she had a thousand questions but was keeping them to herself. Finally, mercifully, the door opened and Boyd walked in.

"We're going to bring Colin in," he said. "I know you all know him as Jonah, but he's asked to be called Colin. It's the only name he remembers being called by." Hadley saw a stricken look cross Lisa's face. "Remember, we will need the results of the additional tests to confirm he is your son, but based on the preliminary evidence provided by the private detectives, you have reason to celebrate today. Last thing, we are still searching for the suspected kidnappers, and I'd appreciate it if you did not bring that up with Colin. Any questions?"

When no one said anything, he turned back to the door and opened it. Agent Trotter walked in, followed by Colin.

Jenny and Lisa both shrieked with joy, and once again, Jenny bounded forward. She wrapped her brother in a hug. "We've missed you," she said, tears streaming down her face. "We've missed you so much."

Colin hugged her back with a stiff, uncertain embrace. Hadley knew that though he was now free from TerraPure and could begin living a more normal life, there was a part of him that would always be there.

Lisa moved in next. She held him tight. "Jonah," she whispered over and over. He grimaced at the sound of his birth name, now a foreign label in his ears. He put both arms around her, and the embrace seemed more natural, though he still looked uncomfortable.

Neil stepped forward and offered him a handshake and a half-hug, slapping his back. "Glad to see you back," he said, as if Colin had merely been away for a week or two.

Finally, Sara rose from her chair. She was shorter than Jenny but also slender. She shuffled forward and took both of Colin's hands in hers. He towered over her. She looked him in the eyes and they stood silently for a moment, before she let go of his hands and hugged him. He hugged her back, and for the first time Hadley sensed a genuine affection.

"I'm sorry," Sara said. "I'm sorry for what happened to you."

"You didn't do anything," Colin answered as they pulled away. "It was a long time ago, and you were a kid. We both were. There's nothing anyone could have done to make it turn out any differently." He surveyed the group, shifting from one foot to another as he appraised them. "I'm glad you all found me," he said, casting his eyes on Hadley, Vince, and Eddie. "And, I want to get to know all of you," he said, looking at his birth family. "But, it may take some time to get used to the idea of having a different family."

# CHAPTER 44

*November 15, 2023*

It felt good to be back in their normal office again. Having received no further threats from Scott Flanagan or TerraPure and with no one lurking around the office or Hadley's home, the agency returned to normal operations. Vince celebrated by bringing in Caruso's coffee for everyone. Eddie promptly set his aside in favor of his trademark sludge in a "new" coffee maker that looked like it had at least 100,000 miles on it. Hadley guessed it came from a second-hand store or garage sale.

"Heard anything from Jenny?" Vince asked.

"We talked for a minute last night," Hadley said. "It sounds like things are going okay. Still a lot of transition."

Hadley admitted to herself that she was putting a positive spin on what was proving to be a difficult situation. The DNA test results had confirmed that Colin was really Jonah Davidson, and that Lisa was his mother and Scott Flanagan his father. Given the unknown whereabouts of Scott, a judge awarded temporary custody of Colin to Lisa. The family that longed for the return of their son for 15 years got their wish overnight and was caught completely unprepared.

The transition had been rough. Jenny had moved back home with Lisa, and Sara was staying with them for a while, too. Battling illness, Lisa found herself back in charge of a house full of her children. While they were adults now and could take care of themselves, Jenny told Hadley that it was hard for everyone not to slip back into a traditional role, and she worried that it was wearing on Lisa.

Learning the truth and reuniting Colin with the Davidsons was the right thing to do—Hadley would never be convinced otherwise. But, she added the rocky transition to the list of offenses Scott and Mary had committed.

"How's Colin doing?" Vince asked, bringing her out of her thoughts.

"About as well as can be expected. Jenny said he keeps to himself a lot. Refuses to answer to Jonah. He's talked about testing for his GED. He has no interest in going back to school. He turns 18 in June. My guess is he'll be out on his own pretty quick after that."

"Not quite a storybook ending," Eddie said, slurping his coffee. "But, at least the family has some closure. So, there's that. I'd love to help collar the kidnappers, but they could have left the country by now."

They sat in silence for a few minutes. Unlike other cases, this victory was hard to savor.

"Hey!" Vince exclaimed, looking up from his phone. "We're trending on Twitter."

"What?" Hadley asked. Vince thrust his phone toward her. After the DNA tests were confirmed, the FBI had put out a press release about Colin's recovery and reunion with his birth family. On top of everything else, the Davidsons had been subjected to daily press coverage that had finally started to dwindle. The agency's role had not been disclosed. Until that morning.

"Ugh," Hadley said. "Someone leaked our information to the press."

The first phone call came in two minutes later, a local newspaper looking for comment on the case. That was followed by inquiries from every television station in town, as well as several radio stations and a multitude of bloggers and online news personalities.

Within a couple of hours, the photographers lined up outside the agency, double parking and blocking driveways. Eddie locked the door and turned out the lights. The three of them huddled in Hadley's office, listening to the knocks and the shouts from outside. The agency phone rang constantly.

"I wish we had a back door," Hadley said. "We're never going to get out of here."

"It should be good for business," Eddie said. "First Batson and now this. That's a couple high-profile cases. Our marketing for the year is done."

Vince's cell phone buzzed and he looked at it and gave a wry smile. "Trotter says, 'You're famous. Congratulations or something.'" They laughed as the knocking and ringing continued.

"We're going to have to make a statement," Vince said. "Any volunteers?"

"I'm not exactly dressed for the occasion," Eddie said. He had a point. He wore jeans and a stained silk shirt, missing its top two buttons, which Eddie never used anyway. Vince and Hadley had both worn sweaters.

"Maybe they'll go away if we keep ignoring them," Hadley said.

Eddie shook his head. "One thing I learned on the force is that when there's a big case like this, they won't go away until they get what they want. You have to feed the beast, or it keeps getting bigger and hungrier."

Hadley opened her laptop to write a statement when her cell phone rang. "How did they get this number?" She ignored the call and started typing. Seconds later, a text message came in from the same number. "Vince, can you finish this? I actually need to take this call."

She moved from her chair and crossed the outer room to Vince's office. She tapped on the number that had texted. Danielle Knowles answered on the first ring. "Hadley," she said, her voice barely a whisper, "I can't talk long. If my mom finds out I'm telling someone this, she'll go ballistic."

"What is it?" Hadley asked. "Is everything okay?"

"I think I know where Scott and Mary are."

"Have you told the police? We have a contact at the FBI you can call."

"No, I can't go to them. You'll think I'm as paranoid as my mom, but I don't want this pointing back at me. You're the only one I trust."

Hadley sank into Vince's office chair, the exhaustion from the investigation overwhelming her. Her shoulders felt heavy. She wanted to go home and take a nap. But, she couldn't leave the office because of the horde outside.

"Hadley, are you there?"

"I'm here, Danielle, but you need to talk to law enforcement."

"I can't. But, listen to what my mom told me. She said that she and Cara, I mean Mary, used to talk about what they'd do if they weren't at TerraPure. Mom always said that she didn't have any other options. But, Mary told her she owned a cabin near Divide. She bought it cheap as a fixer-upper after college. My mom told me Mary said she and Scott would still go there every year or so to check the place out."

Hadley scribbled notes as Danielle talked. "Do you have an address?"

"No, but it was probably in Mary's name. I have to go. Thanks."

Danielle clicked off the call. Hadley returned to her office as Eddie said, "I think it looks fine, but you should add something about how we're open for business. If we're going to get free advertising, we might as well make the most of it." He saw

Hadley in the doorway. "Everything okay? You look... concerned."

She recounted the conversation with Danielle. "If it's true, it's obviously a big lead. I'm thinking we call Trotter and let him investigate it."

Vince nodded. "Definitely. How reliable do you think the tip is? Not that Danielle would lie, but it's been a few years since Donna had contact with Mary."

"Can you look up property ownership in Divide? If we can get an address, that might be more convincing."

"Give me a second," Vince said. He scurried off to his office. Hadley returned to her chair and read the statement Vince had written. She sent it to the printer and dreaded going outside to face the vultures.

The phone continued ringing. As soon as one caller would give up, someone else would try. The voicemail indicator pulsed continuously as new messages came in. Hadley went back to Vince's office, where he stared at the screen in frustration.

"No properties in Mary's name," he said. "Nothing for Scott Flanagan, either. Costas owns a lot of property, but nothing in Teller County."

Hadley thought about her interview with Donna, and how Donna had told her they had to give up their truck when they came to TerraPure. Would Mary have had to surrender her property?

"Can you look up Mary as a seller?" Hadley asked. "See if she gave up the cabin to TerraPure 15 years ago."

Vince squinted at the screen and entered new search parameters. He sat back and smiled, the tension easing out of his shoulders. The printer on his desk came to life. "Mary deeded a property to CF Enterprises about six months after Jonah disappeared. Remember, there was no TerraPure yet; the land had belonged to Costas Energy until Costas sold. I'm guessing the CF stands for Costas and Flanagan. The property is listed as

800 square feet on three acres. Depending on the condition it was in and the money she was making, I could see her being able to afford this."

He took out his cell phone and dialed Trotter's number. He put the phone on speaker. The agent picked up on the third ring. "Vince, this better be good," he said. "We're buried in leads about where Scott and Mary might be hiding."

"I have one more for you," Vince said. He told the story, not giving Danielle's or Donna's names.

"So, these former TerraPure residents," Trotter said and paused. "You don't think I can figure out who that is? How bad of an agent do you think I am?"

"She's spooked," Hadley said. "She's worried the tip will get traced back to her, so she won't call it in herself."

"I get it, but it doesn't help. As I said, I'm buried in leads here, and we're trying to figure out what's real and what's not. There are only so many agents and so many hours. You know I hold your work in high regard, but you're basically relaying hearsay right now. Hearsay from an anonymous source who can't give us any specifics."

"I found the address," Vince said. "The part about Mary owning a cabin in Divide checks out. That should count for something."

"I appreciate the call," Trotter said. "And, we'll look into this. But, I have to triage it with everything else we're looking at and prioritize where to send resources."

"So, you're saying..." Vince didn't finish his thought, so Trotter picked it up.

"I'm saying we will get to it in good time. Let us do our job, and you can keep busy doing media interviews or something. Seriously, though, thanks for calling this in instead of looking at it yourself this time. Gotta run."

Vince pocketed his phone. The office line continued to ring.

"We're not going to get any work done here today," Hadley said.

"Probably not for a couple days until this blows over and there's another big story to cover," Eddie said from Vince's doorway.

Vince shook his head. "I think I liked it better when you two disagreed all the time. You heard Trotter. We can't go out there."

"Vince, look at your detective's license," Eddie said. "It says you're a private detective. You're not a fed. You don't take orders from Trotter."

"What's the harm in taking a little field trip?" Hadley said. "If we see signs of Scott and Mary, we can tell Trotter." She did her best impersonation of the FBI agent: "He can reprioritize his resources."

Vince smiled but didn't look convinced. "If you come with us, I'll read the statement to the wolves out there," Eddie said.

"No way," Vince said. "We can't trust you with the media."

"Fine. If you come with us, I won't read the statement."

Vince picked up the statement from Hadley's printer. "For the record, this is a terrible idea."

He started toward the door. Hadley winked at Eddie and they followed him out. As soon as the door opened, a throng of reporters and photographers ran their way. Eddie and Hadley slinked around the edge of the crowd. Hadley's Jeep was blocked in by a news van, so they'd need to take Eddie's.

Vince held up his hands for quiet. "I have a quick statement. I won't be taking questions." Someone asked him to spell his name. He did, then read from his paper. "The Fleck, Collins, and Marcotte Agency was recently hired to investigate the abduction of Jonah Davidson, a crime that occurred 15 years ago. We are pleased to say that our efforts, in conjunction with a law enforcement operation, led to the reunification of the Davidson family. We're proud of the results of our work."

He folded the paper in half and stepped away. A reporter shouted, "Do you have any role in the ongoing hunt for the kidnappers?" Another yelled, "Who hired you? Was it the Davidson family?" Yet another called out, "How did you know where to look for Jonah? Did you get an inside tip?"

Vince waved the questions off and joined Eddie and Hadley, the reporters following close behind. The three of them jogged to Eddie's Wrangler and piled in. Eddie pulled away from the curb as the reporters continued to shout questions.

"Well done," Hadley said. "I think we've found our official agency spokesman."

"Better you than me," Eddie said. "Hadley, I'm assuming you have gear and gadgets at your place we'll need to pick up on the way?"

"On the way?" Vince repeated. "You seriously want to drive out to Divide right now?"

"No time like the present. Maybe we'll get back in time for you to see yourself on the 10:00 news."

# CHAPTER 45

The wind whipped around them as they headed west of Colorado Springs, the temperature dropping as they gained altitude. A few minutes later, snow started falling, a few flurries at first but steadily getting heavier. By the time they reached the town of Woodland Park, visibility had dropped and snow blanketed the earth in near-blizzard conditions.

Eddie slowed the Jeep as the road grew slicker. He showed no signs of turning around, and Hadley was glad. They had driven two and a half hours; they might as well find out if anyone was staying at Mary's cabin. And, she had invited back-up.

"We'll get to the turn-off for the cabin before we get to Divide," Eddie said. "If anyone needs to stop, there's a gas station up here."

"Let's stop," Hadley said. "We can wait for Brad, and he can follow us in."

"Brad?" Vince asked. "The lab guy?"

"Yeah," Hadley said. "I asked him if he wanted to come. He's interested in the citizen detective world, and I've been mentoring him. I thought some hands-on experience would be good."

"I can't believe we're just now hearing about this," Eddie said. He pulled up next to a pump and looked over his shoulder at her. "You're not trying to trade me in for a younger model, are you?"

Hadley laughed. "I don't think we can get rid of you that easily."

Eddie grabbed his coat from the back of the Jeep while the gas pumped. Hadley had picked one up at her place on the way out of town, and she was glad she did. The wind slammed against her as she walked toward the convenience store, kicking up a wave of sand and grit. She turned away from the onslaught, closing her eyes to keep the debris out.

They huddled in the Jeep, looking at the terrain images on the maps on their phones. Eddie squinted at his screen and zoomed in until everything pixelated. "This is no help," he said. "These maps don't show anything useful. We'll be going in blind."

"The good news is with the weather, if they're there, they'll probably be holed up in the cabin," Vince said.

"And, the bad news is that the snow will make us easy to track," Eddie countered.

"There's Brad," Hadley said, looking out the back windshield. A Ford F-150 diesel rumbled into the parking lot. Hadley climbed out of the Jeep, and Brad rolled down his window. "You have the address?" she asked.

"Yeah."

"Follow us in. When we get there, we'll split up. You can go with Eddie and see how a former cop approaches a scene. Vince and I will stick together."

He grinned and gave her a big thumbs up. "This is so much cooler than sitting in the lab all afternoon."

"Well, get ready for disappointment," she said. "About 90 percent of clues don't pan out. I'd be shocked if we find anything."

Twenty minutes later, they wound their way through numerous twists and turns until they found the driveway leading to the cabin. It went up a steep hill. It reminded Hadley of her time in Wyoming with Dan, but she forced herself to focus on something else.

She wondered if Eddie's ancient vehicle would make the climb in this weather, but he didn't attempt it. Instead, he pulled off the side of the road under the cover of a stand of trees.

"It's a bit of a hike, but we're probably less likely to draw attention if we go up on foot," Eddie said. "We don't know how close to the driveway the cabin is, so we'll have to survey the area when we get up there."

Brad parked behind them, and the four of them started up the hill. The snow made finding footing difficult, and they took it slowly. Hadley slipped a couple of times, and once she thought she'd slide down the hill, but Brad caught her.

The driveway had old pine trees on either side. With the snow, it looked like a Christmas postcard. The cold bit her cheeks as she made it over the top of the hill and looked at the expanse in front of her.

The driveway continued about 150 yards beyond the rise and ended abruptly in front of a log cabin with green shingles peeking out here and there from the snow. A detached garage stood next to the cabin, the door closed, and any tire tracks previously made had been covered by the snowfall.

Eddie motioned the group into the pine trees at the driveway's edge. The trees would give them visual cover, as well as protection from the bitter wind. Hadley peered through her binoculars at the cabin.

"The windows are frosted over," she said. "And, in this light, it's hard to tell if there are lights on inside or not."

"Vince, are there any other buildings on the property?"

"Hard to say, since the last sales listing is so old. But, at the time, all that was listed was the cabin and garage. That doesn't mean there isn't some kind of shed or other structure on the property."

"Vince and I will cross back over the driveway and circle from the right," Hadley said. "Eddie, you and Brad wait here in case someone comes out. We'll meet up here and search the rest of the property if we come up empty."

Hadley and Vince darted across the driveway and disappeared into the trees on that side. They crept through pines and spruces until the woods cleared out in front of them. The cabin looked small, probably a one-bedroom, maybe two. There was no smoke in the chimney, and from their current angle, Hadley was convinced there were no lights on inside.

Hadley nudged Vince and motioned to move forward, toward the cabin. The driveway was to their left, and they approached at an angle. About 15 feet before they reached the building, Hadley heard the chugging of an engine. A second later, headlights cut through the snow. The truck, it looked like one of the beaten up numbers from TerraPure, crunched to a halt on the snow-covered gravel. The tall, thin frame of Scott Flanagan jumped from the passenger seat and sprinted toward them, his trench coat billowing in the wind behind him. He raised his hand, and Hadley saw the glint of gunmetal.

"Run," Vince said, grabbing Hadley's arm. They took off in a zigzag, entering the trees as the first shot rang out. Bark and pine needles exploded nearby. They ran deeper into the woods, the sunlight diminishing the further they went. They didn't have much daylight left to begin with, and Hadley hoped they'd be able to find their way back out in the dark. Scott thrashed behind them.

"You can't get out that way," he yelled. "The only way back is to follow the driveway."

Paying him no heed, they pushed forward, turning to the left, then doubling back to the right in the hope of losing their pursuer. Hadley had no idea where they were in relation to their entry point into the woods and hoped Vince was tracking their movements and could lead them back to the driveway. There'd be time to figure all that out later; at the moment, the most important thing was getting away from Scott—and his gun.

Vince ran a few steps ahead of her and to her left. He swerved to the right, and she tried to follow, but lost her footing and went down hard. Her right knee drove into the ground and she felt a shudder of pain through her thigh and hip. She pushed herself to her feet and bolted forward but did not see the branch directly in front of her. It whipped against her face, and she felt a welt form on her cheek. Her eyes watered and instantly stung in the bitter wind.

She stumbled forward, rubbing her eyes with her sleeves to clear her vision. When she lowered her arm, she saw the cabin in front of her, the truck in the driveway still running, headlights on. They had completed a circle through the woods. The prudent thing to do would be to race down the hill to the vehicles and call Trotter to let him know they'd found Flanagan.

She heard rustling in the trees to her right and saw Vince rush out of the woods a few yards from where she'd come out. He must have had the same idea because he pointed toward the driveway, and as he caught up to her, they both turned toward it. Her heart raced and sweat trickled down her face from under her wool beanie, turning to an icy liquid. She hoped Eddie and Brad had already gone down the hill.

They started running again, but as they neared the truck, Hadley heard the unmistakable sound of a shotgun click. Mary Taggert stood between them and the descent, a double-barrel in her hand, pointed directly at them.

They stumbled to a halt. Hadley raised her hands instinctively. "Don't shoot, Mary," she said. "We can talk this out."

"You've done enough talking," Scott said from behind them. He breathed hard. Hadley turned her head to look at him and saw pine needles stuck to his coat and hair. "Let's take them to the garage."

Mary kept the shotgun pointed at them, and Scott, still gripping his pistol, led them forward to the detached garage. He fumbled with his key ring when they got there, but a moment later, he rolled the wide door open on its track.

There were no vehicles inside. The garage was stuffed with a variety of tools and odds and ends, with just enough room for the pickup to pull in. Scott grabbed some rope and bound their hands behind their backs.

"You don't need to be here for what happens next," he said to Mary, his voice low and grim. Mary glowered at them beneath the glow of the exposed lightbulb in the middle of the structure. She returned to the truck and cut the engine. Hadley heard the jingle of keys once again followed by the front door of the cabin slamming shut.

Scott paced in front of them. It only took a couple of his long strides to cross the open area before he'd turn and cross back. Hadley noticed his boots and thought back to TerraPure and that same footwear on her neck pressing down before the merciless kick. This time, he had a gun and no witnesses. She swallowed hard and tried to keep a clear head.

"You've caused me a lot of trouble," Scott said, still keeping his voice down. "I heard about Colin and that other family. They're probably filling his head with nonsense about how they're his real family." He stopped pacing and drew his mouth into a tight frown. "I was going to forget about you and just focus on how to get Colin back. But, you showing up here today changes the equation." He leaned in close to them and Hadley smelled the whiskey on his breath. He grabbed Vince's arm and shoved him toward the garage door. "We'll do you first," he snarled.

Vince stumbled out of the garage, and Scott shoved him toward the woods. Hadley crept to the edge of the garage, terrified to watch and terrified not to. Scott looked back at her, a cruel smirk crossing his face. He turned back to Vince.

As soon as he raised his pistol, Hadley bolted. It was hard to sprint with her hands behind her back, but she only had to cover 20 feet. She lowered her shoulder and crashed into Scott's back. The weapon clattered to the ground as Scott stumbled forward.

He regained his balance and wheeled on her, rushing forward and shoving her down. His eyes darted around the ground until he spied the gun. As he bent to pick it up, Hadley struggled to her feet. She ran away from him in a semi-circle. He raised the gun and followed her path with its muzzle, chuckling at the feebleness of her attempt.

A thousand thoughts rushed through Hadley's mind as she prepared to take her last breath. She had no doubt Scott would pull the trigger. She kept moving, turning her body sideways to create a smaller target. The chuckle stopped, and Scott stepped forward a few feet, still trying to hold her in his sights. Vince charged him from the other side, but Scott, ready this time, raised a leg and landed a solid kick to his chest. Vince crumpled to the ground.

Scott stood between the pair, looking indecisively from Vince to Hadley. He squared his jaw, turned his body to face her, and assumed the Weaver position, a perfect push-pull grip on the handgun.

The shot rang out, echoing through the wooded hills. It went wide of Hadley, and her first impulse was to hit the ground, but she knew she had to keep moving and be as hard of a target as possible. He continued to follow her with the gun, moving his upper body only; his legs remained in their shooting stance.

Hadley heard a rumble coming toward her as the second shot rang out. Something slammed into her body. She flew across the open space and landed a few feet from Vince. She wondered if she'd been shot, but then she heard the screams coming from where she had just stood and realized Eddie had saved her.

Scott looked perplexed, as if unsure how he had not accounted for the possibility of there being others in the woods.

He faced Hadley and Vince once again. "Run," Vince whispered. "Opposite directions."

They both scrambled to their feet and took off as Scott raised his weapon once more. Hadley ran toward the woods. Over her shoulder, she saw Vince running at Scott.

Before Scott could fire, another shadowy figure grabbed him from behind and slung him to the ground. Hadley stopped running and watched as Brad jumped on top of Scott and tore the gun from his hand. He smashed the handle into Scott's temple. He cocked his arm back and did it again with a sickening thud.

Hadley and Vince both stumbled toward Eddie. Brad untied Vince's hands followed by Hadley's. He ripped off his jacket and shoved it at Hadley, who tried to stanch the blood pooling in a widening circle in the snow beneath them. In the twilight, it looked like a shadow swallowing up the white earth.

Brad and Vince ran to the cabin. As they reached it, the door swung open and Mary Taggert stood, the light from inside shining around here, the shotgun in her hands and raised to her shoulder.

The two men slowed to a stop, standing just feet away from her. "Scott's okay, Mary," Vince said. "But, my friend is injured and we need to get him to a hospital." Mary didn't move, a statue in the cold night. "Shooting us won't fix the situation," Vince said. He took a few steps sideways, and she followed him with the barrel. Vince raised his hands.

Hadley watched the scene in horror, tears pouring down her face as she kept applying pressure to Eddie's wound. Mary lowered the gun, then abruptly raised it again, and Hadley was sure she had Vince square in her sights.

With Mary's attention focused on Vince, she didn't notice Brad take a step forward. He grabbed the shotgun by the barrel, jerked it from her hands, and flung it away. "Go inside and get towels," he barked at Vince. When Vince was inside, he said to Mary, "Get me the keys to your truck. Now!"

Mary ran inside as Vince came out. He and Hadley gingerly lifted Eddie's shoulder to reveal a second wound. The bullet had gone straight through. Eddie was in a state of semi-consciousness, murmuring as they bound his shoulder with towels.

Brad and Vince moved Eddie to his feet and dragged him to the back of the pickup. As they lifted him into the bed, Brad told Hadley to collect the guns. She found the shotgun a few yards away. Brad had dropped the pistol next to the spot where Eddie had been shot.

Mary handed Brad the keys. "I'll be back for you in a minute," he said.

He drove carefully down the driveway, Vince in the back with Eddie and Hadley in the passenger seat. He pulled next to Eddie's Jeep. "Do you have his keys?" he asked Vince.

Vince reached inside the pocket of Eddie's jeans, Eddie moaning in pain as he did. "Yeah," Vince said. "Should we move him, though? Why not just keep him in the back of the truck?"

"He'll freeze to death before you get him to the hospital," Brad said. He and Vince moved Eddie to the back of the Jeep. Hadley checked her cell phone and still did not have a signal.

"Start driving toward Woodland Park," Brad commanded. "As soon as you get a signal, call 911 and tell them what's going on. If an ambulance meets you on the way, great. If not, I saw a sign for a hospital at the exit. I'm going back for the other two."

He left the pickup parked on the side of the road and took his F-150 up the driveway as Vince took off. "Drive as fast as you can," Hadley said, "but don't slide off the road." She sat in the back seat with Eddie, cradling his head in her lap and holding the towels in place. The bleeding appeared to have slowed down, but Eddie looked pale and weak.

Hadley kept as much pressure on the wounds as she could, checking her phone for a signal every few seconds, and praying that he'd pull through.

# CHAPTER 46

*November 16, 2023*

"We have way too many cases that end with one of us in a hospital bed," Eddie said.

"It's only happened twice," Hadley said.

"That's too many if you ask me," Eddie answered. For the first time Hadley could remember, he didn't have a trace of humor or sarcasm in his voice. He looked older than he had in the office the previous morning. The doctor said the bullet had made a clean entry and exit; it hadn't hit a bone or nicked an artery. The damage was limited to soft tissue. He'd be sore for a while but would make a full recovery.

"Did you get any rest last night?" Vince asked.

Eddie rolled his eyes. "In a hospital? Are you kidding? They came in every hour to take a reading or change a bandage and then told me to get some sleep."

"Sounds about right," Vince said.

Eddie took a long sip of water from a plastic cup on a tray beside his bed. He made a face. "I don't know what they filter their water through but it tastes like garbage. You should have smuggled some coffee in."

Hadley smiled. That was more like the Eddie she knew. "Hopefully, they'll let you out soon," she said.

Eddie put the cup back on the tray, wincing with the movement. "I know I've said this before, but I think this is it for me," Eddie said. "I'm ready to retire for real."

"I'll believe that when I see it," Hadley said.

"Remember when you fired me on this case?" Eddie asked.

"I didn't fire you…"

"Sure you did," Eddie interrupted. "Water under the bridge now. But, know what I did with my time until you called me back? I went fishing. I didn't worry about finding new cases or doing surveillance on a cheating husband. I caught trout. Sounds like a better use of my time than getting shot."

"I don't think you need to worry about searching for new cases," Vince said. "They're coming to us now. I checked the agency's voicemail earlier, and the calls didn't stop while we were out yesterday. It's going to take us a week just to return them all."

They sat for a few minutes. Vince broke the silence. "What's the deal with Brad?" he asked.

"What do you mean?" Hadley said.

"The way he sprang into action and took charge. Not your typical lab tech."

"He was a paramedic in Chicago," Hadley said. "He saw a lot of trauma cases. And, he does some MMA fighting and ninja obstacle course races in his free time. Kind of an adrenaline junkie."

"So, the anti-Vince," Eddie said.

Hadley allowed herself a small laugh. Her stomach still turned from the events of the previous evening. "The anti-Hadley, too," she said. "I tried to tell him detective work is actually quite boring, but there's no way he'll believe that now."

A light rap sounded at the door, which immediately opened. A nurse stepped in. She reset one of the monitors hooked up to Eddie and made notes on his chart. "The doctor will be in to see you in a bit," she said. "We should be able to discharge you after that." She looked at Vince and Hadley. "You have a couple more guests. I'm supposed to limit the number of visitors to two at a time, but I'll make an exception this time. When the doctor comes in, visitation is over."

With that, she buzzed out of the room, the model of efficiency and competence. She left the door open and Brad Cummings walked in, followed by Will Trotter. Brad wore the same clothes he'd had on the day before. Trotter wore jeans with a long-sleeved button-down shirt and a sports coat. He wore a serious expression and shook his head as soon as he saw Eddie.

"I'm glad you're okay," he said. "But, I warned you all something like this could happen. Why didn't you wait for my people to check this out?" He glared at Vince.

"Don't blame him," Eddie offered. "It was my idea."

"You're lucky it turned out as well as it did," Trotter answered.

"We can thank him for that," Eddie said, nodding toward Brad. Brad smiled but held his hands up.

"I didn't do anything that anyone else with my training wouldn't have done," he said.

Trotter looked at each of them. "I'd say that if you plan on continuing to take cases like this one, you'd do well to make sure you always have a paramedic with you." Vince laughed, but Trotter cut him off. "I'm not joking. And, you're lucky no one died."

"We get it," Vince said, and Hadley heard the annoyance in his voice. "Message received. Now, what ended up happening with Scott and Mary?"

"Your friend here took them to the Woodland Park police station yesterday," Trotter said, "and the police contacted us. We picked them up for processing. Scott has been uncooperative. He demanded a lawyer, and even with his lawyer present, he's provided few answers to any of our questions."

"What about Mary?" Hadley asked.

Trotter finally smiled. "Mary's a different story. I guess she got tired of keeping secrets, because she told us the whole story. You've probably pieced it together by now but it started when she reconnected with Scott Flanagan and Jeremy Costas after college. They were starting this anti-government commune. According to Mary, the politics were all Scott. Jeremy was interested in setting up something off the grid as a proof of concept for his technology.

"Things turned romantic between Mary and Scott. She went out to the commune a few times and wanted to move out there with Scott, but he was on the fence. Apparently, he wasn't as invested in the relationship as she was. But, one night, he'd had a bit too much to drink, and when Mary mentioned that she was cleaning houses in Park Hill, he let it slip that he'd had an affair with a married woman who lived there and had fathered a child with her. He gave the woman money to keep it quiet, but he said his one regret in life was not being able to raise his son at TerraPure.

"Mary fantasized about reuniting Scott with his son, and she got to know the kids in the neighborhood."

"Creepy Mary," Vince said.

"Exactly," Trotter continued. "When she worked the birthday party for the Davidsons and saw Jonah, she thought for sure she had a match. She took his picture, so she could compare it to a photo Lisa Davidson had sent to Scott a year earlier."

"Did Scott know what she was up to?" Hadley asked.

"No," Trotter said. "Not at that point. He found out when Mary and Jonah showed up at the commune."

# CHAPTER 47

*March 27, 2008*

Mary knew she could be working a desk job, behind a computer, and not on her knees scrubbing someone else's toilet. Her choice of employment was worth it, she reminded herself, for the freedom it afforded her and keeping her independent from the government and corporations. She smiled as she thought about the discussions she'd had with Scott about that very freedom and how passionate he was about building an independent life at TerraPure.

She finished the toilet and went to the kitchen sink to fill her mop bucket, detouring through the living room on the way. She despised the people she worked for. She hated the fact that they wasted money on something they could so easily do themselves. It exemplified everything wrong with America, she thought.

She also hated the way people reacted when they learned what she did for a living. There was an artificial power structure based on who made how much and who paid whom. A house cleaner, Mary had learned, fell on the wrong side of the equation on both of those counts. She knew the people who hired her felt superior to her. She also knew that they had no clue that she had an exit strategy, while they'd be toiling away in the same rut for the rest of their lives.

She peeked out the blinds and looked at the street in front of her. Her heart caught in her throat as she saw the family from next door. The girl was riding her bike, and the boy played with a ball in the grass, both under the watchful eye of their mother. The girl meant nothing to her. The boy was another story altogether. She watched for several minutes, then grudgingly toted the bucket to the sink.

She filled it halfway with hot water, steam floating up from the surface, and added a mopping solution that was supposed to be specially formulated for hardwood floors. She doubted the solution was any different than average dish soap, but she charged her customers extra for it.

She set the bucket down and fetched her mop from the corner when she heard the scream. The little girl had been shrieking all morning, with the boy joining in occasionally. This time sounded different, though. This cry had an urgency to it—a call of distress.

She went back to the window and watched as the mother rushed out of the yard and down the sidewalk. She returned a moment later, the girl bleeding in her arms. The mother bolted past the boy, who continued playing with his ball, oblivious to the chaos around him.

Mary stepped onto the porch and looked at the house next door. The woman had run inside, leaving the door open. The boy's ball rolled away from him toward the house Mary was at, stopping right at the edge of the yard.

Mary made her decision. She ran from the porch to the yard, reaching the ball at the same time as the boy. In one deft move, she scooped him into her arms and kicked the ball back to his own yard. He cried out, and she clamped a hand over his mouth, running back inside, checking over her shoulder to make sure no one was watching.

Inside the house, she threw the deadbolt into place and leaned back against the door, her chest heaving. The boy squirmed and cried, and she set him on the floor. She wanted to keep him quiet, so she rushed back to the kitchen and looked in the pantry. She had no idea what a child would like or could even eat. She saw a package of graham crackers and hoped that would do the trick.

She handed the boy a cracker. He inspected it carefully before taking a tentative nibble. The crying stopped and he smiled, shoving a corner of the cracker into his mouth and sucking on it.

She had to move quickly. She exited through the garage and opened it, driving inside to hide her car. She heard voices from next door calling for the boy, but they hadn't made their way to the alley yet.

Back inside, she dumped the mop bucket in the sink and collected her supplies. She took them out to the car. She took a tentative peek through the front window, barely moving the slat in the blind to see out. Both the mother and the older daughter were out there, but they ran back inside. Mary knew this had to be her moment.

She gathered the boy, who started fussing again, and took him to her car. She was sure she was supposed to use some sort of baby seat or carrier, but that was the least of her concerns. She buckled him into the back and handed him another graham cracker.

She pulled out of the garage into the alley. She had to get out of the car to close the garage door using the external keypad. She held her breath, hoping no one would come into the alley while she was back there.

Fortune was on her side. The garage door came down, and she made it into the car and out of the alley without encountering anyone. Steeling her nerves and maintaining the speed limit, Mary made her way through the neighborhood. The boy seemed to enjoy the car.

She had made it out to one of the main roads when she heard the sirens. She took a deep breath and kept her foot on the gas pedal. Her hands trembled on the steering wheel as she drove. She turned up the radio and thought about what it would be like to show up at TerraPure with Scott's son. She smiled as she thought about how he would react to having the chance to fulfill his dream life. In her heart, she knew she was doing a terrible thing, but she also knew it was her one chance to be a part of Scott's wishes.

A couple of times, she thought she should call the whole thing off and turn back, but she pushed the thoughts aside and pressed on with her plan. With each mile she put between herself and the boy's home, she felt calmer and more sure of herself, less concerned about the lives she was changing forever.

# CHAPTER 48

*November 16, 2023*

Agent Trotter left first, followed by Brad. Vince and Hadley remained in the room with Eddie. His head lolled to the side, his eyes closed. Hadley was about to suggest they leave him to rest, when he looked up and fixed his eyes on her.

"I wasn't completely wrong," he said.

"What are you talking about?" she said. "You're not hallucinating are you?"

"I'm fine. I mean other than having holes in my body I didn't use to have. I'm talking about my theory on the case. Remember what I told you at the beginning? Most child kidnappings involve a family member. I said we needed to focus on the father. Turns out, he was the key to the whole thing."

"We just didn't know who the father was," Vince said.

"I hardly think you can take credit for that," Hadley said.

Eddie smirked, then grew serious. "There is one lesson I learned on the force that I should have shared with you before now. When we have an unsolved case like this, there's a chance someone you trust isn't telling you the whole truth. If Lisa had come forward sooner about her affair with Scott..." He trailed off.

The door opened, and a doctor walked in. The doctor on duty the night before had been young and energetic, with perfect skin and teeth. He looked like he came straight out of an advertisement for a "date a doctor" web site. He'd been replaced by an older doctor, with gray hair and sagging cheeks. He looked like a half-starved version of Richard Nixon.

"I'm Doctor Harvey," he said, and Hadley wondered if it was his first or last name. She wouldn't find out. He squinted at the two visitors and said, "I'll need to speak with my patient now."

Vince and Hadley walked down the stairs to the cafeteria for some coffee. Vince picked one up for Eddie, too, convinced he'd be joining them momentarily.

"It's off to San Antonio for you, then?" Hadley asked.

"Yeah, and I know the timing's not great," Vince answered. "I'll have plenty of down time while I'm there, so I can do leg work on the new cases. Whatever research you and Eddie don't want to do, just send it my way."

"Do you really think Eddie's going to be working any more cases?" Hadley asked. "Even after he recovers?"

Vince sighed and took a long sip of coffee. He made a face. "This stuff is terrible. Eddie will love it." They both laughed. "I think he's serious about retiring this time."

"Where does that leave the firm? I mean, we're losing one of our partners, and we suddenly find ourselves with a pipeline bursting with potential cases. I'll go over them this week and prioritize the money makers, but we're going to over-extend ourselves quickly."

"We probably need to take on an associate," Vince said. "I can put out an ad. Maybe post it on our web site or Facebook or something like that."

"Actually," Hadley said, drawing the word out. "I have someone in mind already. Someone we know we can trust."

"I don't know," Vince said. "Brad seems like a great guy, and we can certainly always use extra muscle, but he doesn't have any experience."

"Neither did you when Eddie brought you in as a partner."

"And he wants the job?"

"Sitting in a lab all day isn't exactly the best environment for an adrenaline junkie."

Vince drank from his coffee again, making the same face as before. "Since I don't know the first thing about hiring an associate, let's do it."

An hour later, they were back in Eddie's Jeep, Vince at the wheel, Hadley riding shotgun, and Eddie dozing in the back seat. The weather had cleared, and they were greeted by a brilliant blue sky and excessive sunshine. Hadley scrolled through the agency email, moving media inquiries to a new folder and marking the more interesting sounding cases for follow-up.

After a while, she put the phone away and settled back into the seat to feel the warmth coming through the window and enjoy the ride. She closed her eyes and let relief wash over her.

"This case almost cost us everything," she said, opening her eyes.

Vince nodded, staring at the road ahead. "Was it worth it?"

She thought about the Davidsons, TerraPure, Danielle and Donna, and eventually her mom and Heather. She thought about Dan, still in prison in Cañon City. She thought about Scott and Mary and their awaiting justice.

"Definitely."

# CHAPTER 49

*March 1, 2024*

They had agreed to meet at Caruso's at 9 a.m. By 9:15, Hadley was convinced he wasn't coming and was ready to go back to the office. As she gathered her things, a shadow fell across her table. She looked up to see the lanky frame of Colin Jonah Davidson.

"Sorry," he said. "I'm still not used to driving and parking in the city."

Hadley bought him a coffee and they sat on opposite sides of the booth. He looked different than the first time she'd seen him. Wiser, perhaps, and less frantic and anxious.

"How have you been?" she asked.

"Good," he said. "Things are getting better with the Davidsons. With Lisa and Jenny, at least. Sara hasn't been around much. And, I think things will always be weird with Neil."

"It's a big change," she said. "I can imagine it's hard to settle in."

"I took the test for my GED," he said. "I'm looking for jobs. I'd like to get my own apartment when I turn 18, but Lisa was showing me how to make a budget, and I'm not sure tought I can afford." He swirled the coffee around in his cup and inhaled its aroma before continuing. "You're probably wondering why I wanted to talk to you." He paused and rested his chin on a fist. "You told me you'd been kidnapped. Was it hard when you came back?"

Hadley didn't answer right away, and Colin seemed content to wait. Finally, she said, "It was different for me. I wasn't gone for nearly as long as you were, and I was older when I was taken. I didn't fully understand what had happened, but I knew I belonged back home with my mom. But, yeah, it was hard. The things I couldn't wait to get back to when I was gone—riding my bike, playing with my toys—I didn't want to do when I came back. I'd gotten so used to Dan's rules about not being able to leave the house or do anything that he hadn't approved, it was like I was still a prisoner even after I got back."

Colin nodded. "That's exactly how I feel. I get that things at TerraPure aren't like in the real world, but when that's all you've ever known, it's hard to adjust to anything else. I find myself wishing it was still there, so I could go back."

"Have you considered talking to a therapist?"

"I've tried, but they don't know what it's like. That's why I wanted to talk to you. See if you had any advice for me."

"I'm probably the wrong person to ask," Hadley said. "It was just a few months, but there's not a day that goes by that I don't think about being held captive. If I dwell on it too much, it's like I never escaped."

She reached across the table and took his hand. She looked him straight in the eye, and his gaze matched the intensity of hers. "Experience shapes who you are, but it doesn't have to limit you. Move forward, one step at a time, and get the most you can out of each day. You've been given a gift of freedom. Don't waste it."

They said their goodbyes, and she watched him walk down the street where he had parked Lisa's car. She walked around the corner to the office, eager to see what new cases awaited and determined to follow her own advice.

# ACKNOWLEDGEMENTS

I owe a debt of gratitude to many people for their support and encouragement of my writing. Bringing these stories to you would not be possible without them.

Jen, you've been with me every step of the way, and I can't imagine taking this journey without you. Carvin and Miles, you've cheered me on and kept me going when I needed an extra boost. Mom and Dad, Bernie, Kay, Ron, Laura, Todd, Kyla, Todd, and Holly, thank you for believing in me and always being there.

I owe a huge thank you to my agent, Cindy Bullard, at Birch Literary. You wouldn't be reading this book without the hard work she puts in behind the scenes. The same is true of Reagan Rothe and the entire team at Black Rose Writing. From editing to production to marketing, they've breathed life into my words.

As I've said before, the best stories are stories of redemption, and I'm grateful that my redeemer continues to write my story. Thanks to all of the readers for investing your time in this book. A special thanks to all of you who've taken the time to write reviews, recommend my books to friends, and offer encouraging words through social media.

I always love hearing from people who read the books, and you can find me at www.travistougaw.com

# ABOUT THE AUTHOR

Travis Tougaw is a writer and editor. He earned degrees in English from Angelo State University in Texas and the University of Nebraska at Omaha. An Air Force veteran, Travis has worked in a variety of roles including English teacher, employee educator, and health care administrator. Captives is his second novel, following *Foxholes*, the first Marcotte/Collins Investigative Thriller. In his free time, Travis enjoys reading, playing musical instruments, trivia, and spending time with his family. He lives in Colorado with his wife and children.

TRAVIS
TOUGAW
FOXHOLES
MARCOTTE AND COLLINS INVESTIGATIVE THRILLERS - 1

# NOTE FROM TRAVIS TOUGAW

Word-of-mouth is crucial for any author to succeed. If you enjoyed *Captives*, please leave a review online—anywhere you are able. Even if it's just a sentence or two. It would make all the difference and would be very much appreciated.

Thanks!
Travis Tougaw

We hope you enjoyed reading this title from:

# Black&Rose
## writing™

www.blackrosewriting.com

Subscribe to our mailing list – *The Rosevine* – and receive **FREE** books, daily deals, and stay current with news about upcoming releases and our hottest authors.
Scan the QR code below to sign up.

Already a subscriber? Please accept a sincere thank you for being a fan of Black Rose Writing authors.

View other Black Rose Writing titles at www.blackrosewriting.com/books and use promo code **PRINT** to receive a **20% discount** when purchasing.